colors

of

TRUTH

PAULA PAUL

Colors of Truth

©2021 Paula Paul

print ISBN: 978-1-09838-472-2

ebook ISBN: 978-1-09838-473-9

CHAPTER I

Caroline

Looking back from a vantage point of more years than I like to admit, I would say that the New York Store in Morton, Texas, was the thing that set my life in a new direction. Mother had a rule that we weren't to go inside that little store on the north side of the square in Morton because it was owned by a Jew.

I went inside anyway. It was the summer after I graduated from high school, ready to start college in the fall and far too young to imagine just how many changes were in store for me.

Mr. Rabinowitz was the Jew who owned the New York Store. It was never explained to me why that made the place undesirable. Although Mother was a Southern Baptist, she wasn't the religious kind who blamed all the Jews for killing Jesus. However, being a Jew was akin to being an Italian or Greek or Mexican or anybody else that was not a southern white. They were all suspect. Besides that, Mr. Rabinowitz's store was kind of shoddy, and everything in it was cheaper than it was at St. Clair's Department Store across the street. Mr. Rabinowitz was a single-owner businessman competing against a chain store.

That was a long time ago—the 1950s. Back then, the store was kitty-cornered from the Cochran County courthouse which, as in most small towns in Texas, sat in the middle of the square. Next to the store was the drug store and then the Rose Theater. On the day I entered the store for the first time, the marquee on the theater advertised *Rear Window*. It was a picture show from last year, but the Rose was always a little late getting the new latest movies. I still hadn't seen it.

Our pickup was parked in front of the forbidden store, in the only available parking space. I sat alone in the cab, waiting. Mother had gone into St. Clair's to buy a new pair of nylons for church. My sister, Dotty, was with her. Junior, our little brother, was at home with Daddy. It was late June and hot, the air rich with the aroma of green things. Bordering all sides of Morton were fields of cotton and maize. The crops were all green shoots now, too early in the season to be anything more.

The forbidden store's name was painted on a dry, splintery board mounted across the top front. A relentless west Texas sun had faded the letters, making them hard to read. Most people referred to it as the Jew Store anyway. In my mind, the owner had given the store its fancy name and had the sign painted because New York hinted at sophistication and elegance.

I could see the store's front window clearly from my seat as I waited in the pickup. The store was anything but elegant. Its window display was cluttered, featuring a mannequin with a face cracked from constant sun exposure. She wore an ugly plaid skirt and a loose-fitting blouse. Scattered around her feet were a pair of men's work shoes, a wicker sewing box, two flashlights, a clock, a wooden statue of a horse, and a doll with a porcelain head and a cloth body. I saw dust on top of the doll's head.

As I was staring at the messy display, my attention was drawn away by someone walking into the store. I recognized the girl, Pearlie, although I didn't know her name at the time. She was a negro girl, or colored, as we said in those days, probably close to my age—that is, around seventeen. She and a few other coloreds rode the same school bus that I rode. Instead of sitting at the back of the bus, however, Jasper Hutchinson, the bus driver, made the coloreds sit at the front of the bus. He said that made it easier to keep an eye on them in case there was any trouble. White kids were dropped off at a nicely appointed brick school in the middle of a cotton field. It was called Three Way, so named because sometime in the 1940s after the war, three country schools were consolidated by the Texas Department of Education to create a bigger school. Black children stayed on the bus and attended school in a dilapidated building about ten miles away in Morton.

No one called the bus driver Jasper. He was always known as Hutch. He had graduated from Three Way High School several years before. Seems the only job he could find was the bus-driver job, and he still lived with his mama. He was a big man with dense fireplug arms bound with ropy veins. The view of his wide back as he was driving the bus always reminded me of the thick, hard cornerstone of the Three Way Baptist Church located just across the road from our school. A bull neck stuck out of Hutch's khaki-covered back and was topped with a surprisingly small head sprouting strands of hair the color of dead grass. When he spoke, his high-pitched voice was hard to understand over the din of voices on the bus.

A few weeks back, just before school was out for the summer, I had spoken to Pearlie. She and her family lived in an old run-down shack about two miles from our house and were our nearest neighbors. The whole family worked for various farmers around the county. Daddy had hired them a few times to work in our field. This girl and two little boys, whom I assumed were her brothers, had only recently started riding our bus to the colored school in Morton. It had something to do with a state mandate. Before that, I don't know how they got to their school that was supposed to be one of those separate but equal schools that coloreds attended.

On the bus, all the colored kids stared straight ahead with stony faces and wary eyes. I recall Pearlie sitting on the outside edge of the seat with her arm around one of the little boys next to her, while her free hand fiddled with her hair. The dark, curling strands were stretched and twisted into two thick plaits winding around her head. I couldn't keep my eyes off of those braids, since my own light brown hair was too fine to stay in a decent braid. I was also fascinated by the slender arm draped around the little boy. Her arm reminded me of black silk, exotic and alluring. The protective way her arm encased her brother's shoulders captured my attention as well.

I wanted to start a conversation with her because I was curious about her. My sister said I was nosey because I ask a lot of questions. Curious is a much nicer word, so I stuck with that. There were several things about her that aroused my curiosity. I wondered what it was like to be black here in west Texas. I'd heard of Emmitt Till and what happened to him a little over a year ago. They say he was lynched for flirting with a white woman. I didn't think that would happen here since, as far as I knew, all of our coloreds knew their place, and we all got along just fine.

Grandma said they were God's children like white people, but still they were not the same as us, so she said. Besides their color, they were morally deficient. They had babies out of wedlock, stole from white people, and murdered each other at an alarming rate. Looking at the girl in front of me, remembering those strange eyes that I always noticed when I got on the bus and saw her sitting in the front seat, it was hard to imagine her doing any of those things.

On that day, I tapped her on the shoulder to get her attention, but it didn't work. She didn't move a muscle. "You have pretty hair," I said. At the sound of my voice, she moved her feet a little into the aisle and half-way turned around to look at me. Her face was blank, but her eyes danced with something I didn't understand.

"What's your name?" I asked.

Her face remained stony for the first few seconds before she cut her eyes toward Hutch's broad back and whispered, "I can't talk to you." She turned away from me. At the same time, I thought I saw Hutch raise his eyes to give us a quick glance in the rearview mirror.

Raylene Propps, who was sitting next to me, punched my arm, and a giggle spewed out of her mouth. "You're an idiot." she said.

"I'm not an idiot, and what are you laughing at?" I snapped without looking at her. My eyes were on the colored girl's fat braids.

"Hey, I didn't mean that in a bad way. I meant idiot-funny, not idiot-dumb." Raylene snickered again. "I know you were trying to get her in trouble."

"I wasn't trying to get her in trouble. I just wanted to talk to her."

"Yeah, sure." Raylene said.

I turned to look at Raylene, keeping my voice low so no one else could hear me. "I'm just curious. I wanted to talk to her. Besides, I feel sorry for her."

Raylene giggled again. "I guess I feel sorry for them myself. Too bad they had to be born niggers. I'm just glad I wasn't."

The girl's shoulders stiffened, and I knew she'd heard us. I wanted to say something to her to lessen the tension of the moment, but all I did was open one of the books I held in my lap and mumbled something about needing to study for the test. I buried my head in the book so I wouldn't have to talk to Raylene and wouldn't see Hutch's faded blue gaze flicker toward me again and again. I pretended to be absorbed with my book, but I was still wondering about the girl. She and the other coloreds must have been told not to talk to the white kids. Maybe it was for their own good. Maybe Hutch was afraid some white smart aleck would try to start a fight with one of the colored kids.

"That's a history book you're looking at." Raylene said after a while

"So?"

"The test today is in Algebra."

I didn't answer her. Instead, I went back to looking at the words on the page. Just as I was getting off of the bus when we got to school, Hutch stopped me.

"Caroline." he said just before I reached the door. When I turned to look at him, he said, "Leave the niggers alone."

"I don't know what you mean. I wasn't bothering anybody."

Hutch laughed. "Nice girl like you got no business with 'em. Don't talk to 'em no more."

The look on his face made my blood boil. "You can't tell me who I can talk to and who I can't."

The kids behind me, still waiting to get off the bus, were laughing. Someone shouted, "Why you want to talk to niggers anyway? Just sit by me. I'll give you something to talk about." The voice belonged to Kent Dunlap and I didn't bother to turn and look at him. He thought he was something special, and loved harassing girls with suggestive remarks. Raylene was dying to date him because he was co-captain of the school's six-man football team. The other captain was my boyfriend, Doug McCalister, who lived on the other side of the school and rode a different bus. Kent wouldn't have dared say what he did if Doug had been there.

His remark brought more laughter.

Speaking over the clamor, Hutch said, "Don't sass me, young lady."

"I wasn't sassing. Just mind your own business. You got plenty of it to mind, from what I hear. Stuff your mama doesn't know about, but everybody else does." As soon as the words were out of my mouth, I was sorry I'd said them. Mother would skin me alive for gossiping if she found out. It was true, though, that some people said Hutch had a girlfriend in Morton and that he took her out to the Cotton Club in Lubbock. That was a place where you could drink liquor if you brought your own. You could even dance. To Baptists like Hutch and most of my family, dancing was as bad as drinking. As for drinking, Cochran County, Bailey County, Lubbock County, and just about every other county around us had laws against selling liquor, including the counties across the state line in New Mexico.

"I'm reporting you to the superintendent." Hutch got out of the driver's seat, and I backed away. It was an automatic reaction on my part. I truly didn't know whether or not he was about to attack me.

A shout came from the back of the bus. "Leave her alone, you bastard!" It was Dotty, my fourteen-year-old little sister. She used her skinny arms to shove her way through the crowd of students behind me in the aisle.

"Who you callin' a bastard, Dorothy Campbell?" Hutch's face turning white to red, like the bloom on a cotton plant.

"You son of a bitch!" yelled Dotty.

I was suddenly afraid for her. "Shut up, Dotty."

"You're both going to see the principal." Hutch said, shoving his way off the vehicle. The bus was quiet now, everyone was absorbed with the drama.

"I wish you were dead!" Dotty shouted after Hutch.

"Dotty! Don't say stuff like that," I said.

There was a murmur from the crowd, but before it could reach a crescendo, Dotty spoke again. "Well, I do wish he was dead. If I could, I'd kill him myself. By this time, Dotty had shoved her way up the aisle and was next to me. Her face was as red as Hutch's, her eyes glistening with angry tears.

That was a few weeks ago, just before school was out for summer. Dotty and I did get reported to the principal's office but got off with a warning. I think the principal had his mind more on the end of the school year and his chance to get away from us for a while. His feeble punishment made Hutch mad as a wet hen, but there was nothing he could do about it.

Now I was staring at the entrance to The New York Store, wondering what the colored girl was doing in there. Mother had told me the merchandise in the store was second-rate, and it catered to poor people. That was a strange thing for her to say since we weren't exactly rich.

It was getting hotter in the pickup, even though I'd rolled down both windows. I opened the passenger door, my eyes still on the display window of the store. I moved closer to better see the display. There was a package of wooden spring-loaded mousetraps I hadn't noticed earlier next to the mannequin's left foot. A framed picture hung crooked on the east edge of the display cubicle that had been hidden from my view. It was a sun-faded depiction of "The Last Supper."

My gaze was drawn beyond the display window to the few people milling around inside the store. Two Mexican women tried to keep a little boy in check as they examined something on one of the shelves. Two other people stood near the back.

One was Hal Fitzgerald. He wasn't from around here, and didn't seem to have any family. I'd heard he came from Levelland a few miles east, but had recently moved here and did jobs for farmers. He wasn't much older than I was—I would say about nineteen. Daddy hired him once to drive the tractor. People said he'd been in jail, but no one knew why.

I leaned closer, almost against the glass. At the back was the colored girl. Next to her was the owner, Mr. Rabinowitz. I'd seen him several times standing outside his store, one foot propped up behind him against the building while he smoked a cigarette that he held in a hand that was badly deformed.

"That's the old Jew." Mother once said when she'd seen me looking at him. It was odd she called him old. He looked to be about her age.

Now he stood close to the colored girl, speaking to her in an animated manner while she looked down at the floor. I continued to watch as he reached his hand toward her and tilted her face up, forcing her to look at him.

Was she crying?

She shook her head as if saying "no." He briefly put an arm around her, then reached in his pocket and handed her a handkerchief. She refused it and turned away, standing with shoulders slumped for a moment before walking away. He reached out as if trying to call her back.

I backed away from the window, did a quick glance around to make sure no one was watching, and pulled the long handle on the glass door to let myself in The New York Store.

The little Mexican boy plowed into me as he ran through the store with a red toy car in his hands, making motor noises with pursed lips.

"*Roberto! Deja de correr!*" one of the women called out. She hurried toward him and yanked him away with a rough jerk of his arm. Without looking at me, she walked away, pulling the boy behind her.

Mr. Rabinowitz had disappeared into a room in the back of the store, but I saw the girl with her back to me standing near one of the display racks. Two electric fans, one just outside the front door and the other closer to the center of the store, made *richity, richity, richity* sounds as they moved stifling hot air around the room. I walked to a display table and pretended to inspect a white blouse with a lace-trimmed collar. It was surprisingly pretty. I kept my head down as if I were looking at the blouse, but raised my eyes to watch the girl. She turned around and came toward me. Up until today, I'd never seen her standing since she boarded the school bus before I did and was always sitting in the same seat at the front. She was still sitting there when all of us who went to the white school got off, and was again in that same seat when we later boarded the bus after school.

Now I could see that she was tall, several inches taller than I am, and thin like a stalk of maize. But she had a bosom that had ripened well beyond my own which were no more than two handfuls of wheat.

When I saw she was headed toward the exit, I stepped into the aisle, pretending to be surprised to see her.

"Oh, hello!"

She glanced at me with a startled expression and quickly looked down at the floor, mumbling something incomprehensible that I supposed was an acknowledgement of my greeting. She quickened her pace toward the door, leaving me staring after her.

I was still watching her hurry away when another voice startled me. "Can I help you with something?"

I whirled around. Mr. Rabinowitz stood beside me. He had a long face, thinning hair and darkish eyes. I was surprised to see he looked like one of my uncles. By that, I mean he wasn't any color but white.

"No. No, thank you. I ... I was just looking."

"I saw you admiring the chemise."

What's a chemise? I wondered. I was incredibly nervous.

He picked up the blouse I'd been looking at, letting it unfold and holding it up in front of me. "I think I have it in your size." The blouse or chemise or whatever he had called it, was pretty, but I saw its fabric was thin and cheap-looking.

"Thank you, but I have to be going."

"I see you know Pearlie." he said just as I turned to leave.

"Pearlie?" Looking at his face, his eyes weren't brown as I had thought, but an odd gold color.

"The girl who was just here."

"Oh, you mean the colored girl."

"The colored girl." he said, repeating my words in a way that signaled disapproval.

"I don't really know her. She rides my bus." My gaze drifted toward the window as I kept an eye out for Mother and Dotty coming out of St. Clair's.

"You spoke to her." It sounded almost like an accusation.

"Well, I was just trying to be nice."

Mr. Rabinowitz's expression changed to something sad. "Nice." he said, leaving that one word hanging as if that were a bad thing.

"Why was she crying?" I blurted out.

"Why don't you ask her?"

I opened my mouth to speak, but after an intake of breath, all I said was, "I gotta go."

He called to me as I hurried away. "Pearlie could use a friend."

That stopped me in my tracks. I turned, and finally managed to say, "I'm always nice to people. Even coloreds."

His frown made me uncomfortable.

"I gotta go." I repeated. By the time I got to the door, I felt the presence of someone near me. It was that ex-jailbird Hal Fitzgerald reaching around me to open the door for me.

"Hi." he said.

"Hi." I said, startled.

"You're Caroline Campbell."

"Yes." He had unusual eyes—grey, with dark circles around the iris. We were standing outside the door by now. An outside fan above the entryway was blowing hot air, tossing my hair into my face.

He introduced himself.

"I know who you are." Raylene had told me about seeing Hal Fitzgerald around town. She thought he was cute.

He offered a crooked smile that made me blush. "Word gets around, I guess."

"I have to meet my mother and sister." I said awkwardly. "See ya."

"I hope so," he said to my back as I rushed back to the pickup.

CHAPTER 2

Caroline

"I saw you coming out of the Jew store." said Dotty later at home, when we were unloading groceries from the back of the pickup. Behind us the windmill groaned as its blades turned and sent the sucker rod plunging into the innards of west Texas. "Don't play like you didn't hear me. I saw you and you know it." She jumped from the back of the pickup, her small, thin body hardly making a sound when her feet hit the ground. A grocery bag of Post Toasties, sugar, flour, and syrup was the only thing that gave her enough weight to make a sound. She stood, sack balanced on one bony hip and dress hiked up on that side all the way to her thigh. Dotty gave me a mischievous grin, which I interpreted as evil.

Jesus, our mongrel part-Collie, romped around us, happy we were home. Junior was responsible for naming the dog. Mother had protested that calling a dog Jesus was sacrilegious, but somehow it stuck.

Junior came up with the name when he was almost three years old. Our preacher, known as Brother Rodgers, sprinkled his sermons liberally with the name he pronounced Jeee Zus. Junior, sitting on Mother's lap at church one Sunday blurted out "Jeee Zus!" during the sermon. At first the rest of the congregation was stunned, but then one of the deacons, Mr. McCalick, let out a loud "Amen."

After that, Junior was almost considered a saint. We got our dog a few days later, and Junior called him Jeee Zus as soon as he saw him. Before long, Mother was calling him Jesus—even "Jesus Christ!" when she was especially upset with the dog.

"So what if I went inside The New York Store?" I said in response to Dotty's accusation.

"If Mother knew, you'd be in trouble.

"For what?"

"You know for what. For going in that store when she told you not to."

I jumped out of the back of pickup with my sack of groceries. "You didn't see me. You're just trying to get me in trouble."

"I did to see you."

"Lying is a sin," I said.

"I'm not lying. Just ask that colored girl that rides our bus. You know, the one you tried to talk to and got us both in trouble. I saw her come out of the store too. I bet you went in there to talk to her. Or was it that boy—Hal something or other?"

"You're crazy. I did not go in the store to talk to her or anybody. And I didn't get us both in trouble. You managed that yourself with that dirty word you used."

"'Bastard' is not a dirty word."

"Of course it is," I said. "And so is 'son of a bitch.'"

"'Bastard' is in the dictionary. How could it be a dirty word if it's in the dictionary?"

"Forget it." I said, heading for the house.

"I'm just trying to keep you out of trouble." Dotty said. "I don't know why I bother because you sure don't appreciate it."

I turned around to look at her, consumed with guilt. She had been trying to defend me when she called Hutch a bastard and a son of a bitch. I had started the incident by sassing Hutch when he made me angry. I had denied everything to him, but couldn't deny it to myself. "Dotty, I …"

Before I could get out my apology, Daddy came out of the house to help with the groceries. When he disappeared back into the house, Dotty started again. "You know everybody thinks you were talking to that colored girl on the school bus because you were trying to get her in trouble for talking to a white. I'm surprised the principal didn't bring that up when we got called in to his office."

I stopped and faced Dotty. "I was not trying to get her in trouble. I was just trying to be friendly."

"With a colored?"

"What's wrong with that?"

Dotty shrugged. "Nothing's wrong with it. I just wanted to see what you'd say. You're such a snob."

"Don't call me names, you brat."

Dotty laughed and put the grocery sack she was carrying on the ground as if it were too heavy. "I know you're not friends." She was still giggling. "I know you. You're just nosey. You always need to know everything about people, especially if they're different. Get out of here, Jesus." she added when he started pulling bananas out of the grocery sack.

"That's not nosey. It's being interested. Want me to carry that?" I pointed to the grocery sack still on the ground.

"No!" Dotty snatched up the sack again.

"What are you two doing out there? Mother stood in the doorway, holding open the screen. "Stop lollygagging and come on in the house and help me put away the groceries." Behind her, chewing on something and peering around the skirt of Mother's dress, Junior stared at us.

"Hey, y'all." Junior said, scurrying around Mother to hug Dotty and me around our legs as we held onto the grocery sacks

"Hey, yourself." Dotty said. I managed to shift the grocery sack to my hip so I could ruffle his hair with a free hand.

"Did y'all buy me a surprise?" asked Junior.

"With what?" Dotty asked. "You think we got money? Ha!"

Junior looked up at both of us, his face crumpling. Jesus immediately went to his side.

"Don't worry," I said, "Mother got you something. I was with her when she bought it. Ask her what it is."

Junior smiled and ran away to coerce Mother to give him his surprise—a small metal truck, blue, like our pickup. He played with it in the yard with Jesus while Dotty and I went inside and helped Mother put away sacks of sugar, cans of spinach and green beans, and jars of pickled beets. Mother complained about the price of each and every can.

"If we just had enough water on this God-forsaken place to plant a garden we could save a little money." she said, speaking more to herself than to me or Dotty. These complaints about the lack of water were nothing new.

Dotty and I didn't speak until Dotty bumped my arm with a big can of molasses she was pretending to put away.

"Ow!" I screeched. "You did that on purpose."

"No, I didn't."

"You lie, and you know it."

"I don't lie." Dotty said with an air of sanctimony. "Lying is a sin. Seems like somebody told me that."

"Like you care about sin."

"More than you do."

"What's that supposed to mean?

Dotty cut her eyes toward Mother. She leaned close to me and whispered, "You think I don't know what you do with Doug?"

"That's none of your business, you brat," I said.

"You try to make everything your business, Miss Nosey. You even try to make colored people like Pearlie your business."

I stopped what I was doing. "How did you know that's her name?"

"What? You didn't know?"

"No, I didn't. Seems you're even nosier than I am."

"Quiet! Both of you!" Mother said. "I have a headache, and in no mood to listen to y'all fussing at each other."

I shoved a sack of flour inside a cabinet door. Dotty dumped a bag of apples in the sink to be washed. When all the groceries were put away, I left the house through the back door, letting it slam behind me. I walked at a rapid pace toward the chicken house and the livestock tank. I was almost to the dairy barn, with Jesus silently following along, when Dotty caught up with us.

I slowed my pace as Dotty came even with me, and we walked side by side for a while, headed toward the pasture, neither speaking. The short grama grass had begun to dry since the last rain several weeks ago. It crunched beneath our feet as we walked. Pale green mesquite brush dotted the pasture, along with ground-hugging cactus plants. We were careful to avoid the sharp spines of the cactus, but purposefully brushed against the mesquite so it would waft its spicy fragrance our way. In a little while I glanced at Dotty. Her face was screwed up into a frown. It struck me how small and thin and vulnerable she looked. In spite of our bickering, I had always felt protective toward her. I even had a small scar under my right eye because of a fight I got into several years back when we were both in grammar school, and a boy on the school bus was teasing her about being so small.

"Hey, Dotty."

"Yeah?"

"Sorry I called you a brat. You're not a brat, really."

After a pause, she said, "Well, I'm sorry I tried to make you feel bad about talking to Pearlie." When I didn't reply, she added, "It's okay to be nice to coloreds. I mean, we're supposed to love everybody, aren't we?"

"I guess so."

We walked for a while before Dotty spoke again. "But you *are* nosey. You're always asking people stuff. Like with Pearlie."

"I'm just curious. And interested."

Dotty stopped. "That's the same as nosey, and it can get you into trouble."

"I don't see how just trying to start a conversation can get a person into trouble."

"Give me a break. You got sent to the principal's office."

"That was Hutch's doing. He's a jerk."

"No kidding." said Dotty and giggled.

I'd started the walk with no particular destination in mind, but once Dotty joined me, it was clear where we were headed. There was a big draw behind the barn that fascinated her. The dry gulch had attracted Dotty since she was old enough to walk. As we drew closer, she broke away and ran toward the draw—a moth flitting toward a flame.

Blackwater was the name of banks, real estate companies, coffee shops, and small grocery stores. It was also the name of our chasm that Daddy told us was an extension of the big Blackwater Draw. It gouged the earth from Lubbock into New Mexico, draining the Great Plains.

Dotty had scoured every library in the region looking for information about the draw. She'd found nothing in the school library or the public library in Morton. She hit the jackpot when she convinced Daddy to take her along when he went to buy a cow and a calf in Portales, New Mexico, thirty miles away. The public library there had some of the information she craved. She'd found other bits in newspapers and magazines.

"Did you know all of this used to be wet lands a long time ago?" Dotty said as we walked. I did know because she talked about it all the time. "There used to be pine trees growing here." she said. "Now there's not a tree in sight. Just these old mesquite bushes."

"Yeah," I said. "It would be nice to have trees."

"Prehistoric people camped along our draw when it was a real stream."

"Yeah, I know." I said again. "They left all those spear heads and stuff you're always digging up."

"People were here around 9500 B.C.," she said, still talking as if she hadn't heard me. "That's almost ten thousand years before Jesus was born!" she said. "Now that's a long time ago. I can hardly imagine that."

Dotty knew the names of all of the now extinct animals that once lived along the draw and where their bones had been found. Dotty, who barely eked out Cs in school, knew all of this.

I reached the edge of the draw just in time to see her slide down the side toward a shovel she'd left stuck in the ground at its bottom. She'd used it to dig a hole that was almost three feet deep in the hard, rocky ground, hoping to find mastodon bones. Dolly had abandoned the quest when she hit solid rock and learned she'd need dynamite to blast down at least fifteen feet. More recently, she'd been on the look-out for arrowheads. She'd found two different types. At least she said they were different. They just looked like regular old arrowheads to me.

"I wish it would rain." she said, kicking the ground. "Maybe it'd soften the ground up a little. Make digging easier."

I sat on the ground at the bottom of the draw and leaned against the sides, trying to position myself in the shade of a squatty mesquite bush. "You going to start digging again?"

"Maybe."

"If you'd spent as much time studying as you do out here digging, you might make better grades," I said.

She gave me a defiant look. "I make passing grades."

"And you're satisfied with that?"

She shrugged. "Just because you make As doesn't mean you're smarter than me."

"Oh, Dotty, nobody says you're not smart."

She'd lost interest in our argument, picking up the shovel and scraping the ground.

"Dirt looks soft here." she said, more to herself than to me.

She stayed out there the rest of the day, long after I went back to the house. When Mother sent me out to tell her to come in and help with nightly chores, Dottie had a hole almost as wide as the one she'd abandoned.

"Find any mastodon bones?" I asked.

She looked up, her sweaty face smudged with dirt. "No, but I found this." She proudly held up what looked like a broken spear point.

"A lot of work for nothing, huh?"

She threw down her shovel and scowled, following Jesus and me back to the house.

CHAPTER 3

Caroline

Once the rain finally started, Daddy planted cotton. Farmers, like those closer to Morton, had their own irrigation wells and already had a good stand of small cotton plants turning their fields into luxurious green-striped carpets. Dry-land farmers like Daddy had to wait for nature's rainy permission to plant the fuzzy white seeds. Our crop was younger.

Although the field was half a mile west of the house beyond the pasture, the ground was so flat I could see beyond the windmill all the way to the miniature dust storm created by Daddy's tractor as he plowed the rows of plants.

Dotty walked past the windmill toward the field in freshly-ironed lime green pedal pushers and a white starched cotton shirt. She was going to ask Daddy for permission to take the pickup to visit Joanie Sommor who lived six miles away down by the Stegall Gin. She wanted to practice a piano duet she and Joanie were scheduled to play for church Sunday after next. Mother had already said yes, and I was sure Daddy would too. Mother was happy when Dotty's attention diverted from digging for bones and spear points.

"You're a strange child." Mother had once told her. That was last year when Dotty's passion for digging was growing. "I wish you wouldn't do things like all that digging."

"It's not strange." Dotty countered.

"Good way to wear out a shovel." Daddy had said.

Dotty's indisputable answer had been, "Well, what are shovels for if not for digging?"

Our parents were right, though. Dotty was wearing out a perfectly good shovel, and I could see why some folks thought she was strange. She lived in her own world of old bones and arrow heads. She had so far shown little interest in a social life at school and preferred jeans or her pedal pushers to the ruffles and starched petticoats that were popular then. Plus, unlike me and my stone ear and clumsy fingers, Dotty was a natural at the piano. Mother hoped that would be her saving grace and managed to come up with a few dollars to pay for lessons. Dotty ignored the lessons and taught herself chords and picked out her own tunes. Daddy called it playing by ear. Mother called it a waste of money, but then glowed with pride when Dotty agreed to play piano at church.

Returning from the field, Dotty climbed into the pickup and rolled down the window to call out to Mother who was watching her from the front step. She told Mother she'd be back in a few hours. I was still at my perch at the window when she drove off. She'd only recently learned to drive, and still didn't have her license, so she only drove on country roads. I turned away before she was out of sight—bad luck to watch someone until they disappear, Grandma said. It means they'll be dead before you see them again. I knew it was a crazy old wives' tale, but I followed the rule, especially with Dotty.

I felt a stab of loneliness. Dotty and I were as different as two sisters could be, neither of us adverse to pointing out each other's perceived faults or yelling insults. But we had spent our lives on a remote farm, twenty miles from our country school, and thirty miles from the nearest town, so we'd learned to tolerate one another. Well, okay, we more than tolerated each other, and, as I mentioned, I had the scar to prove it. Whoever coined that phrase, "Blood is thicker than water." probably had a sister like Dotty.

Mother was busy at the kitchen table writing the Three Way Community News for the *Morton Tribune*. She wrote it out in long hand and mailed it in each week. It contained little tidbits like, *Mr. and Mrs. Aubrey Nathans had visitors from California last week. Mrs. Nathan's sister, Patricia Ledbetter and her husband, Charles, arrived Tuesday and will be here a week. Mrs. Nathans said she hopes the weather stays pretty for the visit.*

Another announced that *A baby shower for Mrs. Oliver Hanbury was hosted by Cora Matthews at her lovely home on Friday. The living room was decorated with pink and blue strips of crepe paper. Punch and cookies were served, and Mrs. Hanbury went home with a bounty of gifts for the expected arrival of her third child in October. She hopes this one is a girl.*

Beneath the table on the rug, Junior had fallen asleep sucking his thumb and his arm around Jesus, so I went to read in the bedroom I shared with Dotty. I was a few chapters into *The Catcher in the Rye.* The book intrigued me, mostly because everything seemed so foreign, and not just the idea of someone being in an insane asylum. Living in Manhattan and going to a private school were equally exotic. Nor had I ever met anyone as sophisticated as Holden Caulfield.

This time, however, when I read, Holden seemed more annoying and whiny than intriguing. I put down the book and stepped out on the front step. It was warm outside, but it was the time of year when the sun was still too shy to be brutal and only wanted to caress. Dressed in shorts and a T-shirt, I sat on the step, elbows propped on my bare knees, chin in one hand, while I let the warmth embrace me.

In front of me the flat plains of west Texas stretched as far as I could see. The panorama was featureless except for the windmill and the swirl of dust made by Daddy's tractor to the west and another swirl to the southeast. That one caught my attention. It was a moving storm at least a mile away and meant a car was approaching on the dirt road. Whoever it was had already passed our nearest neighbor, the shack two miles away where Pearlie lived. It was too early for Dotty to be returning, so we had company coming. Living in such a remote corner of the county meant visitors were rare.

I watched the car make the turn toward us. The driver slowed and stopped on the dirt driveway in front of our house. I didn't recognize the car, but once it was stopped, I recognized Hal Fitzgerald's face through the car window.

"Hey." he said, getting out of the car and walking toward me as I sat on the porch. He swaggered as he walked, squinting his black-rimmed eyes against the sun. I couldn't have been more surprised to see anyone, but I stayed right where I was, my hand still resting on my chin as I watched his approach.

"Hey yourself." I said, hoping Mother wouldn't come outside and run him off. She wouldn't want a person like Hal showing up. He wasn't from around here and was therefore suspect. Plus, I didn't want her to run him off because I wanted to study his face, his lopsided grin and short, compact build. Raylene was right, he was kind of attractive, but he didn't seem interested in any of the girls in the area. Raylene assumed he had a girlfriend back in Levelland. She was probably right. He wasn't as handsome as my boyfriend Doug, and Doug was several inches taller and had a solid, powerful build. Still, there was something about this guy that made me want to get to know him better.

"I'm Hal Fitzgerald." he said.

I nodded.

"You're Caroline Campbell."

"How'd you know my name?"

"I asked somebody."

"Like you said, word gets around."

He grinned. "Mr. Campbell around?"

Standing, I brushed the dust from the porch step off of the back of my shorts. "He's working in the field. Plowing." I pointed to the cloud of dust half a mile away. There'd been a fleeting moment when I'd thought he might have come all this way just to see me.

"Thanks. I'll drive out there." He didn't turn back to his car, though. He just stood looking my way.

"What?" I said finally.

"I should have told you when I saw you in town. You. . .Well, you seem like a special kind of person."

"Me?" It was dumb reply, but he'd caught me by surprise.

Hal nodded. "I heard what happened when you talked to that nigger girl on the bus a few weeks back."

"Good Lord, is it all over the county?"

He shrugged.

"Well, anyway, nothing really happened."

"I heard you got a good ass chewing and that you took the blame for it so Pearlie wouldn't get in trouble."

How did everyone but me know her name? "I didn't take the blame for anything that wasn't my fault," I said.

Hal looked at me with those squinty eyes. I couldn't tell if it was just the sun or if he thought I was lying. "You didn't do anything wrong." he said, and started walking toward me.

For some reason, I felt I had to sit again. I dropped to the porch with my legs straight out in front of me.

Hal spoke. "I said, what's wrong with talking to Pearlie?"

I shrugged, answering without looking at him. "It's against the rules."

"Rules are made to be broken."

Looking up, I saw he was grinning. "That's a cliché," I said.

"Now what does that mean?"

"It's French for a word or a sentence that's overused."

"You speak French?"

"No." I turned and stared at the earth tank across the road, south of the house and several hundred feet away.

He laughed. "Well, I tell you something in English. If sentences are overused, it's probably because they're true. I'll tell you something else that's true—that Hutch is a son-of-a-bitch."

I looked up, and couldn't keep from grinning myself. "Dotty would agree with you at least," I said.

"How about you?"

I stifled a snicker. Hal saw it on my face, making him grin before saying, "You can talk to anybody you want to. It's a free country."

That was another cliché. "Obviously, coloreds can't talk to anybody they want to."

"Well. . ." He sat next to me.

"Well, what?" I was surprised at how close Hal's face was to mine. I was looking at the little rings around the outside of the irises of his eyes. They looked like black halos.

"Well, nothing." He had nice full lips that looked a little pursed.

"I'll bet you were going to say it's different when you talk about colored people," I said. "You think they don't have the same rights as we do."

Something flared in those odd eyes. "You know what I think, do you?"

"I don't know. I mean, no."

"I think you don't know your ass from a…" He blushed a little and turned away. "Sorry, I shouldn't have said that."

"What? Ass? You think I haven't heard that word before?"

"No. I mean I shouldn't have gotten so defensive." He was silent for a moment. "So what do *you* think? Should niggers have the same rights we do?"

"Don't use that word. Say coloreds."

"What's the difference? They mean the same thing."

"Well, colored sounds nicer."

He rolled his eyes. "Okay, do colored people have the same rights we do?"

"In a perfect world. they would." I tried to inch away from him.

"But the world ain't perfect."

"No." I said. "It isn't."

"That's what I meant. *Isn't.* I can see I have to watch my words around you."

"Don't make fun of me."

"I'm not making fun of you." Hal said. "You're a smart girl. And a nice girl. Besides that, you're kinda cute. But in spite of all of that, there ain't nothing … there isn't nothing you can do about what rights colored people have or don't have."

I bit my tongue to keep from correcting the double negative.

"You're looking at me funny." he said. "I guess I used another wrong word."

I answered with a shrug.

He looked uncomfortable for a second or two before he spoke again. "I gotta tell you something, sweetheart. Try not to cross old Hutch again. He's bad news. He could hurt you."

His words shocked me. "What are you saying?"

"I wouldn't put it past him." said Hal. "I'll tell you this much, somebody ought to beat the sh—beat the daylights outta him."

"That sounds extreme." I was remembering Dotty saying she wanted Hutch dead, but I didn't mention it.

"You don't know some of the things he's done."

"Like what?"

"Bad stuff."

"Oh, please. I can take care of myself"

He was trying not to laugh.

"What's so funny?"

"Sorry," he said, but he couldn't keep a grin off his face, which irritated me beyond words. "Listen, I gotta go," he said. "Been nice talking to you."

"Wait!" I said just before he turned away. "How did you know that girl's name is Pearlie?"

"She told me."

"You mean you talked to her?"

"Sure. Why not?"

"Well, I just didn't think..."

"It's only on the school bus that coloreds ain't allowed to talk." The frown on his face made me feel dumb. "If you want to talk to Pearlie so bad, get Rabinowitz to introduce you."

He had called me sweetheart and said I was a special kind of girl. I didn't know whether to be angry or flattered. I might have eventually found my voice if we hadn't been interrupted.

"Hello. Can I help you?"

Both of us quickly turned to see Mother standing in the doorway. Hal was the first to speak. "Hello. You must be Miz Campbell."

She studied his face for a moment. "Oh! You're that new boy. Fitzsimmons or something."

"Fitzgerald," he said. "Halick Fitzgerald."

Mother looked at him unsmiling and silent for a moment before she said again, "Halick? I knew some people with the last name Halick when I was in school. I think they were from Levelland."

"My mama's folks are the Halicks."

"I see." Mother said. I definitely got the idea she didn't approve of the Halicks. "Can I help you?" she asked again.

"I come to see Mr. Campbell." Hal's voice was surprisingly steady and self-assured.

"He's in the field. Plowing."

"Yes, ma'am. I know where he is." He glanced at me and then at Mother. "Nice to meet you, Miz Campbell." He walked to his car and got in. He waved to me as he left.

Mother watched him until he disappeared in the dust stirred up by his car. "How long has he been here?" she asked.

"Just long enough to ask me where to find Daddy."

"You must have given him a real long answer." she said, disappearing back into the house.

I sat on the porch a while longer, watching to see if Hal would come back by the house. He stopped his car at the edge of the field and waited for the tractor approach. They talked for a little while, until finally I saw Daddy's tractor start down the cotton rows and Hal's car moving away, headed toward the section line southwest of the house. The roads were laid out in square sections with a crossroad every mile. It would have been half a mile out of his way to come back by the house.

I kept an eye on the roads a while longer, hoping I'd see Dotty coming back from practice. I finally gave up and went inside to help Mother with the ironing and then to find my book to read. Dotty still hadn't returned when Daddy came in for supper, driving the tractor.

CHAPTER 4

Caroline

"Where's Dotty?" asked Daddy. Junior was on his lap while he cut his fried steak into bite-sized pieces. We sat in mismatched chairs at the big square oak table in the dining room. An overflowing bookcase lined one of the walls, and a chest-type freezer stretched across another. The top of the freezer offered itself as a space for folded laundry, clean canning jars waiting to be filled, a few books, and an old chiming clock that had belonged to Mother's grandmother.

"She's still over at the Sommors' practicing her music." Mother said. "You're the one that let her take the pickup."

"She's got no business being gone this long." he said, spooning white gravy over the cut-up pieces of meat.

"Didn't you tell her how long she could be gone?"

"Nope." Daddy refused to react to Mother's accusatory signals.

When supper was over, the dishes done, and Junior was asleep cuddling next to Jesus, Dotty still hadn't returned.

"If we weren't so far out in the country, we could have telephones, and I could call the Sommers' house to find out if Dotty's still there." Mother grumbled to herself, standing on the front step to watch the road for an approaching pickup. "Maybe she had trouble with the pickup, George." she said to Daddy through the screen door. "A flat tire maybe. Or Dotty could have run out of gas."

Daddy was inside watching the news on one of the two TV channels we could get. I sat on the couch trying to read while the Camel News Caravan blared out a story about President Eisenhower's recovery from a heart attack. Ordinarily, I would have been propped up on the bed in the room I shared with Dotty, but her unexplained absence made me want to be surrounded by the rest of the family.

"She'll be all right." Daddy called to Mother through the screen from where his chair was positioned near the front door. "The pickup's full of gas and she knows how to change a tire."

Mother stayed outside with her eyes on the road at least a half hour longer before she came inside and went to the bedroom and closed the door. By this time, I'd tossed my book aside and slipped out to take Mother's place on the front steps.

The sky was partially covered with a gauzy, thin night curtain, and a few stars had to push their way through as the opening acts for what, in a few minutes, would be the spectacular sparkling show of a summer night. Dotty and I sometimes sat on these steps together, watching the sky, trying, mostly without success, to identify constellations. Dotty insisted the Milky Way was misnamed because it looked more like a melting snow drift than spilled milk.

I watched the road for a distant headlight, waiting for the sound of a motor. There were no lights and no sound except for the *clank, clank, clank* of the windmill and the occasional mournful call of a coyote near the earth tank across the road. Jesus joined me on the steps, resting his head in my lap. The night sounds around us were too familiar for Jesus to stir or even open his eyes. It would take a distant approaching motor to awaken him.

He slept soundly until I disturbed him by standing up to go inside the house to escape swarms of mosquitos. I washed my face and my feet, then put on my pajamas and got into bed. It was an odd feeling to have the bed I shared with Dotty all to myself. I lay on my back staring at the dark ceiling and listening to the windmill, still hoping for Jesus's bark signaling a coming car. A cow called for a missing calf and was answered by the tank-dwelling coyotes, but there was no other sound until the old clock on the freezer chimed twelve times.

Soon after, I heard the door to Mother's and Daddy's bedroom open and heavy footsteps moving toward the kitchen. Was Daddy setting out on foot to look for Dotty? I slipped on old sandals and ran through the back door to follow. He headed toward the barn with a flashlight in hand. By the time I reached him, he had emerged from the barn carrying a saddle.

"Go back to bed, Caroline." he said.

"You taking Sargo to look for Dotty?"

"Yeah. Now, do like I said and go back to bed."

"I thought Sargo had a lame leg." I said, referring to the cutting horse Daddy used to work the cattle. The beautiful sorrel had cut his leg on a piece of wire. The vet had said it would heal in time but he shouldn't be ridden while the cut was healing.

"I'll take care of this." He turned away from me and walked toward Sargo who was sleeping next to the corral fence. Looking for Dotty on horseback in the dark wasn't a practical solution, but I was as desperate to know she was safe as Daddy was. I knew better than to argue.

He had not yet reached the horse when we heard Jesus barking. Looking toward the road, I saw the headlights, still at least two miles away.

"Dotty?"

I couldn't see well in the darkness, but I heard the *pshh, pshh* of the brush as Daddy rubbed it along Sargo's back in preparation to place the blanket and saddle on him. The brushing stopped.

"That's her." he said. "I know the sound of our pickup motor." With the flashlight, he headed back to the barn to put away the saddle. "Go inside. Don't wake your mother." There was no mistaking the sharp tone of his voice. I went to the house.

My eyes were wide open, staring into the darkness of the bedroom I shared with Dotty when I heard the pickup pull in the driveway. There was the thud of the door slamming and muffled voices. Before long, I heard Daddy's footsteps and the bedroom door opening and closing.

Dotty would be in soon, and she would tell me everything.

I fell asleep, waiting. When early morning sunshine flowed into the bedroom window and splashed on my face, I sat up in bed, realizing Dotty still had not come to bed. I got up and ran to the living room, still in pajamas. Dotty wasn't there, and Mother was sitting in Daddy's chair with a writing pad in her lap, scribbling her news reports. Daddy had already gone to the field to work.

"Where's Dotty?" I asked.

"Out in the back somewhere." Mother said.

Outside, I looked for Dotty. The pickup was in its usual place, but she was nowhere in sight. The most likely place to find her was her was the draw behind the barn. I heard the sound of a shovel against rocky dirt as I got closer. Dotty was down in the interior, hidden by the steep walls of the wash out. But she was not digging. Instead, Dotty had filled in the wide hole and was now smoothing its surface with the flat end of the shovel.

"Dotty, what are you doing?'

"Digging." She threw down the shovel and started climbing up the sides.

"It looked like you were covering up something."

"Well yeah, I decided to fill in that old hole and dig someplace else. I didn't want to accidently fall in it or anything." She climbed over the side and stood beside me, slapping her dirty hands together to rid them of dirt.

"That's weird." I said. "You never filled in any other holes you dug."

She shrugged. "So what? I guess I'm maturing." She walked away.

"Where are you going?"

"Back to the house."

"Where were you last night?" She didn't answer, so I ran to catch up to her. "You were late getting home last night."

"So?"

"Daddy was worried." I said.

"He shouldn't have been. I got home okay."

"So where were you?"

"Nobody likes a nosey busybody."

"Tell me, Dotty."

"It's none of your business." She hurried away from me. By the time I followed her into the house, she had locked herself in our bedroom. I pounded on the door, but she wouldn't open it. Didn't even bother to tell me to leave her alone.

"Are you trying to tear down the house?" Mother had put away her writing pad and stood behind me.

"Dotty's in there and she won't open up." I banged the door again.

"Stop that racket. It's giving me a headache." Mother put her hands to her temples. "And you've got company." she said in a quieter voice. "Go see what he wants, but. . ."

"Who is it?" People in the area were so widely scattered that I seldom saw friends during the summer except for Saturday nights when we would all gather in town.

"It's that Fitzgerald boy." Mother said, speaking in a whisper. "Get rid of him as soon as you can. He's not the sort you should be hanging out with."

"What's wrong with him?" I said, trying to smooth my hair.

"Just get rid of him."

I ducked into the bathroom in the hallway on my way to the living room and glanced at my reflection in the mirror over the sink. I was met with a dreadful, hopeless sight, but if I took too long Mother might make Hal leave.

"Hi." I said, entering the living room.

He was sprawled on the couch reading one of Dotty's *Archie* comic books.

"Oh!" He stood, running his eyes over me. "You're looking good."

"Sure, I am." I said, my attempt at sounding sophisticated.

He smiled then glanced toward the kitchen where Mother had retreated. "Wanna go outside?" he asked, motioning with his head toward the front door.

"Why not?"

He opened the door for me and followed me out. We walked to the windmill and sat on its bottom rail.

"Are you surprised to see me?" he asked.

I shrugged. "Kind of." I stared straight ahead at two long rows of fence posts lining the road, but I sensed him looking at me. Turning, I was surprised to see he was frowning. Hal looked worried.

"I just wanted to see if you were okay."

That surprised me. "Sure, I'm okay. Why wouldn't I be?"

"How about Dotty? I was wondering about her."

I stood and looked at him. "Why would you be worried about Dotty?"

Finally, he let out a long breath and said, "Never mind."

When he started walking away, I grabbed his arm. "Wait a minute. You're not getting away without telling me why you're worried about Dotty."

He shook his head, a funny look on his face. I couldn't tell if it was worry or fear or something else. "If she didn't tell you, then it's not my place to—"

I gripped his arm harder. "Tell me!"

His eyes grew wide at the harsh sound of my voice. He glanced toward the house, then back at me. "I saw her in Morton yesterday, and—"

"Morton? But she was supposed to be over at Joanie's, practicing for the church program."

"I don't know where she was supposed to be, but I saw her in Morton." His voice took on a sound of urgency. "She was upset."

"About what?" A band of anxiety tightened around my chest.

"About old Hutch. He was giving her a hard time about Pearlie."

"That colored girl? Hutch was giving her a hard time because of me talking to her?" My mind was spinning. Dotty sneaking away to Morton. Getting in trouble because of me?

"It didn't have anything to do with you." Hal sounded nervous. "It was because he saw Dotty talking to her. They were standing outside The New York Store."

"That can't be! Dotty's not supposed to go near that store. She wouldn't do that."

Hal shook his head. "Look, sweetheart, all I know is what she told me when I saw Pearlie crying her eyes out. Dotty was crying, too."

My fear reached a new level. "Why were they crying?"

Hal gave a nervous glance toward the house. "I can't talk about it now. I'll come over later, Saturday night. I'll pick you up like we're going to the picture show in Morton."

"I can't do that." I was about to tell him I always went with Doug to the show on Saturday night, but before I could get the words out, Mother stuck her head at the door and called.

"Get in here, Caroline. I need help getting supper on the table. You expect Dotty to do everything?"

I paused long enough to look at Hal several seconds while I tried to think of another way to meet him.

"Caroline! I said get yourself in here!"

"Coming!" I said, still looking at Hal, still not knowing how to solve my problem. "I don't know if I can—"

"Caroline!"

I turned away, hurrying toward the screen door Mother was holding open with one hand and a furious look.

"Saturday night. Pick you up at six." Hal said.

I turned to try to tell him one more time that I couldn't go, but he was already in his car. I watched him drive away, and kept watching until he was half way to the section line.

I heard the sizzle of chicken frying in the kitchen as soon as I opened the front door. The smell, sweet and meaty, permeated the house. Dotty was in the dining room setting the table with the white dishes that came buried in every box of oatmeal we bought. She placed mismatched metal knives, forks, and spoons on each side of the plates just as we had both learned to do in home economics classes at school. Every girl enrolled was required to take four years of the classes whether she was interested in becoming a housewife or not. The school had to keep up enrollment in the classes in order to qualify for state funding.

I grabbed a handful of paper napkins off the freezer chest and began folding them to place under the metal forks—also something we'd learned in home-ec. "Are you in trouble?" I whispered to Dotty.

She'd kept her head down, ignoring me.

"I heard you were in town, talking to Pearlie." I said, whispering.

This time she responded with a hiss. "Shut up!" Dotty disappeared into the kitchen and returned with a bowl of mashed potatoes. She set it on the table and left, heading back to our bedroom. I wanted to follow, but Mother called me into the kitchen and told me to make the gravy.

"Leave Dotty alone." Mother said. "George will handle it."

Metal clicking against crockery plates made an eerie sound in the almost silent dining room as our family ate supper. The only other noise came from Mother cautioning Junior to behave when he blew bubbles in his milk. I stole glances at Dotty who had emerged from our room and saw that she ate almost nothing, even though fried chicken, mashed potatoes, and gravy was her favorite supper.

After we'd finished eating, Dotty and I started clearing the table, stacking dishes to take to the kitchen. Neither of us was surprised when Daddy spoke.

"Dotty, come with me." he said, moving toward the back door. Dotty followed, and Mother glanced at me with a knowing look.

"I'm going to watch television." she said. "*Matinee Theatre* Is on tonight."

Daddy and Dotty went to the back porch to do their talking. I finished with the dishes and waited for her in our room, sitting up in bed, trying to read *Catcher in the Rye* and not comprehending anything. I put down the book when Dotty entered the room. She glanced at me briefly before turning away and getting ready for bed.

"Dotty. . ."

She pulled her shirt over her head and threw it at the dresser. It missed and fell on the floor. "He chewed me out. I can't have the pickup for two weeks. Is that what you want to know?"

"I want to know what's going on. Why did you talk to that colored girl?"

Dotty pulled a pair of pajamas from a drawer. "Her name is Pearlie. And I talked to her because I wanted to. Just like you did."

"Did you sneak off to town just to talk to her?"

Dotty crawled into bed and faced away from me without answering.

"It can't be anything that important." I said to her back. "I mean, so important you had to sneak off without telling anybody."

"You might think you know everything, Caroline." she said, "but you don't know anything at all."

She didn't speak to me again that night, and she was out of bed before I woke up. I found a note on the dresser. It was short. All she had written was, *Don't tell Mother and Daddy about me talking to Pearlie.*

CHAPTER 5

Pearlie

Pearlie was feeling poorly that morning when she awoke at five o'clock. She thought it was because it was her time of month to have the curse. Mama said the curse was punishment for what Eve done with that apple. Tempted Adam with it. That made no sense to Pearlie. For one thing, she'd never tempted anybody with no apple or anything else, and she'd never met a soul who claimed to be Adam. As far as she was concerned, whatever Eve done back in the old times was Eve's problem, not hers, so there was no cause for God Almighty to curse her.

She didn't have cramps yet, and there was no blood, but she sure felt bad. Kinda tired. Feeling that way made it hard for her to put up with Mama's nagging her about them two white girls. *I catch you talking to either one of them Campbell girls again, I'll blister your behind,* she said. Pearlie would never think of telling her about talking to that youngest one in town and that she had probably said too much. Neither had she ever tried to tell Mama it was the one named Caroline who had started the talking on the bus, and that she had only given her short answers and tried to get away. Pearlie never told, because if she did, Mama would say she was talking back and smack her for it. Them little swats she gave her on the butt never hurt none, but that didn't mean Pearlie liked it, and she definitely didn't like being told she was talking back when all she wanted to do was tell Mama the way it was.

It wasn't her place to set Mama straight. Pearlie knew that, but it sometimes made it hard to talk to her. Lord knows she wished she could talk to her now. No telling what Mama would do if she told her what was troubling her. Have a fit. Faint. Both probably.

As close as she'd ever come to talking to anybody about it was when she let something slip to Mr. Rabinowitz in The New York Store He had seen how troubled she was the last time she was in there, and had asked if she all right. If it'd been anybody else she would have said yes, everything is just fine, or maybe just walked off without saying anything. But there was something about him, the way he looked at her, maybe. Or it could be on account of what she'd heard about him. Old Uncle Thaddeus—that was Mama's uncle—told her Mr. Rabinowitz was tortured during the World War. Bad as Jesus was, Uncle Thaddeus said, except he wasn't hung on no cross. They beat him, same as they did Jesus, and they took his wife and children and put 'em in a German prison and tortured them until they died, and there wasn't a thing Mr. Rabinowitz could do about it. Uncle Thaddeus said the Nazis did that to a lot of the Jews across the ocean. Uncle Thaddeus wasn't one to tell lies, and besides that, you could see in that Jew's eyes that something bad had happened to him.

Anyway, at the time, Pearlie needed to talk to somebody, so she told Mr. Rabinowitz. Now she wished she hadn't.

What happened had hurt Pearlie's soul. It ate away at it like a maggot on a piece of rotten meat. Trouble always passes, Mama says. Pearlie wasn't so sure Mama was right unless a person takes things into her own hands to make sure trouble passes. She'd been giving it lots of thought. Pearlie had to do something before that old maggot ate her soul plumb up. She just wasn't sure how or even what to do.

Caroline Campbell might come up with something, thought Pearlie. Everybody said she's smart. Caroline was kinda like Uncle Thaddeus, always wanting to find out about something. But Pearlie knew the world could end before she'd ask a white girl for advice. Especially Caroline Campbell.

Feeling as she did, Pearlie didn't want to think about Caroline or anybody else. If she had her way, she'd take a nap. But she had work to do, hoeing weeds outta somebody's cotton patch. She'd be out there working with Mama and Papa and her two brothers and Uncle Thaddeus if his rheumatism wasn't bothering him. They worked for all the farmers around the county. Last week, they'd worked in Mr. McCalister's cotton field. Then it would be somebody else for the next few weeks. Whoever it was would be there to pick them up to take them to the field soon as it was daylight. Best to get started before it got too hot, that's what Papa said. Pearlie could never see what difference it made, since they worked right through the hot part of the day anyway. That was hard work, hoeing cotton. Pearlie wished she was rich so she wouldn't have to do it. Mama would laugh at her if she heard her saying something like that. She might even swat Pearlie's behind.

The sun already had a good start at prowling up the edge of the sky before the pickup arrived to take Pearlie and her family to the cotton field. Pearlie looked at the pale morning sky and knew it wouldn't be long before it would pour its pot of blazing fire upon them.

All of them, Pearlie, Mama, Daddy, and the boys, Luthy and Todd, along with Uncle Thaddeus, were waiting in front of the shack when the pickup drove up. At first, Pearlie didn't recognize the man driving. He was just another farmer in khaki pants and shirt and a big western-style straw hat. When she got a better look, she recognized his eyes. White man's eyes, blue. Not ice-blue like most white men but more like blue flames. It was George Campbell, Caroline and Dotty's daddy. He motioned with his head that they were all supposed to get in the back bed of the pickup. Pearlie wrapped her dress around her legs as much as she could so nothing would show when she climbed up. Times like this made her wish she was a boy so she could wear overalls like Papa and Uncle Thaddeus and the boys, but Mama said no girl of hers was wearing britches. Didn't matter that white girls wore blue jeans even to school. Mama said it wasn't natural.

There were eight hoes in the back of the pickup. The way they had been sharpened made Pearlie think of stars shooting off of the silvery edges. That was a good sign. Some farmers let the edges get dull so it took twice as long to chop a weed and finish up a field.

Reaching the Campbells's field, Pearlie saw people already walking along the straight chocolate-colored rows, chopping at weeds. She climbed from the back of the pickup feeling a little bit woozy but managing to stay on her feet. When Pearlie looked up and saw who was working the row of cotton next to her, her heart dropped into her stomach. It was Caroline Campbell.

CHAPTER 6

Caroline

When she saw me, I was almost at the end of the row, looking straight at her. Her eyes grew wide, and she got a funny look around her mouth, like maybe she was going to be sick. It was clear she didn't like me but I didn't know why. I'd never done anything except try to talk to her.

"Hi, Pearlie." Dotty's voice came from behind me. Pearlie glanced at her and mumbled something before quickly turning and grabbing a hoe out of the back of the pickup. She walked away without looking back at us, the hoe slung over her shoulder like a soldier off to battle.

"Get back to work, girls." Daddy said, and went over to the coloreds to give them instructions. Dotty and I always worked in the cotton field in the summer, except we didn't get the twenty-five cents an hour that the other hands got. Daddy had promised us it wouldn't take more than a week or two to finish the field this time because he'd hired a crew to help. I hadn't guessed Pearlie and her family would be the crew.

As I worked, I kept glancing their way and Dotty was doing the same. After a while, Daddy left in the pickup, heading to the north field to finish plowing.

"Don't start bothering Pearlie." Dotty skipped some plants to catch up with me, several nightshade plants untouched by her hoe. With pale leaves glistening in the sun, in Texas they're known as white weeds.

"I'm not going to bother anybody." I said, pretending to be intent on my work.

"Ha!"

"And just why do you think you have to protect her from me?"

Without answering, Dottie put her head down and chopped at a little shoot of a weed, then another and another until she was several feet ahead of me on her row. Pearlie was back behind me, and I could hear the *scrape-scrape* of her hoe chopping at wayward weeds that were trying to sap precious water from our cotton. I could tell she was moving fast. If I slowed down, she'd soon be even with me.

She got there sooner than expected, but I kept my head down, pretending not to notice. My eyes were turned toward her, but I was sure Pearlie couldn't tell I was looking at anything other than my row of cotton. I had on one of the homemade bonnets Mother insisted Dotty and I wear. It kept my face inside a calico tunnel. I must have sped up a little because I stayed even with her for several minutes, our hoes grabbing at roots in an odd counterpoint rhythm. Each strike produced a different scent—tumbleweeds were earth and metal, blue weeds smelled like skunks, and those ground-hugging crawlers Daddy called careless weeds smelled oily and pungent.

"Why you watchin' me?"

Pearlie's voice startled me. "What?" I stopped working and stared at her.

She was holding the end of the hoe suspended above a fallen weed. Emphasizing each word, she asked, "Why... you...lookin'... at...me?"

"I wasn't looking. I was minding my own business." I brought my own hoe down with a hard thrust, forcing up something by the roots.

She shook her head. "You tore up three or four a them cotton plants back there. I say you got your mind on something else." Her eyes were dark, fiery liquid moving from side to side, front to back, searching. She was afraid of being caught talking to me.

I looked behind and saw the sad cotton plants I had gouged out of the row.

"Your daddy ain't goin' to like that." she whispered, keeping her own head down as she started working again.

"No, I reckon he won't." I said, wishing I could think of something else to say to keep her talking. But I came up short. There was only the rasping of metal against soil for a long time. I worked faster than normal to keep up with her. By the time I got to the end of the second row, my arms ached. I wasn't sure why I was so curious about Pearlie, except that I'd never gotten to know a colored person before. Colored people were different from white people, and I wanted to know what they thought about, how they felt about things. I wanted to know if they had a natural sinful nature like some people said, and if that were true, why they seemed so religious at the same time. Mother said they were confused about the true religion. She said all that shouting and dancing and waving arms that took place in colored churches was like they were at a party instead of church, and that was undignified. About all us Southern Baptists do is voice an occasional *Amen* during the service, and that's only the men. Women are supposed to stay quiet in church, which was fine with me.

Did Pearlie shout and wave her arms at church? Did she like to read? What sort of books did she like? Would we have things we could talk about?

Pearlie went to the water jug at the end of the row and poured out a dipper full. The coloreds had their own jug identical to the one Daddy had set out for Dotty and me—both big bleach bottles Mother washed out to get rid of the bleach taste, then wrapped in a damp feed sack in a losing effort to keep the water cool.

I watched as Pearlie shook out the last drops from the tin cup and wiped her mouth with the back of her forearm before handing the cup to one of her brothers. Once again, I was watching while pretending not to. Pearlie ambled over to pick up her hoe at the end of a cotton row. As she bent down, she stumbled and fell to her knees. Dropping the tin cup in my hand, I ran to her side. Dotty was behind me, calling out, "Pearlie! What's wrong?"

By the time we reached her a woman I guessed to be her mother was squatting next to her. She pulled Pearlie's head close to her bosom.

"You still feeling poorly, baby?" Her voice was low and gentle, and she rocked Pearlie as she held her close, her plump body moving from side to side. "Tell me what's wrong, Pearlie girl. You been sickly too long."

"I be okay, Mama." Pearlie's voice sounded weak, but she pushed herself away from her mother. "Just got too hot, that's all."

Pearlie's mother stood, pulling Pearlie to her feet. She looked at her with an expression either worried or angry. "We best get back to work." she said.

Before they could move away, I piped up, "Pearlie can rest if she wants to. I mean, if she's sick."

"Don't need no rest." Pearlie said, not looking at me. She dragged her hoe to the end of the row and started chopping weeds.

When I started toward her, Dotty grabbed my arm. At the same time, Pearlie's mother spoke up. "She fine. We all just fine." Her words came out like she was mad, as if she were blaming Dotty and me for Pearlie feeling sick.

"What do you think is wrong with her?" Dotty asked me in a quiet voice as we returned to our work.

"I don't know." I said. "I just hope it's nothing serious."

Dotty glanced at me, then got back to work. "Sorry." she murmured. "I know you're worried about her, but I'm more worried than you are. You don't know what I know."

That stopped me. "What don't I know?"

"None of your business."

I reached across her cotton row to grab her arm. "Dotty Campbell, don't get high and mighty with me."

She jerked her arm away. "I'm not high and mighty!"

"Dotty!"

She glanced up at me, and I could see through the tunnel of her bonnet that she wanted to tell me.

"It's just that Jew told me he thought she needed someone to talk to, that there was something wrong with her."

"You mean Mr. Rabinowitz?"

"Well, he's the only Jew we ever knew, isn't he?" Dotty said. "Well, except Jesus."

"What else did Mr. Rabinowitz say?"

"Nothing." Dotty was silent after that, walking along the row, looking for weeds. I was thinking about what Mr. Rabinowitz had also said something to me about Pearlie needing someone to talk to.

What Dotty said next caught me off guard. "Do you think she's pregnant, maybe?"

"Good lord, Dotty! There's no reason to think that." I was thinking of Mother a few years ago when she told us she was going to have a baby. There'd been no observable symptoms at first, at least not to Dotty and me, not for several months until her waist thickened, then her middle grew round and big. Mother said it was an easy pregnancy. All she ever complained about was an occasional backache just before Junior was born.

Dotty walked away, chopping weeds. In a little while, as I worked behind her, I could hear her sniffling.

"Dotty, what's wrong?" I asked.

She started chopping weeds faster than ever, determined to get away from me.

We worked several hours longer, and the coloreds seemed to be doing their best to stay away from me as well. I could hear Pearlie's daddy singing as he worked. His voice was good enough to be on the radio. He was trim and muscular, with a scar on his face that might have been a burn scar.

"His name is Johnny." Dotty said when she saw me watching him. "Daddy told me that."

"So you finally decided to speak to me again." I said. "Why don't you tell me why you were crying?"

"And why don't you just mind your own business?" she said, moving away from me again.

Johnny moved toward one of the two little boys working beside him. They seemed too young to be doing such hard work. Johnny squatted next the boy and lifted his bare foot, gently removing a sticker before they all went back to work. I'd pulled plenty of stickers from Junior's feet myself. He always screamed like he'd been stabbed. The little colored boy didn't make a sound.

We quit working in the field around six o'clock while there was still plenty of daylight. By the time we took Pearlie and her family home to their shack and got back to our house, it was six-thirty.

As our truck pulled up in front of our house, I was surprised to see Hal's car parked in front.

"Drive around to the back!" I said

Daddy gave me a surprised look. "Why would I do that?"

"I have to go in the back door." Even if he wasn't my boyfriend, I couldn't let Hal see me in sweaty work clothes and my hair plastered to my head because of that stupid bonnet. My plan was to sneak in the back door and hurry to the bathroom where I could make a quick attempt at making myself look better.

Daddy looked at me like I had lost my mind. "You have to go in the back door? That doesn't make sense."

Dotty didn't say a word, which was unlike her.

It was too late anyway. Daddy had already stopped the pickup in the front driveway, and I saw Hal and Mother sitting on the front step.

"It's that Fitzgerald boy." Getting out of the pickup, Daddy glanced at me and shrugged, mumbling something like "Sorry."

Mother was leaning toward Hal while he talked, as if she was completely entranced by what he was saying. She put a hand on his shoulder. "Well, as you can see, she's back."

I didn't want to get out of the pickup, but Hal was walking toward me. "Hi." he said, opening the pickup door for me.

I turned away from him. "I look terrible."

He laughed. "No, you don't. You're beautiful."

"Well, you're a liar." I said, but his ridiculous comment made me laugh. Not to mention how it made my heart beat a funny rhythm. No boy had ever called me beautiful.

Taking my hand, Hal pulled me out of the pickup. "Get yourself cleaned up, and I'll take you to the picture show in Morton."

"The picture show? You said we'd go Saturday. Today's Wednesday."

"Yep. It's Wednesday."

"But…"

"They have shows during the week. Not just on weekends."

"But…"

"But you've never been in the middle of the week? You've got to live dangerously."

I stared at his crooked grin, the shock of dark hair falling at an angle across his forehead, his full lips. All of it made him look a little dangerous. Then I remembered how I looked, and ducked my head down, hurrying toward the house.

Dotty followed me into the bathroom. "You going out with him?" she asked while I ran water into the tub.

"No." I tested the water and began shedding my clothes.

Dotty grinned. "But you want to go out with him." I welcomed that grin. She was the old Dotty again.

"Who says I want to go out with him?"

"I can tell." Dotty cocked her head at me. "What's it like having two boyfriends? Doug *and* Hal. I only have one."

"You do not have a boyfriend. You're too young."

"I'm almost sixteen."

"You're not even fifteen."

"Go!" I wrapped a towel around my body and shoved her out the door. "Hey!" I called before she disappeared. "Exactly who is it you think is your boyfriend?"

"Make it quick in there because I want a bath before supper." she said, ignoring my question.

I made no attempt to hurry. In the full tub, I filled a pitcher full of water and poured it over my head, the best means we had to wash our hair without a shower. I was still rinsing out shampoo when Dotty opened the door and stuck her head in.

"He's still out there." she announced.

My first inclination was to submerge myself underwater and stay there. Instead, I sprang out of the tub, dried off quickly, slipped into my thick chenille robe, and wrapped a towel around my hair. With any luck, I could make it down the hall to our bedroom without being seen. The only way Hal might see me was if he were in Daddy's chair against the wall that provided a view of the hallway. No one ever sat in that chair when Daddy was around, so I was safe.

"Hey!"

I felt my heart drop to my stomach. If I'd been smart, I would have kept walking, but I turned to look. Hal was in Daddy's chair. Daddy was nowhere in sight. I was so embarrassed I couldn't speak—a good thing, or I would have said something stupid.

"Looking good." He flashed that crooked grin my way.

My face flushed as I hurried to the bedroom and slammed the door behind me. In a few minutes, I was dressed in clean jeans and a fresh shirt. My hair was still damp. The only way to make it look decent was to wind it up in pin curls secured with a bobby pin and wait several hours for it to dry before I brushed it out. There was no time for that. I started for the door, knowing I looked like a sad wet dog. I turned back into the room to paint my lips with Royal Red lipstick.

I steeled myself with a deep breath and marched into the living room. "Oh, hello, Hal. You're still here."

He got up from the chair, grinned again, and shrugged. At the same time, Dotty said, "You knew he'd still be here."

How long had she been in the living room with Hal? What had she said to him? I gave her the most withering look I could manage before I spoke to Hal.

"I'm sorry you waited so long for me because I can't go out with you. I already have a boyfriend."

"You belong to him or something?"

"Of course not."

"Well." he said. "I'm not asking you to marry me. I just want to take you to the picture show."

"But my hair is wet."

He laughed. "It'll be dry by the time we get to town."

"But it won't be pretty. I can't go out without fixing my hair."

"You're full of excuses." he said.

"Hello, Hal." Daddy said, coming into the living room at just the right moment to keep me from having to come up with another lame excuse. He had been in the back, probably checking on the cattle before he came in the house.

"Mr. Campbell." Hal said, offering his hand.

"You still looking for a job?" Daddy asked.

"Got one." Hal said. "I'll be driving a tractor for Mr. Sommers for a while."

"Sommers, huh? He's a good man. He'll treat you right." He glanced at me then back at Hal. "You two going someplace?"

"No." I said and at the same time Hal said, "We were going to the show but it's too late. Now I guess we'll just get a hamburger for supper at the drive-in."

"Have fun." said Daddy.

"Thanks, we will." Hal grabbed my hand.

"Don't forget, Caroline, you got to get up soon as the sun is up." Daddy called to me as Hal pulled me toward the door.

Once outside, Hal turned to me. "Look, I gotta say, if you really don't want to go, I'm not going to force you."

I looked at him for several seconds then surprised myself. "You said you'd buy me a hamburger."

His face lit up. "Let's go." he said, opening the car door for me.

We drove away parallel to a gaudy red-orange sunset streaking on the horizon. It had burnished the entire atmosphere to the color of watery wine that, along with a day of physical labor, left me feeling giddy. I forgot to be angry with Hal for showing up and at myself for being seduced into going with him. I sensed him stealing glances at me as he drove.

"I hear you're going steady with Doug McCalister."

"No." I answered,

"Everybody seems to think…"

"I don't care what everybody thinks." I said, interrupting. "I'm not going steady with him. We just. . .go out sometimes."

"Okay."

I glanced at him and saw that a little grin played at his lips, but he turned his eyes back to the road.

"I suppose Dotty told you I was going steady with Doug." I said.

"No, she didn't. She and I talked about arrowheads and digging up old bones, stuff like that."

"Dotty's favorite subject."

"She knows a lot of stuff. I'll bet she's going to be famous one of these days. You know, writing books, digging up new discoveries."

"Dotty? Writing books? She won't even write the stuff she's supposed to for school."

"Don't sell her short."

"I wouldn't think of it." I said, although the direction of the conversation surprised me. I would never have expected Hal Fitzgerald to be defending my little sister. Of course, I loved her, as I've said earlier, and would defend her against any kind of harm, but I mostly thought of her as a little brat, even though she was barely three years younger than I was. Doug thought that of her as well.

She'd been acting differently lately, though.

"We talked about Pearlie, too." Hal said. "She told me how curious you are about her."

"Did she?" Now that was the Dotty I knew—telling things she had no business saying, especially to anyone I dated.

"She seemed kind of concerned about her."

"Mmm." I said, thinking a noncommittal response was best. I didn't want to start gossiping about one of Dotty's half-baked notions like the possibility of Pearlie being pregnant. I'd heard colored girls were always getting pregnant when they weren't married.

"I take it you don't share her concern." Hal said.

"You don't know my sister. I'm not sure there's any reason to be concerned."

"Could be you don't know your sister." he said.

I felt a little jolt of alarm. "What do you mean by that?"

"She's not a dummy" he said

"I know that."

"Just don't let anyone hurt her." he added.

"I've protected her all my life." I said, sounding defensive.

He gave me an odd look as he reached to turn on the radio. "Let's see if we can find a station that's playing songs by Elvis Presley. I like his music."

"Like? I *love* him. He's playing at the convention center in Lubbock in two weeks, but I don't think Mother's going to let me go."

By the time we'd made the drive to town, I'd forgotten about the mystery of Dotty's behavior, and our conversation had given way to trying to remember all the lyrics to "Blue Moon of Kentucky." My hair was dry by the time we got to town, just as Hal had said it would be. It was falling in ringlets because of the permanent wave I'd gotten a few weeks earlier.

"You look like a movie star." Hal said while we waited for the carhop to bring our burgers. I looked down at my hands and felt my face grow warm. I was just grateful that there were no other cars at the drive-in filled with people my age to see my hair not styled. There was only one other car, parked several feet away that appeared to have two adults in it about my parents' age. "You're blushing." Hal said.

"How do you know?" I asked, managing a laugh. "It's too dark to see anything."

"I got Superman eyes." he answered. "I can even see who's in that car over there. It's Mr. Burleson and his wife."

"Burleson?" I leaned forward. "You mean the algebra teacher?"

"I didn't know he taught algebra, but that's him."

"No way, he's too uptight to be seen at a drive-in." I tried to see better, but I was momentarily blinded by the headlights of another auto pulling into the parking lot. When the lights were turned off, I clearly saw the occupants of the dilapidated pickup.

"What?" Hal asked, watching my reaction.

"That's Pearlie's parents in that pickup!"

Hal was skeptical. "How do you know that?"

"I saw them today. Daddy hired Pearlie's whole family to work in the field with us. That's her mama." I said, pointing, "and her daddy."

"You sure?"

"Positive. The side of his face? It's all scarred up. I'd know him anywhere."

"Oh yeah." Hal said. "I heard he got burned in the war."

"Where'd you hear that?"

"Mr. Rabinowitz told me."

"You mean that Jew?"

Hal's eyes were still on the colored couple. "He said Mr. Davis got burned rescuing soldiers trapped in a building."

"Mr. Davis? That's his name? I never heard anything but Johnny."

"Johnny Davis." Hal said. "Mr. Rabinowitz says he risked his life to save two young white soldiers. Said he deserves the Medal of Honor. Mr. Davis was in an army hospital for six months or more."

"Well, that was brave of him.'

"He'll never get a medal, though." Hal said as if he hadn't heard me. "I guess they don't give it out to niggers."

"You mean coloreds."

"Yeah, whatever."

"But if he saved two white men… "

I didn't finish the sentence, but Hal didn't seem to notice. His eyes were on the wide window of the drive-in. The restaurant's two carhops were sitting on stools, staring out at the Davises. Behind them, a man in a greasy apron was talking in an animated way, gesturing toward the Davis' car, shaking his head.

"They're not going to come out and take their order." Hal said.

"I guess they're not supposed to." I said.

Hal turned his head suddenly to look at me. "Not supposed to on accounta they're colored." Hal was silent a moment, still looking toward the Davises. "I wonder if those two soldiers cared if it was a nigger that was rescuing them."

I didn't reply. There *were* rules about who could sit or eat where or drink out of which water fountain—rules I never questioned. I turned my gaze back to the Davises' pickup, trying to see more clearly the awful scar on his face.

Instead, I saw Mr. Burleson get out of his car. He was in a hurry, and he almost knocked down the food tray attached to his window. He walked toward the Davises with long, quick strides. Tapping on the window of the old pickup, I heard him shouting. "Roll down the damn window!"

Lights from the interior of the drive-in glared like an obscene sun showing too much truth, and I could see round-as-moons faces pressed to the window. Johnny's and his wife's faces were turned away from me, all of their attention on Mr. Burleson. He was talking to Johnny, but had lowered his voice so I couldn't make out what he was saying. He flung his arm in an exaggerated gesture toward the street, and Johnny's wife reached her hand toward her husband. He briefly looked at her, then started the pickup and backed out of the parking spot.

Mr. Burleson watched them go, hands on his wide hips until the Davises' pickup was on the street, headed toward the outskirts of town.

"Shit." Hal said.

"Johnny should have known they don't serve coloreds here. I mean most places don't, you know."

Hal turned to me, an odd look on his face. "Yeah. I know." He sounded almost angry. "Real Christian, huh?"

His tone made me defensive. "Nobody says they're not children of God, just like we are. They're just different, that's all. God made us different, and we're supposed to live our own..."

"Bullshit!" Hal said. "Where'd you come up with that crap?" He took a cigarette from his shirt pocket and lit it with the car's lighter.

"Hal, it's what everybody says, the preacher, my mother, even the teachers at school..."

"You don't have to believe it just because they say it. How are they different?" Hal demanded. "How, besides the color of their skin?"

I shook my head. "Don't be ridiculous. You know as well as I do that coloreds are different from us in more ways than their color. Like Mr. Rabinowitz."

"We're all different." Hal said in a calmer voice, the cigarette dangling from his lips. "I'm different from you. You're different from your mother. That doesn't justify hate or prejudice."

"Good lord, Hal, you sound like a Yankee. I don't hate anybody. I just know the way things are."

"You have no idea of the way things are, sweetheart. No idea at all." He honked the horn to signal the carhop to come pick up our tray.

"Don't be condescending to me." I said.

Hal gave me a look that almost frightened me. But then he smiled and said, "Okay."

We drove home in an awkward silence until Hal made a lame attempt to return things to normal. "So what did you do all day besides work in the cotton field?"

"Nothing." I said and added, "Unfortunately." I was thinking of my second feeble attempt to talk to Pearlie. I was trying to be nice. Didn't that prove I wasn't filled with hate or prejudice? The silence between Hal and me was growing longer, so I made my own attempt to alleviate the awkwardness. "Dotty thinks Pearlie may be pregnant."

I regretted the words as soon as I spoke them. It sounded like gossip. I'd spoken without thinking. My words lingered, polluting the space between us. I knew Hal had felt the shock of the words when he suddenly said, "Why does she think that?"

"I don't know." I tried to laugh, hoping it would signal I didn't take the possibility of Pearlie's pregnancy seriously.

"Don't go spreading stuff like that around." he said.

"I wouldn't do that!"

"You just told me."

I turned away from him, looking out the window into the darkness. I'd never felt lower. What I had said was nothing more than gossip, and beyond that I'd managed to make Hal think I was full of hate and prejudice toward colored people. But that couldn't be true, so why did I feel so awful? Why were tears filling my eyes and running down my cheeks?

"You just don't know, sweetheart." he said, eyes on the road. "You have no idea the way things really are."

CHAPTER 7

Pearlie

S he felt better the next morning. Not that she felt great. She still
hadn't started her period or, as her mama called it, had her visit
from Aunt Flo.

A few days back Mama had started in on Pearlie wanting to
know if she was upset about something. Pearlie told her no, nothing
was wrong, but she wouldn't let up. Mama kept at it for three days,
wanting to know what's wrong. Pearlie wasn't about to tell her. She
knew better than that, on account of Mama would have a hissy fit,
cause trouble with certain people, then things would be even worse
for Pearlie.

The only person she'd spoken the truth to was Mr. Rabinowitz,
and she only told him because he was so nice—kind and gentle. Like
Jesus. The Bible says Jesus was a Jew too. Pearlie wondered if kind and
nice came natural with being a Jew. If it did, then she couldn't help
wishing everybody was a Jew.

Pearlie could tell by the way he was treated that some people
didn't like Mr. Rabinowitz just because he was a Jew. People wouldn't
go in his store, and would even cross the street so they wouldn't have
to come in contact with him when he was out and about. Pearlie
couldn't figure out what difference it made to people if somebody

was a Jew. He wasn't colored. As far as Pearlie could tell, the reason white folks don't like black folks was because they are colored. When she thought about it, that didn't make sense neither. It made her head hurt to ponder it.

While she waited with her family to be picked up and taken to a cotton field, she vowed she wasn't going to dwell on it so she could enjoy feeling just a little better.

It was only a few minutes later when Mr. Campbell dropped her and her family off at his cotton field to hoe weeds. The two Campbell girls were already working when Pearlie and her family arrived. Dotty, the kind of strange one, was walking along chopping at weeds like they were snakes fixing to bite. Caroline, the nosey, dreamy one, lagged behind, chopping in a haphazard way, like she didn't have her mind on it.

Pearlie was feeling so good she even said good morning when she came up alongside Caroline on the row next to her. "Good morning, Miss Caroline." she said real low, but Caroline heard her.

Caroline looked at her, surprised, and said good morning back.

Pearlie kept working and managed to get ahead of Caroline, but she could tell Caroline was still watching.

Pretty soon Caroline caught up with her. "Hey, Pearlie. It's okay for us to talk out here in the field."

Pearlie didn't answer.

"That time on the bus?" said Caroline. "I wasn't trying to get you in trouble. I hope you know that"

Pearlie nodded.

"I was just trying to be friendly, Pearlie." said Caroline, a serious look on her face.

"Why you trying to be friendly to me?"

Pearlie was aware of Caroline stopping, letting Pearlie get farther ahead. "Why not?" Caroline asked. "Why wouldn't I want to be friendly with you?"

That made Pearlie think for just a minute maybe Caroline was weak minded. Pearlie turned around fast, and snapped at her. "On accounta I'm colored."

Caroline gave her a funny look, which Pearlie ignored. Instead, she started chopping away at the patch of blue weeds she'd found herself in. Pearlie could feel some kind of powerful mood coming off of Caroline, but couldn't tell what it was. Couldn't tell if Caroline was mad or if her feelings were hurt or if she was just looking down her nose at her.

After a while, Caroline said from behind her, "I'm sorry, Pearlie. I didn't mean to upset you."

When Caroline said that, Pearlie felt a catch in her throat and chest. She didn't reply, though. She just kept on chopping weeds, mostly because she didn't know *what* to say.

It pretty well ruined Pearlie's day though. She couldn't get her spirits back up, so she just kept working as hard as she could until it was time to go home. Pearlie knew she ought not to let a white girl get her down like that. Especially when, if she told herself the truth, Caroline hadn't really done or said nothing bad to her. Maybe it was true she was just trying to be friendly. But the two of them couldn't be friends. There had to be something up with that girl.

Still feeling down after supper, when she came back to the house and after she'd finished helping Mama clean up the kitchen, Pearlie decided to take a walk.

The long stretch of dirt road seemed to go nowhere. All a person could see on either side of it were fields of cotton. The dryland cotton wasn't tall yet, just about six, seven inches. It was pretty and green, though, and the straight rows were a wonder to look at as she walked along. But Pearlie preferred looking straight ahead, where the road led the way to where sky and earth come together. Pearlie knew they didn't really come together. Still, she liked the idea, imagining she could step right on up into the sky. Right into heaven. Even if that wasn't so, it was nice thinking about going to heaven where everybody treated you good. It would be even nicer if you didn't have to die to do it. There'd been times when Pearlie had wished she were dead, but right now wasn't one of them.

The sky on the horizon was turning red, streaked with yellow and a purple so dark it was nearly black. Red sky at night, sailors' delight. Red sky in the morning, sailors take warning. Uncle Thaddeus said that all the time. People were talking about sailing on the ocean when they come up with that old saying. Pearlie had never seen the ocean, and probably never would. She had seen Monument Lake, though. Sometimes when it rained, the lake filled up and white people went there to swim and have picnics on the shore. Sure would be nice to get in a cool lake when the weather was so hot.

Pearlie was walking along thinking all these thoughts when she heard something way off behind her. A car was coming her way, stirring up dust from the road. She moved to the side, out of the way.

It whipped by her like a shiny black bat flying out of hell. She recognized the car, and knew it meant trouble. Sure enough, the car stopped a little ways up the road, its tires making a scrubbing sound against the hard-packed dirt. The motor squealed as the car backed toward her. She moved farther off the road so that she was walking in the ditch. The ditch was full of tall Johnson Grass that made her legs itch, and there were a lot of Goat Head stickers chewing into her bare feet. Still, there was no way she was getting out of the ditch.

It was less than a minute before she realized how much of a fool she's been to think staying in the ditch would help. When the car stopped, he opened the door and got out. "Hey Pearlie! Hey nigger girl! Ain't no use in you running." He was laughing and chasing after her. In no time, he caught her and grabbed her arm. She tried to jerk free, but lost her balance and fell into the Johnson Grass and stickers. She wanted to cry because the stickers were biting her legs and arms, even her neck. But she wouldn't let him see her tears.

"Now you shouldn't run from me." he said, jerking Pearlie to her feet. "I ain't going to hurt you. I'm gonna treat you nice."

"No! I ain't going with you no more." she shouted while he pulled her toward the car. She tried to plant her feet, but it did no good. He pulled her by her arms, her feet dragging behind her, scraping her toes until they bled. By the time he got her into the back seat, Pearlie had lost her battle with her tears.

"Shut up, bitch!" he yelled.

The first time it had happened she'd just gotten off of the bus he drove at the colored school on the edge of Morton. He'd grabbed her from behind and forced her into a car. As the car drove away, he had talked to her in a voice he must have thought sweet, but it made her sick to hear it. "It's okay, Pearlie. I ain't going to hurt you. I just want some a that sweet black pussy."

She remembered how the car had slowed down and headed off the road, bumping across a pasture until they stopped in front of an abandoned boxcar.

She was there again, the same boxcar. He pulled her out of the car. She tried to hold back, but her feet were bleeding and hurting from the stickers. They were hurting even more as she was dragged across the pasture's dry grass.

He slid open the boxcar door, and she saw the dirty old mattress on the floor that she'd seen the other time. The boxcar had been used in the past to house field workers like her family. Sometimes it was Mexicans that came up from New Mexico to work, and sometimes it was coloreds. The floorboards were beginning to break down and there were long cracks in the walls.

He threw her on the mattress and held her down with his knee. Then he was on top of her. She tried not to cry. She tried to think about walking to the end of the road where it leads on up into heaven.

CHAPTER 8

Caroline

"I think Nigger Johnny tried to kill him." Sheriff Homer Maylock said to Mr. Rabinowitz one day when I was in the New York Store.

Sure, I wasn't supposed to be in there, but Raylene Propps had come by in her daddy's new Nash on a Thursday afternoon and asked if I wanted to go to town with her. Since we were finished with working the field for the time being, Mother said I could go as long as I was home by dark. I dressed up in a full gathered skirt over two mesh petticoats to make it stand out and flounce when I walked. I wore bobbysocks and saddle oxfords. I'd polished both the white and brown leather until the shoes gleamed. I'd even soaked the shoestrings overnight in bleach. My hair was curled and brushed as close to perfection as I could make it. Once we were in town, I told Raylene I wanted to go to The New York Store.

She smirked. "There's nothing in there to buy. Let's go to St. Clair's. They have poodle skirts. I'm dying to get one."

"They'll be expensive."

"How do you know? Have you even looked at them?"

"No, but..." I grabbed her hand and pulled her toward The New York Store. "Just come with me. I just want to look around. No more than five minutes, I promise. Then we'll go to St. Clair's."

"You are so weird." Raylene grumbled. "It'll be embarrassing if anybody sees us." Nevertheless, she let me drag her into the store. We were standing together looking at celluloid Kewpie dolls, and Raylene was going on about how cheap-looking they were. "Nobody but Mexicans ever buy these things." she said.

Just then, I saw the sheriff and Mr. Rabinowitz come out of the back where Mr. Rabinowitz had his office, and Sheriff Maylock said those words about Johnny. I knew he meant Pearlie's daddy. Raylene heard him too. She nudged me and signaled with her eyes toward the men, then looked down at the tiny doll in her hand, pretending not to listen.

The sheriff said something inaudible to Mr. Rabinowitz and hurried from the door. Mr. Rabinowitz wore a grim look on his face as he moved toward the interior of the store.

"Let's get out of here." Raylene said.

I ignored her and purposely intersected Mr. Rabinowitz. "Who was he talking about?" I asked.

Raylene pulled on my arm. "Good lord, Caroline! Come on!"

Mr. Rabinowitz looked at me with interest. "I think you heard him. He was speaking of Mr. Davis."

"No, I mean, who does he think Johnny Davis murdered?"

"Caroline!" Raylene hurried toward the front door without me, utterly embarrassed.

Mr. Rabinowitz shook his head. "No one was murdered, and the sheriff doesn't have any proof of anything."

"But…"

"Your friend is waiting for you." he said, gesturing with his head toward Raylene. Through the front window, I could see she was walking toward the drugstore. Mr. Rabinowitz left to greet another customer.

When I managed to catch up to Raylene, she was seething. Grabbing my arm, she pulled me toward Turpin's Drug. "If you *ever* do anything like that again, I'll kill you." she said, between clenched teeth.

"Do what? I don't know why you're so upset. Don't you wonder…?"

"No, I don't wonder about anything. Probably just another nigger he tried to kill. You know they're always murdering each other."

"I don't think Johnny Davis would want to hurt anyone."

"Smart as you are, Caroline, you don't have common sense. You don't know Johnny Davis any better than I do—which is not at all. How could you possibly know him? He's a nigger." She pulled at my arm again. "Come on. I want to see if Turpin's has any Chanel Number Five."

"Really?" I said. "That smells like something my grandma would wear."

"No, it does not. It's a sophisticated, cosmopolitan scent."

"Where'd you get that idea?"

"I read it in my mother's *Redbook*."

Our conversation degenerated further after Raylene asked Alma Turpin, the store owner's wife, for the perfume along with several others with names like *Je Reviens* and Shalimar and Evening in Paris. Wearing a bored expression, Alma supplied samples, commenting now and then. "This one is very nice for young women," or "Here's a classic scent." Raylene kept dabbing her wrists and the inside of her arms as well as mine with the various samples until I felt I'd completely lost my sense of smell. The entire time, I kept my eye on the open door where a fan whirled overhead just outside the entrance. I watched the sidewalk and street just in case I saw the sheriff dragging Johnny off to jail.

Mrs. Houser entered the store, fanning herself with a handkerchief and dressed in a shirtwaist dress of light blue printed cotton. A little blue hat topped her curly grey hair. Mrs. Houser was the girl's Sunday School teacher at the Baptist church Raylene's family and mine attended.

"Oh, hello, girls." she said when she spotted us. "Are y'all here alone?" Before we could answer, she added. "Better get home. Awful news, isn't it?" She glanced toward the back and called out to Rob Turpin, the store's owner. "My prescription ready, Robby?"

"Hello, Mrs. Houser." Rob said without looking up from whatever he was doing behind the counter.

Mrs. Houser started toward the back, her cotton dress swishing around her ample hips, her black purse swinging from her wrist. She turned around just before reaching the prescription counter and admonished us. "Get on home, girls. I wouldn't want a daughter of mine out at a time like this."

Seeing the puzzled looks on our faces, Alma said, "She's right, you know."

I knew Mrs. Houser was talking about the same thing Homer Maylock had mentioned, but I wanted to pry more information out of anyone I could. I asked Alma, "What did she mean by what's going on?"

"Y'all haven't heard?" Alma gave us a surprised look. "She's talking about Jasper Hutchinson. Some nigger tried to kill him."

"Hutch?" I said, shocked.

"Oh, my Lord." said Raylene.

"I don't know when he was attacked." Alma said, excited now to share the news, "But the sheriff said Hutch's mama claimed he never came home last night. The sheriff found his car out east of town on the Levelland highway. It had blood all over it. They found him in the hospital. Somebody dumped him there in the front while it was dark and drove off. He was unconscious when they found him."

"Why does the sheriff think a colored tried to kill him?" I asked.

"When he woke up, Hutch told him it was Johnny. On top of that, Homer claims he saw Hutch and that nigger Johnny yesterday, arguing out on the courthouse square." Alma said, motioning toward the courthouse with her head. "Johnny tried to kill him later last night."

"But if he dropped him off at the hospital, maybe he never meant…"

"Probably got scared because he couldn't finish the job fast enough." said Alma.

"Is there any proof it was Johnny?"

Alma shrugged. "That's who Hutch claimed done it."

I felt both sick and scared at the same time. Johnny Davis attacking someone? He couldn't possibly have. I'd worked in our field with him for more than a week, never more than a few rows of cotton away from him. I'd seen him comfort a crying child, heard him singing in his beautiful voice. He was a war hero.

"Well, Homer will have him in jail pretty soon, so he won't be a danger to any of us." Raylene said.

Alma wearily shook her head. "I swear, sometimes I think they ought to lock 'em all up. It's just plain scary the way they're always killing somebody."

"Always?" I asked. "We haven't had a murder around here in a long time."

"Honey, we don't always know when they kill each other. Mostly we just hear when they try to kill a white person. They murder each other all the time."

"I just can't believe that's…"

"She's right." Mrs. Houser said, plodding toward us and interrupting me. Her plump hips made her walk like she was treading through mud. "You never know about coloreds. Some of 'em may be Christian, but they're not like us. They're just different. That's why I'm telling you girls to go on home. Things could blow up into trouble here in town."

"Johnny might be a colored, but he's no troublemaker." I said.

"Caroline, we've got to go home." Raylene said, interrupting again. Her voice was unusually loud, and she gave me a look of warning before starting for the door. Before I could protest, she giggled nervously and looked at Alma, shaking her head and rolling her eyes. "I'll be back later." she said and moved her eyes toward me as if to say I was something to be dealt with. "I still want the Chanel, but I'll just get it later."

"Y'all come back and see us, hear?" Rob called from the back.

"What did you do that for?" I asked when we were out on the sidewalk. Anger sliced my words.

"Don't get huffy." Raylene said. "I just saved you from looking stupid in front of Alma and Rob and Mrs. Houser."

"I wasn't about to look stupid. I was just trying to make a point."

"It was the wrong time to make a point." she said. "Now, come on. Let's get to St. Clair's before old lady Houser comes out and sees us and tries to make us go home again."

"Aren't you going to buy the perfume?"

"I'm not going to pay that ridiculous price. I'd rather buy it in Lubbock next time Mother goes. I'll probably get better quality there anyway."

I followed Raylene to the department store, annoyed she was so bossy and unreasonable, but also annoyed at myself for being at her mercy, since we'd come to town in her car. I was in no mood to shop for anything, although I'd wanted a poodle skirt for weeks.

Hutch being attacked and Johnny being accused of it weighed heavily on my mind. I sat in the store's shoe section while Raylene tried on a poodle skirt. She flirted with Troy Bannon at the cash register when she bought it. Troy was a Morton boy who worked at St. Clair's after school and during the summer. His twin sister, Joy, dated a boy from our school.

"You're gonna look great in that skirt." Troy said, punching the cash register keys.

"You think so?" Raylene asked, pretending to be shy.

"Sure, you will. You're even cuter than that little puppy dog that's embroidered on there."

Raylene giggled and let her hand linger on his when she took her change.

"You sure you don't need shoes to go with that skirt?" Troy asked. "We got a shipment of ballerinas in yesterday."

"Ooo, I'd love to have a pair of ballerinas, but not today." cooed Raylene. "I'll be back, though. I'll buy 'em later."

"I hope so." Troy said. I had to admit, even from where I was sitting back in the shoe department, the way he smiled at Raylene looked kind of charming.

She called to me to come on because she had to get home. She turned back to Troy and giggled again. When I followed her out, Troy winked at me as I walked past him.

"Why are you so quiet?" Raylene asked as she drove us home. "You're not still mad, are you?"

"No."

"Then why are you sulking?"

"I'm not. I just don't feel like talking."

"You still upset about that old nigger being accused of hurting Hutch?" That sounded like an accusation, as if it was a bad thing to be upset. "There's nothing you can do about it."

"I noticed Troy didn't even mention it." I said, adding, "Maybe he hasn't heard about it."

"Of course, he has. Everybody in town must know about it by now."

"Well, I think it's odd he didn't mention it."

"He's cute, isn't he? I think he likes me."

It seemed like that ride home was never going to end. When we finally arrived, I didn't invite her in. I just opened the door and got out as quickly as I could. All I said was, "Bye. Thanks for the ride. See ya."

Raylene stared at me with a stunned expression when I turned around at the front door and waved before hurrying inside the house.

Our living room seemed a sanctuary as I closed the door and stood a moment, enjoying the quiet. My instinct was to flop on the couch and close my eyes against an approaching headache, but I wanted to see my family. I needed to share the awful news.

I found Mother seated at the kitchen table as usual, writing the news for the weekly paper. She was so intent upon her work, she didn't seem to notice I had entered the room.

"I'm home." I said.

She looked up with a surprised expression. "Oh! I didn't hear you come in." She went back to scribbling and, without looking at me asked, "Did you hear any news?"

"Yes."

She shoved a blank piece of paper at me. "Write it down, and I'll add it to his week's submission."

I found it hard to speak, but Mother didn't seem to notice my silence. Finally, I said, "Somebody tried to kill Jasper Hutchinson. They think it was Johnny Davis."

Mother's pen suspended over the ruled tablet she used to write her news. "Johnny tried to kill Hutch? Who says so?"

"I heard Sheriff Maylock talking about it. Hutch got dumped off at the hospital unconscious. When he woke up, he said Johnny did it."

"Lord,! You girls have been working in the field with that man!"

I nodded and tried to speak again, but my throat was too constricted.

Mother stood up abruptly, letting her pen roll across the table and onto the floor. "I've got to drive out to the field and tell George right now! A coldblooded murderer!"

"Wait a minute, Mother." I called. "Nobody was murdered. Just beat up, and Johnny hasn't been proven guilty. It could be somebody else."

Mother turned. "For heaven's sake, Caroline, if Homer Maylock thinks Johnny did it, I'm sure he did."

"It's not right to talk like that, Mother! Nobody in America is guilty until…"

Her face was red with anger. "You talk back to me like that, and you won't be going out with Raylene or Doug or anybody for a month! Now get outside and find Dotty. Get her in the house where it's safe."

I opened my mouth to protest again, but instead held my tongue, not wanting to get myself in deeper trouble. I followed her outside and walked passed her as she got in the pickup and started toward the field. I was headed to the draw, assuming that was where Dotty would be found.

She was there, but instead of digging for arrowheads as I expected, Dotty sat on the ground, hands and head resting on her knees.

"Dotty, are you all right?" She looked up at me, and I saw her pale face. "Dotty, what's wrong?"

"Nothing." She stood and rubbed her eyes then picked up a shovel and started scraping the ground but without her usual vigor. She'd been digging earlier, though. I saw fresh dirt turned over outside the wide square she'd dug before.

I went down to her, putting my arm around her shoulder. "Tell me what's wrong." She brushed me away and didn't respond. "I came to tell you something about Hutch." I said, desperate to get her attention.

It worked. She abruptly turned to me with a frightened look. "The sheriff thinks somebody tried to kill him. He was hurt bad, and is in the hospital."

I expected her to be shocked but instead she turned away and made a few more scrapes at the ground.

"Sheriff Maylock thinks Johnny Davis did it." She whirled around to look at me with shock, and I had a sense of satisfaction that I'd gotten a reaction. In the next moment, she threw down the shovel and screamed, a sound so eerie and animal-like it scared me.

She scurried from the draw and ran toward the house. I ran after her calling her name, following her all the way to our bedroom. But I wasn't fast enough. She slammed the door and locked it.

I was slumped on the living room couch when Mother came home. I ran to her as soon as she came in the door. "Dotty locked herself in our room and she won't come out." My voice cracked with the alarm I felt at my sister's strange reaction. "I told her about Hutch and Johnny. Make her come out! I'm worried about her."

"Leave her alone." Mother said. "She's the only one acting like she's got a lick of sense. Unlike your daddy. All he said was Johnny Davis wouldn't hurt anybody. Then he said he had to get back to work." Exhaling a heavy sigh, Mother walked into the bedroom she shared with Daddy, slamming the door behind her.

CHAPTER 9

Pearlie

Pearlie knew that what had happened to her those two times wasn't her fault. Still, it made her ashamed. Afraid as well. Afraid he'd do it a third time. Afraid because she still hadn't had her period. Afraid of what was in for her for the rest of her life.

Mama noticed again that she wasn't acting right, and had kept asking what was wrong. When Pearlie said nothing was wrong, Mama said she was acting sulky.

"I don't know what's wrong with you, Pearlie." she said for what seemed like the hundredth time. "You acting strange. You been talking to that white girl again? That Caroline Campbell? I seen you talking to her in the field when I told you not to. I mean it, too. Don't get chummy with no white girl. It'll just lead to trouble. Just mind your own business."

"I ain't trying to get chummy, Mama. I just answer her questions."

"What kinda questions?"

"She asked me what my name is one time."

When Mama didn't speak, Pearlie added, "Then I asked her one time why she be watching me."

Mama's eyes grew big. "Lord, Pearlie, it ain't your place to ask a white girl that."

Pearlie shrugged. "Didn't 'mount to anything. She just said she wasn't watching me, but she was."

Mama shook her head and frowned. "Stay away from her, you hear me? Stay away from that Caroline Campbell."

Mama said it like Caroline Campbell was some kind of dangerous, while Pearlie knew she wasn't. Caroline just didn't know anything about life in the real world, and that was on account of her being a white girl. Most white girls didn't know the way things were. That was just another way they was lucky.

If Pearlie was white or Caroline was black, Pearlie was pretty sure they could be friends. Caroline was nice enough and smart about stuff, but she was also dumb.

Dotty Campbell, on the other hand, knew a few things. Pearlie thought she'd probably learned something from Uncle Thaddeus. People didn't know it, but Dottie talked to him quite a bit. There was this big old draw out behind the Campbell place where Uncle Thaddeus sometimes liked to walk. Pearlie had followed him once or twice.

For some reason, Dotty was fond of digging with a shovel in that old draw. Pearlie had no idea what Dotty was looking for or what she talked about with Uncle Thaddeus. She never got close enough to hear.

Lots of times, Pearlie wished she was dumb like Caroline. It would be so fine if she didn't have to think about what Hutch had done to her them two times.

"Get the lead outta your pants, Pearlie. It nearly daylight." That was Mama yelling at her. They were going to work in Mr. Propps's field this morning because they had gotten the Campbell field and the McCallick field laid by for a few weeks. They'd move on for now, but they'd probably be back at the Campbells's if it rained again and more weeds sprouted.

Everyone was ready to go to work except Pearlie. She was having a hard time getting started because she hadn't slept much for a few nights. All she could do was lie in bed and try not to cry. She also tried not to think about what Hutch had done to her but couldn't push the memory of it away. And even if she could talk to Mama about it, Mama would just tell her to pray about it. Pearlie couldn't do that. How could she pray to a god that let that happen to her?

"Pearlie, you hear me?"

"Yes'm." Pearlie said and glanced at Papa leaning against the door frame drinking his coffee. He looked sad too. He seemed that way a lot. Maybe a person got that way, sad all the time, when they'd lived forty years like Papa. It made Pearlie wonder what kind of bad things had happened to him that he didn't talk about.

So Mama wouldn't yell at her again, Pearlie ran out of the room without tying her shoes. She could tie them on the way to the cotton field. She stopped in the middle of the kitchen when she heard a loud knock at the door.

"Open the door, nigger!"

"Shut up and let me do the talking, kid." another voice said.

Papa spun around and opened the door, coffee cup still in his hand and some of it sloshing over the edge. He met Sheriff Homer Maylock face to face. Another man Pearlie had never seen before was with him.

Maylock glanced at Mama, then at Pearlie and the boys. Uncle Thaddeus was nowhere in sight. He must have stepped out to the privy.

"Step outside, Johnny." said the sheriff.

"Sure." Papa put down his coffee cup. "What this all about, Sheriff?"

"We'll do the questioning." the other man, who must have been a deputy, said. Before the door closed, Pearlie could see the deputy jerk Papa's hands behind his back. Through the shack's thin walls, Pearlie heard, "You're under arrest for the attempted murder of Jasper Hutchinson."

Mama screamed and opened the door, shouting after the men. "He never tried to kill nobody."

Sheriff Maylock looked at her and shook his head. Pearlie didn't know what that head shake meant. All she knew was that the sheriff didn't look happy, like he didn't like what he was doing.

Everyone watched as Maylock and the other man took Johnny to the police car and shoved him in the back seat. Pearlie had to hold on to Mama to keep her from running after them. She was screaming, "Let him go! He never done nothing."

Pearlie could see Papa in the backseat of the car, and that other man, the one she thought was the deputy, was pointing his pistol at him. Pearlie wanted to run out there herself and knock that gun out of his hands. If he shot Papa, what would she do? What would they all do? But she didn't run . She just stayed with Mama.

Seconds later Maylock was back in the house.

"Sit down." The sheriff took Mama's arm and with a gentleness that surprised Pearlie, led her to the bed in the living room that Mama and Papa shared. Mama sat on the edge, frightened.

"Johnny never tried to kill nobody." she said again.

"Where was he last night?" the sheriff asked.

"With me and the kids." Mama said. "We was all here. After we got done working in the Propps's field."

"What time did you get home?"

Pearlie could see Mama trembling. Her brothers Todd and Luthy stood next to the table, wide-eyed, too scared to say anything. Pearlie went to them and put an arm around each of them.

"We come home early." Mama said. "I don't know, maybe seven o'clock. We all got to get up early and go to work."

"What time did Johnny come back after he brought y'all home?" asked the sheriff.

"What you talking about?" Mama said. "Johnny come home with us. Never went out again. He stay in bed with me all night."

"You're lying, Mozelle." Maylock said. "We both know it." He turned to Pearlie and pointed a finger. "That girl your daughter?"

"Yessir." Mama's voice sounded like an out-of-tune string on Uncle Thaddeus's fiddle. "But she been here all…"

"You know Jasper Hutchinson, don't you?" he said, his eyes on Pearlie.

"Yessir." Pearlie's voice was barely audible. Something was terribly wrong. She knew her papa had gone out again last night because Uncle Thaddeus had talked him into taking him to town to get some rheumatism medicine. Uncle Thaddeus's rheumatism medicine was the kind he bought from a bootlegger. She also knew they were late getting home.

"I hear he gave you some trouble on the school bus."

"No sir." I say. "He never caused me no trouble."

Maylock frowned. "That's not what I hear. He told me he had to chew you out for not following the rules. For bothering white kids on the bus."

"No sir." Pearlie said. "I don't bother nobody, and Mr. Hutch never chewed me out."

"Uh huh. And I guess you never came home and told your daddy about it, did you?"

"No sir."

Maylock looked at her for a moment then shook his head and took a deep breath. "I hope you ain't lyin' to me."

Pearlie wanted to tell him she was no liar, but she was too afraid to speak. In the next moment he was asking her where she was yesterday afternoon.

"Workin' in Mr. Propps's cotton field, then I come home."

He paused before speaking again. "You know where that old railcar is—the one on the highway?

Pearlie could feel her heart leaping wildly, and she was sure Maylock could hear it. She looked down at her hands, wondering what he knew and how. "No sir." she managed to say.

"You sure?"

Her mouth felt too dry to speak, but she finally managed to say, "Yes sir. I sure."

The expression on Maylock's face puzzled her. She couldn't tell whether he was sad or just mad. He turned away again and spoke to Mama. "Now you tell me where your man was last night."

"I told you, sir." Mama say. "He at home with me and the kids."

The sheriff gave her a hard look. "Damn, I hope you're right."

Pearlie saw sweat pop out on her mama's forehead, and she was afraid her mother was about to faint. She wanted to tell the white sheriff that her mama didn't ever lie, and that Papa *was* home last night, even though she knew he wasn't. She wanted to tell him not to swear in front of Mama, that Papa never cussed in front of her. But Pearlie didn't speak, afraid she would somehow make things even worse.

"I'm taking your man to jail, the sheriff said to Mama. He looked like he wanted to say more, but he said nothing. He left, slamming the door behind him.

Mama was still sitting on the edge of the bed. Her whole body quivered, making Pearlie think of a string pulled so tight it was about to break. She went to her and put her arms around her, but Mama didn't move. Her body was rigid, and Pearlie could tell she trying not to cry. Both boys were wailing and hanging onto her legs.

"It gonna be all right, Mama." Pearlie said, though she didn't mean it.

Her mama sat for several seconds longer, staring straight ahead. When she got up, she told Pearlie and the boys to go outside and wait for Mr. Propps to come in his truck to pick them up and take them to his cotton field.

CHAPTER 10

Caroline

When Dotty finally came out of the bedroom, she looked upset. "You all right, hon?" Mother asked.

Dotty nodded.

Mother put her arm around Dotty. "I'm sorry, baby. I know you feel bad about this. We aren't used to hearing about people trying to kill each other around here."

"Yeah." said Dotty, pulling away from Mother and sitting in Daddy's chair.

"Try not to think about it." Mother said. "Let's watch TV. That'll get your mind off of things."

She crossed the room to turn on the television. We got our two channels out of Lubbock, and the reception wasn't always reliable in spite of the tall antenna Daddy had installed on top of the house. After a few seconds, a snowy picture emerged. A man's voice came out of the whiteness telling women Tide detergent would get their clothes cleaner. Next came organ music and another man's voice speaking in measured tones that always sounded creepy. "The…Edge…Of… Night."

I tried to watch as a man and woman worked out the plans to blackmail another man, more organ music, more words about laundry soap, a woman walking down a shadowy street. I was having a tough time following the story because my thoughts kept drifting to our own drama.

I abandoned the soap opera and went to the bedroom to find *The Catcher in the Rye*. I had just opened the book to the page where I left off and slumped on the floor, leaning against the chest when Dotty came into the room.

She sat on the floor next to me. "I can't stop thinking about it, no matter what Mother says."

"I know."

"He's a rat."

"Hutch?"

"Yeah. And Johnny Davis didn't try to kill him."

"I hope not."

Dotty stood up and went to the window. The windmill creaked and groaned in the breeze. "I know Johnny Davis didn't do it because I know who did."

"What?" I sprang to my feet. "How could you possibly know. . .?"

Dotty turned around slowly to look at me. "Don't ever ask me."

"Dotty..."

There were tears in her eyes. "I just had to tell somebody that I knew who did it. I knew I could tell you, Caroline, but I can't say any more." She stared at me several seconds, tears streaming down her face, before adding in a whisper. "I know you won't tell. I know I can trust you."

Something as dark and stifling as a March sandstorm swallowed me. I couldn't speak, couldn't move. Coming to my side, Dotty put her thin, bony arms around me. I felt her heart galloping as she pressed against me.

"You. . .you. . .ought. . .to tell me." I stammered.

"Maybe I ought to." she whispered, pulling herself out of my embrace. "I'll think about it."

At just that moment, Jesus started barking.

"Someone just drove up." I said.

Within seconds, there was a knock at the door, and Jesus had stopped barking. Either he recognized the visitors or they had given him a friendly rub between his ears. He was not the world's best watch dog. We could hear male voices along with Mother's. There was a knock on our bedroom door. Without waiting for an answer, Mother stuck her head in.

"Someone here to see you, Caroline."

"I don't want to see anybody." I said.

"It's Sheriff Maylock." said Mother, looking worried.

The stifling darkness around me thickened. "Why?"

"Maybe about. . .you know, what happened to Hutch?"

"I don't know anything about it."

"You'd better talk to him anyway." Mother said, glancing at Dotty. "You feeling better, Dotty?"

"Not so much." she answered.

"I'll bet it's that corn." Mother said. "Every time you eat fresh corn. . .Go on, Caroline. Don't keep the sheriff waiting."

I reluctantly walked into the hall toward the living room as I heard Mother telling Dotty she was going to give her a dose of Pepto-Bismol.

Sheriff Maylock was seated on the couch, watching the end of *The Edge of Night*. He stood when I entered the room.

"Hello, Caroline." He extended his hand toward me. I was seventeen, not used to shaking hands with anyone, but I took his hand anyway. He held it for only a second in a dry, rough grip before letting go. "We can talk outside if you want to." His eyes shifted toward our bedroom where I could still hear the murmur of voices.

Did he think I had something to say that no one else should hear? "No, it's okay. We can talk here." I said, as if to reassure both of us I had nothing to hide.

"Sit down." he said.

I sat in Daddy's chair. Maybe I thought it would give me a little more confidence. The sheriff settled himself on the couch.

"I want to talk to you about Wednesday night." he said.

"I went to Morton with a friend." I said.

Haylock nodded. "Hal Fitzgerald. I know."

It bothered me that he knew that. It made me feel as if he'd been spying on me, but I didn't say anything. I just sat staring at him, hoping he couldn't hear the thunder in my chest.

"You were at the drive-in at the same time Johnny Davis was there."

I shrugged. That seemed better than saying anything.

The sheriff had a hard look on his face. "You want to tell me about it?"

"Nothing to tell." My voice was shaking, and I coughed to try to cover it.

"No need to be nervous." he said, seeing through my ruse. "Just tell the truth."

"I am." I said, coughing again. "I got allergies." I said and faked another cough. "You must have a cat. The hair gets on people's clothes. Makes me cough."

"I don't have a cat." the sheriff said. "Now tell me about Johnny Davis at the drive-in."

"Like you said. He was there."

"Was his family with him?"

"Just his wife"

"Anything else?"

"No."

"How about that old man? The one they call Thaddeus?"

"I didn't see him."

"Other people claim he was there with Mozelle and Johnny."

I shrugged. "Maybe he was in the back seat. I couldn't see into the back seat very well." I was wondering if he'd questioned Hal. I squirmed in the chair. We had to be sure we had our stories straight. But why? There was nothing to tell. Mr. Burleson getting out of the car and telling Johnny to leave and calling him a nigger was nothing. That kind of thing happened all the time.

"Anybody else see Johnny and his wife?" Haylock asked.

"There were other people at the drive-in. I imagine they saw them. And the carhop, of course."

"What about altercations?"

My head was beginning to hurt, so I closed my eyes for a moment and took a deep breath. "No." My heart was a sledgehammer in my chest. "Well." I added. "Mr. Burleson got out of his car and told Johnny to leave, but Johnny just left, so I wouldn't say there was an altercation."

Maylock laughed. "Burleson don't like coloreds, does he?" Then he added, "Where'd you and Hal go after that?"

"Home. Hal had to get up and go to work the next morning, and I have to be home by ten, unless it's Saturday."

"You sure Johnny went home, too?"

I frowned. "How would I know where he went?"

"Mmm-hmm." the sheriff said in a way that made me worry. It was like he was sure Johnny was guilty, no matter what I said.

"His car headed west." I said. "You know, the direction he would go if he were going home."

"You know any more about this?" Maylock asked. "You know what I'm talking about, don't you? I'm talking about who tried to kill Hutch."

I couldn't breathe. Of course, I knew more. I knew someone who claimed she knew who committed the crime the sheriff was trying to pin on Johnny. I finally managed to shake my head.

"You didn't get along with Hutch, I hear." said the sheriff. By this time Mother had finished giving the Pepto Bismal to Dotty, and she came into the room.

"Good lord, Homer, are you trying to pin attempted murder on my daughter just because she doesn't like Hutch? As far as I know, nobody likes him."

Maylock glanced at Mother. "Come on in here, Dorothy." he said, patting the couch cushion next to him. "I thought you'd left the house. Where you been?"

"Had to take care of Dotty." Mother said, sitting down. "She's not feeling good. I think she's allergic to fresh corn. Upsets her stomach every time she eats it."

"Hershel's allergic to watermelon." Maylock said, referring to his son who was the same age as Dotty. Seems like kids these days are sicklier than we was when we was young."

Mother breathed a sigh. "Yeah. I don't think I worried my mama as much as my kids worry me. How's Winona these days?" Winona was Maylock's wife. Mother and Daddy had known both of them all their lives. They'd all gone to school together in Morton.

"Winona's just fine." Haylock said and turned his glance back toward me. "Is it true you didn't like ol' Hutch?" he asked.

"I guess I didn't like him very much." I said in my quivering voice.

"Homer!" Mother said at the same time. "Leave her alone for heaven's sake."

Homer laughed. "You know I don't think she done it."

"It's not funny." Mother said.

"Don't get riled up, Dorothy." Maylock said, getting to his feet. "I had to question her. It's my job, even if I know she didn't have anything to do with it." He smiled at Mother as she stood up next to him. "You always did have a temper, Dot." he said, patting her shoulder. "I remember that all too well."

That made Mother laugh. She walked him to the door and called out to him as he got into his police car. "You and Winona come see us sometime. Don't wait until you got official business."

"Sure." Maylock said. "Y'all come see us too." His car door closed with a thud and he drove away.

When he was gone, Mother turned to me with a question that made my head spin. "What do you know about all this?"

"About Hutch? I don't know anything."

"I want to know what happened Wednesday night. Did you really see Johnny at the drive-in?"

"Yes, he and his wife."

"That's the last time you're going anywhere with that Fitzgerald boy. I've known all along he's nothing but trouble."

"But Hal didn't have anything to do with any of this."

"The last time. Understand?"

CHAPTER 11

Caroline

The next afternoon, I spotted Hal's car from the front window as he pulled into our driveway. I turned off the vacuum cleaner I was running in the living room before Mother saw him. Dotty had obviously seen him too. She stood still with her dust cloth wadded in her right hand as she looked at Hal's car and then at me.

"What are you going to do?" she whispered.

My answer was to hurry to the front door. By the time I had it opened, Mother was outside and walking toward him. She'd come around the side of the house from the back where she'd been hanging laundry on the clothesline. I stood in the doorway watching as she marched with rapid determined steps.

Hal rolled down the window as he saw her approaching. He was wearing a nice white shirt, open at the collar, and contrasting with his tawny skin, making him look even more attractive.

I couldn't hear what they were saying. Mother was talking to him, shaking her head. He said something back that I couldn't hear. He glanced toward me, standing in the doorway, then drove away as Mother walked to the house.

"He won't be coming around again." she said.

"What did you say to him?"

"I told him not to come back." Mother said and moved toward the kitchen.

"But, Mother…"

She turned toward me. "You're not to see him. Is that clear?"

"That's not fair."

"If you hadn't gone to town with him, you wouldn't be involved in any of this."

"I'm *not* involved." I said. "Just because we saw Johnny that night doesn't mean we're involved. It doesn't even mean Johnny is involved. Hutch wasn't beat up until several days later."

Mother shook her head. "I don't think you understand how serious this is, and of course I know you're not directly involved. I just know that Fitzgerald boy means trouble. You know as well as I do he's been in trouble before."

"You don't know that." I took a step toward her. "It's all just gossip."

"Don't talk back to me, Caroline. I said you're not seeing him again, and I mean it. If you give me anymore back talk, you won't see anybody."

"That's not fair." Dotty said when Mother was out of sight.

I didn't reply, afraid of my own anger. Instead, I sat on the couch and leaned my head against the back.

"You don't like him much, anyway, do you?" Dotty asked. "Aren't you still going steady with Doug?"

"Obviously I'm not going steady with Doug if I'm going out with other guys."

"So you do like him? Hal, I mean."

"As a matter of fact, I like him a lot." I was surprised to hear myself admitting it.

"At least he's smarter than Doug."

"How would you know?"

"I know more than you realize." Dotty said.

I brought my head up and looked at her. "No doubt you do." I said. "Like who tried to kill Hutch."

Dotty's face turned white as the window curtain, and she took a long time to speak. "I was lying. I don't know anything, Caroline."

"You weren't lying, but you are now." I said, glaring at her. "If you know something, you should tell the sheriff. Don't let others take the blame."

"I don't know anything." she repeated, then headed outside. I followed and saw her running toward the back pasture. By the time she reached the barn, I caught up to her and grabbed her arm.

"Dotty, what's wrong with you?"

She jerked her arm free and ran away again. This time, I let her go. I knew where she was going, and kept walking behind as she headed to the draw. By the time I got there, Dotty had climbed down to the bottom. I looked over the edge and saw here sitting with her arms on her propped-up knees and her head resting face-down, the same position as earlier.

I slid down the side and sat on the dirt beside her, putting my arm around her thin shoulders.

Dotty was the first to speak. "Sorry about Hal." She couldn't have said anything that would have surprised me more. She nuzzled against me. "I know you like him. I'm glad you do, actually. I like him too. He's nicer than Doug."

"You know what we should really be talking about, Dotty."

She put her head down on her knees again. "I told you not to bug me, Caroline."

"This is serious. If you really know something, you have to tell the sheriff. Otherwise innocent people like Johnny could go to jail for it. Maybe even go to the electric chair."

She raised her head to look at me, her eyes wide. "I don't really know." she said. "I told you I was lying."

"I don't believe you. I don't understand, Dotty. Why are you acting so weird?"

She looked away from me.

"Why would you say you know if you really don't ?"

"It just slipped out. I didn't mean to say it." She sniffed and looked away. When I pulled her closer, she buried her head in my shoulder and cried until her shoulders shook. I sat with my arm around her until the tears stopped. "Old Thaddeus told me about what happened to Hutch." she said. "I'm not saying anymore. Don't ask me anymore! And don't tell anybody what I said. Promise me that! Please!"

I wiped them from her face with my fingers. "All right." I said. "I promise." She leaned against me a second or two longer before she abruptly stood. I stood up too. "Let's go back to the house."

"You go." Dotty turned and picked up the shovel. "I'll be there in a little while. "I want to look for some more arrowheads."

Reluctantly, I made my way back to the house. A knot had formed in my stomach and rose up to my throat, making me feel like I might choke. It was fear, I knew, and worry. Something terrible was gnawing at Dotty, something more than what Old Thaddeus had told her.

I stayed up as late as possible that night, reading until I finished *Catcher in the Rye*. When I finished the last page, I dropped the book to the floor and spent the night listening to the howl of coyotes as they prowled the edges of the earthen tank across the road, thinking of Dotty and Hutch and Johnny Davis and old Thaddeus. Mostly I worried about Dotty. I knew she was having as much trouble sleeping as I was because of the way she twisted and turned, tangling herself in the sheets and pounding at the pillow with her fist.

The windmill squawking in the early breeze awakened me the next morning after only a few hours of sleep. Dotty was already out of bed.

"She's out digging in the draw." Mother said when I asked. "Acting like something's bothering her. I don't know if it's her stomach or what. She hardly ate anything at supper last night. Didn't eat this morning either, just hightailed it out there to her dig. I don't get why she's so interested in all that old stuff she digs up."

"Maybe she's going to be an archaeologist." I said.

Mother laughed. "Not a very feminine thing to do, is it? But she's smart enough." she added. "Both of my girls are real smart." She smiled at me, and I smiled back halfheartedly. I was still angry at her for running off Hal. I couldn't stay mad for too long, though, because as soon as the dishes were done, she had a surprise for me. She showed me the Simplicity Pattern for a poodle skirt she'd bought at St. Clair's, along with a folded swath of blue-green gabardine.

I didn't make any attempt to hide my delight.

"I went to town while y'all were all working in the field." she said, smiling. "There's enough material here to make you and Dotty each one. Dotty got away before I could even show it to her."

"She'll love it just as much as I do."

Mother was beaming. She was always happiest when she was creating something with her sewing machine. "I thought I'd applique the poodles out of this pink material." she said, pulling out a folded piece of pink gabardine.

"I love it." I said, wishing I felt as lighthearted as I was pretending to feel.

With my housework chores done and Daddy not needing us to work in the field for the moment, I looked through our packed bookcase that we kept in the dining room for another book to read, but now that I'd finished *Catcher in the Rye* as well as *Lord of the Flies*, which I'd checked out of the Morton library at the same time, I couldn't find anything in our limited collection that I hadn't already read at least once and sometimes twice. Mother was tired of hearing me complain about not having anything to read, and it was a relief to both of us when she discovered she'd only bought one zipper when she was purchasing supplies for her sewing project.

"Take the pickup and go to town to get me another, and you can go to the library while you're there." she said, "but promise me to stay away from that Fitzgerald boy if you see him."

"I won't see him. He'll be working."

"I said promise me you'll stay away from him."

It took me a moment to say, "I promise."

"Good. Just don't be gone too long in case your daddy comes in from the field and needs the pickup."

When I got to town, I was able to park directly in front of St. Clair's. I'd decided to stop there first so it would give me more time to browse the library.

When I entered the store, Troy was helping a customer in the men's department. He smiled at me and gave me little wave. "Be with you in a minute." he said before turning back to his customer, a woman buying work shirts for her husband.

"It's okay, I can find what I need." I headed for the wall where zippers of various sizes and colors were displayed. I was still looking for one that matched the color and length of the one Mother had sent with me for comparison when Troy came to stand beside me.

"Heard you went out with Hal Fitzgerald." he said.

"Can't keep secrets in this town." I said, searching the display.

Troy laughed. "Guess not. Here." he added, handing me a zipper. "This is what you're looking for."

"Yes, it is." I took it and started for the cash register at the front of the store.

"Heard Maylock arrested old Johnny Davis for beating up Hutch." he said to my back.

I hesitated. "I didn't know he'd been arrested." I said, facing Troy.

"You think he's guilty? Since you're such good friends with Hal, I thought you might have some inside information."

"What's that supposed to mean?" I put the zipper on the counter. "Hal doesn't know any more than I do."

"I'm not so sure of that." Troy said. "He told me yesterday he was sure that nigger wasn't guilty, but he wouldn't tell me why he thinks that."

"Well, I hope Johnny isn't guilty." I said. "He seems like a nice, hard-working man."

Troy shrugged. "You can't tell about niggers. Killing's in their blood."

"People say that." I said. I wondered if it was really true. Could a desire to kill be in someone's blood?

"Did Hal tell you who he thinks done it?" Troy asked.

"No. He didn't tell me anything. I haven't seen him." I wondered where this was going.

"According to Maylock, all the evidence points to Johnny, but Hal says it wasn't him. I just wonder if he's told the sheriff that."

I shook my head, puzzled at what Troy was saying. "I don't know."

"If you don't know, I sure don't." said Troy. "Hal acted like he was so sure Johnny wasn't guilty, made me wonder if Hal done it himself." He laughed and added, "You want this wrapped?" He reached for the roll of brown paper on the counter.

I picked up the zipper. "No need to waste paper." I desperately wanted to leave.

"I wonder if whoever done it will try again." Troy said, closing the cash register.

I left without responding. Once outside, I crossed the street to the courthouse, a square block of cauliflower-colored brick that would all but disappear in a spring sandstorm. It was planted in the middle of the square along with a few struggling elm trees and wooden benches that, on a Saturday, would seat a flock of old men kicking away thin curls of wood that dropped from the piece they were carving. The Spit and Whittle Club, Mother called it.

I climbed the marble steps to enter the courthouse and the small library on the first floor. I'd never been beyond the courthouse's first floor, but knew that the second floor housed Sheriff Maylock's office and the jail cell. If Troy was right and Johnny had been arrested, he was up there now.

The library smell always made me think of almond Hershey bars and dust. Dotty said that was just plain odd. The aroma welcomed me as I opened the thick door that led into the book-lined room.

Elsie Wilson had been the librarian since before I was born. With greying brown hair, tailored suits, and brown oxford shoes, she was as much a part of the room as the high metal shelves and three sturdy tables waiting for me. She glanced up when I entered and gave me a smile and a nod. When I took the two books I'd checked out earlier to the desk, she accepted them without a word.

I had browsed through one row of stacks and was about to make my way up another when I saw Mr. Rabinowitz standing a little more than halfway down one of the aisles between shelves. He held an open book in his battered hand. When he sensed my presence and looked up.

"Hello." he said in a hushed voice. I returned his greeting with a nod. He turned the book toward me. "Have you read this?" he asked.

I looked at the cover. *The Diary of a Young Girl* was printed in stark black lettering. In even larger type was a name. Anne Frank."

"I never heard of Anne Frank."

"She was a Jewish girl who was thirteen when she started this diary."

I reached for the book. "She kept a diary? Sounds interesting. I've thought of doing that." I took the book and read the description. "I've heard of concentration camps. The Germans sent people there during the war. I've heard people talking about that."

"You studied about it in school, I imagine."

I shook my head. "No, I've never heard anything about it in school. But I've heard people say the Nazis put people in them.

He frowned. "You never heard of the camps? Not even in history class?"

"Well, it's not really history, is it? I mean, it only happened a few years ago." When I stopped flipping pages and looked up at him, I saw he had an odd look on his face. "Why would you be interested in reading a young girl's diary?" I asked.

"Well, you see, I had a daughter close to Anne Frank's age."

"Really? I didn't know you have a daughter."

"I *had* a daughter." he said. "Two daughters. But they and their mother died in a concentration camp called Auschwitz."

"Oh! I. . .I didn't know children. . .I mean, I'm so sorry, I. . ."

He was silent for a moment before he spoke again. "Perhaps it's best you don't know all the horror. . ." He shook his head. "No, it's best everyone know. So it never happens again."

"Did a lot of people. . . well, did they die? A lot of them? Like your family?

"Thousands, my dear. Thousands."

"Thousands? I never knew. . . How. . .how did they die?"

"Many people starved to death. By the time they died, they looked like skeletons. Some of them, mostly women, died in gas showers."

"Gas showers?"

"They were told to strip to take a shower, but it was deadly gas that rained down on them. At least they didn't have to suffer long like those who starved." Mr. Rabinowitz turned his face away, and I could see his mouth contorting as he tried not to cry. I wanted to say something, but before I could speak, he spoke again. "I remember the graves, he said. Rows and rows of skeletal bodies in mass graves. They were all. . ."

His voice trailed off, and I felt a knot growing in my stomach. "I've never heard people talk about that part of the war." I said. "They talk about soldiers dying on the battlefield, but I never realized…"

"Read the book." he said.

"Your wife and daughter, were they…?"

At just that moment, Miss Wilson peered around the corner of a row of books with a frown on her face. "The library is not the place for conversation." she said in a hushed voice.

"Sorry." I whispered.

"Read the book." Mr. Rabinowitz repeated. "Then stop by the store sometime and we'll talk."

Miss Wilson frowned at us again. I took the book to the front desk to check it out, as Mr. Rabinowitz left the library.

"He was talking to you about the war, wasn't he?" Miss Wilson asked quietly while I wrote my name on the card I'd slipped from the pocket at the back of the book.

I nodded, not daring to speak, lest she scold me again.

"He talks about it all the time." she murmured. "Try not to encourage him. It will just upset you. He ought to just get over it like the rest of us."

I took the book she handed me without responding and left the library. As I walked down the steps of the courthouse, my eyes were drawn to the row of buildings on the north side of the square. The theater, the drug store, and The New York Store. The theater was closed until six o'clock, so there was no one there. Two customers walked into the drugstore as I watched. The sidewalk in front of the New York Store was empty, making the dingy little store appear even more forlorn than ever. But Mr. Rabinowitz was inside. Mr. Rabinowitz with his awful truth, his awful loss, his mysterious wounded hand.

Of course, I knew that people had died in concentration camps. I even had a vague idea that Jews were treated badly in Germany during the war. But women and children killed? Why had I never heard of that? Anger grew inside me that I'd never been told. If I didn't know, there were probably others who didn't know. Was it because those who did know think the concentration camps should just be forgotten? Should everyone just get over it, as Miss Wilson had said? My steps picked up speed as I reached the bottom of the stairs and walked toward Mr. Rabinowitz's store.

CHAPTER 12

Pearlie

Pearlie knew her mama wanted to go to town to visit Papa in the jail. She had on her Sunday dress and that little greenish hat she wore when she dressed up. She had never driven much and felt unsure of herself, so she asked Pearlie to drive the old beat-up pickup her papa had bought for twenty-five dollars. The last place Pearlie wanted to go was Morton where everyone was talking about her daddy trying to kill Hutch. More than that, she was afraid she might even see Hutch, if he was out of the hospital.

Now she made an excuse. "I got no drivers' license." she told her mama. She didn't add that it took her a while every morning to get past the sickness that came on her as soon as she was out of bed.

She wasn't likely to get a drivers' license ever. Clarence Earnshaw who went to the colored school where she went had told Pearlie it took him twice as long to go through the driving test as it did the white boy that came in with him, and then he even had to go back and do it over again. Pearlie told her mama it would be even harder for a girl.

None of it made any difference. Mama was going to town to see Papa no matter what. Grabbing her purse, she announced, "All right then, I'll drive myself."

"You'll have a wreck, Mama." Pearlie yelled to her back as she headed for the door. "You can't even shift the gears right, and you get the clutch mixed up with the brake. What if you run into somebody?"

Mama's bottom lip quivered just a little, but she didn't speak. Instead, she marched out the door, shoulders stiff.

"Hold on, Mama. I'll drive you."

"Bless you child." She was all smiles now. "The Lord sure knowed what he was doing when he sent you to me."

"You better pray the Lord don't send no lawman our direction." said Pearlie. "Somebody see me driving, they'll pull me over for sure then you'll have two of us in jail."

By now both boys had run up to them, wanting to go to town. Mama ignored Pearlie's last remark and told the boys they couldn't go. They had to stay with Uncle Thaddeus, she said, walking away and ignoring their loud protests.

"Poor little fellers." Mama said as Pearlie turned onto the dirt road. "Won't do to let them go inside that jail and see their papa locked up. Maybe I can bring a little play-pretty back for both of them. I reckon they's probably something I can buy in that New York Store."

On the drive into town, Mama sat with her head turned to look out the window, and Pearlie stared at the road, praying she wouldn't come across Hutch. When they arrived at Morton, Pearlie found a parking spot next to a rundown gas station several blocks off the square.

"We can walk in from here, Mama." Pearlie told her. Mama didn't argue. She understood that Pearlie didn't want anyone to see that she was driving. It didn't pay for coloreds to take more risks than they had to.

The sun bore down on them like vicious sin as they made the long walk to the courthouse. Mama was finding it hard to put one foot in front of the other, and her green hat was slipping down her sweat-dampened forehead by the time they got to the courthouse steps. Pearlie also felt beaten down by the relentless heat.

Walking and sweating in the sun was enough suffering, Pearlie thought, but it wasn't over yet. Caroline Campbell was just ahead of them, walking up the front steps to the courthouse.

"Slow down a little bit, Mama." Pearlie said. "It's too hot to be walking fast." She was doing her best to give Caroline time to get inside so she wouldn't see them. It wasn't that Pearlie disliked Caroline, but as Mama had said, it wouldn't do to get too friendly. Besides, it would embarrass Mama for anybody to know someone in the family was in jail. Of course, Caroline probably knew anyway.

Mama came to a complete stop on the sidewalk, fanning herself with a handkerchief pulled from her purse. She dabbed at the sweat on her forehead. "Law, it's hot!" she said, puffing her breath through her lips. If it would just rain. . ."

"Just take your time." Pearlie said, an eye to the courthouse. Caroline was inside, but Pearlie wanted to wait a few more minutes to give her time to get to whatever office she might be going to.

Mama took a deep breath and grabbed Pearlie's hand, "Come on." she said. "I want to see Johnny." She held Pearlie's hand all the way to the courthouse and up the steps.

Inside, Caroline Campbell was nowhere in sight. Mama's hand tightened around Pearlie's, and Pearlie could see she was scared. "Ask somebody which way to the jail." whispered Mama.

There's no one in the lobby to ask, but Pearlie didn't want to go into one of the offices. They would look at her funny and want to know what she was doing in there. As she looked around, she was grateful to see a big glass frame on the wall with the names and numbers of all of the offices. She found what she needed.

"The jail's on the second floor, Mama."

Mama blew out a long breath. "Is they a elevator?"

"Don't think so." Pearlie pointed toward the stairs.

Mama blew out another puff of air and followed Pearlie up the stairs. When they got to the top floor, Pearlie saw a big brown wooden door with Sheriff's Office printed in big black letters on a frosty window. Next to the door was another sign in black letters spelling out JAIL. A fat black arrow pointed up the hall.

"This way, Mama." Taking her hand, Pearlie led her down the hallway. Opening another marked door, Pearlie saw a man sitting behind an old wooden desk that needed a coat of paint. The man was smoking a cigarette while looking at a magazine. As soon as he saw the two of them, he quickly slipped the magazine off the desk, as if he didn't want them to see what he was reading.

He looked up and frowned. "What y'all want?"

Pearlie waited for her mama to tell the man why they were there but saw Mama was too scared. "We come to see Johnny Davis." said Pearlie.

"Y'all got permission to visit?" When he opened his mouth to speak, Pearlie saw yellow teeth.

"We family." Pearlie said. "We come to see him."

"I don't give a damn if you're family or not." the man said, "You got to go through the proper channels."

"Go through what?" Pearlie could hear the tremble in her voice.

The man snorted. "They's a door up the hall there." He pointed over his shoulder. "It's got Sheriff's Office printed on it. Hell, I bet you can't even read." he said, snorting again.

"Yes sir, I can read." Pearlie told him.

"Then go back there and tell Janice what you want. She's the secretary. She'll decide if you're allowed to visit."

"Yes, sir." Pearlie pulled Mama toward the door. The man mumbled something she couldn't hear and pulled the magazine off his lap, laying it on top of his old rickety desk. Pearlie glimpsed a picture of a naked lady.

In the sheriff's office, Janice sat behind a desk facing the door. A sign on the desk had her name on it—Mrs. Janice Jacobson. As they entered, she looked up from her work.

"May I help you?"

"We come to see Johnny Davis." Pearlie said, this time without waiting for Mama to speak. It was clear by now she wanted Pearlie to do all the talking.

"You kin?" asked Mrs. Janice Jacobson. She didn't smile but at least she didn't sound mean.

"He my papa, and this my mama. He her husband." Taking her mama's arm as she spoke, Pearlie could feel her trembling.

Mrs. Jacobson moved some things around on her desk and came up with a clipboard with a long piece of paper attached. "Sign in here." she said. "Both of you."

Pearlie signed first, then watched her mama sign. Her name was the only thing she could write and it always took a long time. When Pearlie handed the clipboard back to the secretary, she picked up the phone, punched a button, and said, "Visitors for Davis." She looked at the two of them again and said, "Up the hall. There's a sign on the door. Someone will escort you in."

The man looking at the picture of a naked woman had put the magazine away by the time they arrived back at his desk. As soon as he saw the two of them, he grabbed a large ring of keys and told them to follow.

Pearlie saw her papa as soon as a big wooden door was unlocked. Behind bars, he sat on a narrow bed. He stood when he saw them.

"Y'all be careful." said the jailkeeper. "That man's a murderer."

"Johnny!" Mama hurried toward the cell. Papa reached between the bars to take her hand. "Law, it good to see you, sugar." he said. He looked at Pearlie and said, "You too, baby."

Pearlie saw tears in his eyes. That made her want to cry, too, but she wouldn't. It would upset her mama and papa even more than they were already. "You okay, Papa?" she said.

"Fair, I reckon." Papa said. "They got me for trying to kill Hutch."

"I know." Pearlie said. Mama didn't speak. She just held onto Papa's hand and sniffed back tears.

Papa shook his head and turned away from both of them. That made Mama cry even harder

"I know you never done it." Mama said, "But ain't nobody gonna believe us when we say it."

"What you need is a lawyer." Pearlie said. They were speaking in low voices so the jailer wouldn't hear.

"You know I can't afford no lawyer." Papa said.

"They gonna give you what they calls a public defender." Pearlie told him. "That be a lawyer the state pay for when folks can't afford one."

Papa frowned at Pearlie. "The state? Pay for a lawyer for a colored man? Where you get that idy?"

"I read it in a book." Pearlie had found the book *Civic Laws and Practices* on the floor of the bus. One of the white students had dropped it. She'd read as much as she could in the little time she had before the bus dropped her off at the school for coloreds. There were no books like that in her school.

Papa frowned again and shook his head. The jailer, standing by the door, snickered.

"That little nigger's telling the truth." the jail keeper said. "You're gonna get defended at taxpayer expense. Waste a money for a nigger, if you ask me." He had obviously heard everything. The jailer walked toward them. "So that kid a yours is smarter than you are, you dumbass coon. I bet if she was gonna try to kill somebody, she'd at least be smart enough to get away with it."

Pearlie said nothing. She knew the kind of trouble it could cause when a colored spoke her mind.

"Visiting hours is over." said the man. "You niggers get outta here."

"Johnny!" Mama reached a hand toward him. "Johnny, we be back when we can."

"Don't worry 'bout me, sugar. I be just fine." He put his face close to Mama's to kiss her, but the jail keeper jerked her back.

"Come on, now. Y'all don't give me no trouble." He almost dragged Mama to the door. Pearlie took her other arm, trying to help her.

Mama was doing her best not to cry, but Pearlie could hear her sniffling. She wanted to say something to comfort her, but she could think of nothing, feeling so low herself.

When they reached the bottom of the steps outside the courthouse, Mama turned to Pearlie. "That right what you told your papa? The state gonna get him a lawyer."

"That's the law. They has to do it."

"You say you read that in a book?"

Pearlie nodded.

"That don't make it so." Mama said. "Sepcially if you colored it don't."

Pearlie didn't want to tell her the same thought was running through her mind. Instead, she pointed across the street. "Looky, there's The New York Store. We got to go in there and get the boys a play-pretty."

"Oh, I was gonna forget." Mama said, grateful for the momentary distraction. Pearlie was glad to see her quick steps.

Entering the store, Pearlie once again saw Caroline Campbell, this time talking to Mr. Rabinowitz. Caroline was the last person in the world Pearlie expected, and the last person she wanted to see. She turned around to leave the store, but her mama had already gone to the toy aisle.

"Hey there, Pearlie." Caroline said.

Pearlie hesitated, but she knew there was no way she could escape. "Hidee." she said in a low voice.

Mr. Rabinowitz seemed glad to see Pearlie. He smiled and said, "Come in, Pearlie. What can I do for you?"

Pearlie looked down at her hands so she wouldn't have to look at Caroline. "I just waitin' for Mama."

"Well, come on over here to wait. You can join in the conversation. Caroline was just asking me questions. You might be interested."

Of course, Caroline was asking questions. She always did.

"I was asking Mr. Rabinowitz about the war." Caroline said. "I didn't know what all went on in those concentration camps, did you?"

Pearlie noticed an odd expression on Caroline's face. It was like she was worried about something. What did she have to be worried about? Her daddy wasn't in jail.

"Did you, Pearlie? Did you know about concentration camps during the war?" asked Caroline.

The question surprised Pearlie. She didn't know what to say. "I read about them."

"Where did you find the information?" Was Caroline accusing her of making stuff up?

"I don't rightly know." Pearlie said. "Uncle Thaddeus always coming up with stuff to read."

"Well, I never saw or read anything about what awful things happened to the Jews." Caroline said. "I feel as if it was kept from me on purpose."

"I reckon it was pretty awful. Some of it don't even seem human."

Caroline shoved a book at Pearlie. "Have you read this?"

Pearlie saw that it was that diary book. "Yes, ma'am." she said. "Mr. Rabinowitz, he loan me his copy."

Caroline looked at Pearlie, then Mr. Rabinowitz. "You loaned her a copy?"

Mr. Rabinowitz nodded.

"Then why were you..."

"I was checking it out for you" he explained to Caroline. "I wanted you to read it."

Pearlie felt a surge of guilt since she'd never given the book back to Mr. Rabinowitz. It wasn't that she was going to keep it forever. She just wanted to hang on to it for a little while longer.

"Well," Caroline said, "As soon as I read this, we are going to have to discuss the book." She turned to Mr. Rabinowitz. "I can see I have a lot to learn."

Pearlie wanted to tell Caroline she had no idea how much she had to learn, but Pearlie knew her place, and said nothing.

CHAPTER 13

Caroline

I stayed up nearly all night, reading the book and then thinking about what I'd read. I'd slept no more than two hours when Mother woke me, issuing instructions for my chores that day. It took me a while to get out of bed, and that put her in a grumpy mood. That didn't bother me as much as it might have because I felt so numb.

I knew it was more than not getting enough sleep. It was Anne Frank's book. But it was more than that, too. It was truly awful, unspeakable things had happened to people—mostly Jews, according to Mr. Rabinowitz—and I'd never even heard about it! His wife and daughter dying in a concentration camp? The war ended almost ten years ago. It wasn't enough just to be told that Hitler and Mussolini and Tojo were bad guys and we had a war because of them. I should have been told everything.

I had agreed to Mr. Rabinowitz's suggestion that Pearlie and I meet some time to discuss the book, although I didn't think it would happen. Pearlie couldn't even speak proper English, so how could she have deep thoughts about something like this?

If I were honest, I wanted to put Anne Frank out of my mind and think about going out with Hal again and wearing the poodle skirt Mother was almost finished making. All she had to do was applique the poodle on the bottom. Still, visions of concentration camps and people dying and Anne Frank hidden in an attic kept creeping into my mind. Mr. Rabinowitz had given me some of the details about concentration camps—stories of people starving until they looked like skeletons, of images of women being gassed to death when they thought they were taking showers, rows of dead bodies in a mass grave. Anne had not mentioned those things in her book, and she didn't know that was in store for her once her family's hiding place was found. I wouldn't have known either if Mr. Rabinowitz hadn't told me. It bothered me that I didn't know what happened to her after her diary ended.

"Look what you've done, Caroline!" Mother said, looking up from her applique work as I was ironing. "You scorched the collar of your daddy's Sunday shirt." I had the ironing board set up in the living room. Dotty was practicing at the piano across the room.

"Oh! Sorry." I said. "I think the scorch will wash out next time you wash it."

"You were daydreaming again." said Mother, more a statement than an accusation.

"Sort of. I was thinking about a book."

"You can think about your book later. Keep your mind on what you're doing."

"What book?" Dotty asked without missing a beat at the piano.

"It's about a Jewish girl. She died in a concentration camp. I think she almost starved to death before she died of some disease."

"Why on earth would you want to read something sad like that?" Mother asked.

Dotty stopped playing, whirling around on the piano stool to look at me, eyes wide.

"She almost starved to death? Gosh! Can you even imagine?"

"The Jews had worse things happen to them than starving." I said, feeling a perverse pride in my knowledge. "The Germans performed awful medical experiments on them, and some were gassed with poison when they thought they were taking a shower. A lot of them were shot, and they were put in big pits in the ground and buried. Some were so skinny and undernourished, they looked like skeletons. And there were big ovens…"

"For heaven's sake!" Mother let her applique drop to her lap. "Must you talk about such things? It's not good for you to read that kind of book. Find something else to read."

"I didn't learn all of that in this book." I said. "Mr. Rabinowitz told me some of it" I had mentioned him without thinking. I stopped, but it was too late.

Mother was on her feet. "When did you talk to Mr. Rabinowitz?"

"Ummm. A few days ago.""Where did you see him?"

"In his store." I felt a surge of defiance.

"So you went inside the store?"

"Yes." I looked up from my ironing to face her.

"I told you not to go in there." Mother had a fierce look in her eyes.

"There's nothing wrong with going in there. It's not dangerous or anything, and there's nothing wrong with talking to him."

"Don't sass me!" she said.

"I'm not."

She was about to say something to me, but instead turned toward the kitchen. She'd taken only a few steps when she looked back at me.

"I don't like you hearing about things like that. It's not fit for a young girl's mind."

"He's a nice man, and he didn't mean any harm." I said. "Pearlie talks to him all the time."

"She's right." said Dottie "Pearlie's shy with most people, but she likes talking to Mr. Rabinowitz."

"Pearlie? You're talking about Johnny Davis's daughter?

I nodded.

Mother frowned. "Why are you talking to a colored girl?

"It's okay, Mother. Lots of people talk to coloreds, and besides…"

"Caroline!" There was no mistaking the warning in her tone.

"And besides." I continued, even though I knew I shouldn't. "It's important for me and everyone else to hear about those awful things that happened to the Jews. Maybe then we can keep something like that from happening again. Maybe it will make us…"

"Caroline!" Mother cut me off with the same harsh tone. Both of us were silent for several seconds while we looked at each other. The tension between us quivered and thrummed. "Caroline." she repeated, softer this time, "I'm trying to protect you." I was about to tell her I didn't need her protection but couldn't get a word in. "You don't need to swallow the whole world in one gulp. You're still a child. There's plenty of time."

I couldn't resist raising my voice as she walked away. "I'm not a child, and what do you mean by plenty of time? There's not plenty of time. You can't stop me from growing up and learning what I want to about the world!" I left the ironing and fled outside in a whirlwind of anger and self-righteousness.

I sulked on the front steps for a while before I went back into my bedroom and locked the door. I pulled out Anne Frank's diary and read it all the way through again. Dotty kept banging on the door, yelling that it was her room too. It surprised me that Mother didn't intervene and tell me to stop pouting and let Dotty in. It surprised me even more that Dotty finally left me alone.

I finished the book, tossed it aside and buried my head in a pillow. I couldn't possibly understand all that Anne went through, but it left me depressed and with a feeling that I had no idea how to change the world, no matter how badly I wanted to, while it seemed that Anne, had she been given the chance, would know exactly what to do

That wasn't all that bothered me. Anne Frank's diary ended with her desperately wanting to improve herself. I wasn't sure I wanted to improve myself. I just wanted to be left alone and never have to talk to anyone again. Anne's circumstances were a hundred times worse than mine. After all, I wasn't hiding from police wanting to take me away to a concentration camp. These thoughts only made me feel worse because I wasn't grateful for what I had.

I wallowed in self-pity for several minutes, sobbing into the pillow. Finally, I grew tired of the murky world I'd created for myself and sat up. I picked up the book, wishing I'd never read it and at the same time wishing it had gone on longer. I hadn't read all the stuff at the end—the afterword. I often skipped those pages, thinking all the analyzing and pontificating distracted from the story. This time I wanted anything—dry information about the war and concentration camps and liberation policies—anything that would teach me more about Anne's world.

I had been angry the diary had ended so abruptly, but then I read that Anne and her family had been found in their hiding place the very next day! Anne and her mother and sister were taken to Auschwitz, while her father went to another camp. The writer of the afterword said people he interviewed survived by not thinking about what was happening, but Anne, witnesses said, felt everything. She cried when she saw children, heads shaved like hers, led away to gas chambers and cried again when she saw people waiting in the rain for days for their turn in the chamber. She was separated from her mother, who died soon afterward. Anne and her sister were taken to another camp and caught a terrible disease, probably typhus. They died in the spring of 1945 before Anne turned sixteen. That was only eleven years ago. Everything Mr. Rabinowitz had said was true! As soon as I could, I would go back to the store to talk to him.

CHAPTER 14

Caroline

Two weeks passed after I finished two readings of *The Diary of a Young Girl*, and I hadn't yet managed to get in to Morton and seek out Mr. Rabinowitz. I hadn't been anywhere except to church. The days were long, hot, and rainless, and I'd run out of reading material again. Seeking relief, Dotty and I decided to go swimming in the earthen stock tank in the pasture across the road. Mother caught us just as we walked out the door in our swimsuits.

We were forbidden to get in the tank. It was dirty, she said. We could get polio from that filthy water, she said. Finally, Daddy said we had to go back to work in the field again. He didn't hire anyone extra this time, since there wasn't that much to do.

As usual, I hated walking up and down rows of cotton, looking for invading plants and attacking them with a sharp hoe, constantly hot and sweaty, covered with dirt stirred up by the hoe. I prayed for a cloud, even a little one, to pass between me and the sun for just the slightest and briefest reprieve from the heat. Dotty worked alongside me but hardly said a word. I think she was as fed up with the heat and boredom as I was. All I could think of was that when I got to college and then got a degree, I was never going to set foot in another cotton field. I had decided to become a famous scientist and find a cure for polio.

After a seemingly endless week, Daddy declared the fieldwork done, but I was still trapped on the farm. I felt as restless as ever. Doug showed up one day and asked me to go to the picture show in Morton with him Saturday, just three days away. I would rather it had been Hal, but I was desperate to go anywhere besides a cotton field.

On Saturday, I dressed up in my new poodle skirt and waited for him in the living room.

He didn't show up, and I was left sitting in the living room dressed in my new skirt watching *Your Hit Parade*. I watched it all the way through, including all the Lucky Strike Cigarettes commercials. I tried watching *General Electric Theater*. The host was Ronald Reagan. His smooth voice made me sleepy, so I changed into pajamas and went to bed.

It wasn't the first time Doug had stood me up, but he always had a good excuse—his car wouldn't start; his dad came up with a last-minute job for him; he had a cold or an upset stomach. I never had any reason to doubt his excuses. It would have been nice to have been given some notice ahead of time, but that would have required a telephone, something we still didn't have. I went to bed feeling angry that although we had electricity, indoor plumbing, and television reception, we still didn't have telephones. The county was too sparsely populated, we were told. But being so isolated was the reason we needed telephones! Couldn't the county, or whoever was in charge, see that? I went to sleep, disgruntled at the entire world.

The next morning, Mother greeted me with, "I guess you got stood up last night, didn't you?"

I shrugged and mumbled something purposely incoherent.

Mother reached toward me and patted my shoulder. "Don't take it personally. Doug's a nice young man. I'm sure he had a good reason."

"No doubt."

She picked up on the sarcasm in my voice. "Well, he works full-time, you know. Maybe he had to work late."

"Sure."

"Don't be so sullen, Caroline. You're lucky to have Doug in your life."

She wanted me to marry him. I knew that, even though she'd never said it. Doug was a McCalick, son of one of the most prosperous farmers in two counties.

"Doug shares the responsibility of the farm with his dad. He's the kind that will make something of himself." she added.

"Hal Fitzgerald works." I couldn't help saying defiantly.

"He works for one farmer and then another. Not a steady job. That kind never changes. Never settles down."

"Well, I'm not settling down either. I want to meet other people."

"Like Hal Fitzgerald, you mean?"

"Maybe."

She looked at me for a long time without saying a word. Finally, she spoke. "He's not worth your time, Caroline. Before you get hurt, I hope you realize that."

"Why would I get…?" The look on her face made me stop mid-sentence. For a moment I thought she might be about to cry—something my starched-spine mother almost never did. She looked away, though, with no more than pursed lips and an almost imperceptible shake of her head. It made me wonder if something had happened in her past—a boy hurt her, maybe. Someone besides Daddy.

The day started off as bad as my mood. My usual cure for a bad mood was to lose myself in a book but I'd read everything. Perched on the front step with my back against the door, I settled for Mother's *Redbook Magazine.*

I opened it up to a story titled, "How To Keep A Husband Happy." It didn't hold my interest, so I flipped through to "The Best Recipes For Summer Days." I didn't care about recipes, and I still could not shake off the import of *The Diary of a Young Girl.* I threw the magazine in the front door and set out for the draw where I knew I'd find Dotty. She'd recently found an arrowhead in a shape she'd never seen before and was determined to find more. That interested me slightly more than keeping a husband happy, and I was about to walk to the back to find her when I saw someone about a half mile away, approaching on horseback. I recognized the horse first. It was Sal, Raylene Propps's mare, and Raylene was riding her.

It took a while for her to reach our driveway since Sal never moved very fast, but I waited for her until she rode up next to our pickup parked in front.

"Hi, Raylene." I said. Jesus did no more than raise his head and glance at Raylene from his favorite shady spot next to the house. He was used to both Raylene and Sal.

Raylene leaned on the saddle horn. "I'm bored." she said.

"Welcome to the club."

"Why do we have to live in such an uninteresting place?"

I shrugged. "I guess it could be worse."

"Worse?" She sat up straight. "I don't see how."

I thought of telling her we could be in a concentration camp watching people die, but I didn't want to sound stuffy. I shrugged and said nothing.

She got off of Sal and pulled something out of a saddlebag. "I got this in the mail yesterday." she said. It was a big cardboard fan shaped like a tobacco leaf with a picture of Frank Sinatra on the front and lettering that spelled out, "Lucky Strikes presents *Your Hit Parade*."

"Nice." I said, although Frank Sinatra seemed old to me. Buddy Holly and Elvis Presley were my favorites.

"Let's go for a ride." she said.

I breathed out a heavy sigh, wishing I had something more exciting, or interesting, to do. "I'll tell Mother I'm going." I said. "Then you'll have to help me catch Sargo."

"You tell your mother, and I'll ride out to the pasture. Sargo will follow Sal back to your barn." Raylene raised her eyebrows. "Sex is the answer to every problem."

I turned away before she could see that my face had flushed.

Mother seemed more than glad to have me find something to occupy myself and waved to Raylene and Sal out the kitchen window. True to Raylene's prediction, Sargo, though he was a gelding, followed Sal to the barn. Raylene helped me saddle the horse, and we rode off with no particular destination.

I loved the muscular, cutting-horse feel of Sargo, the rhythm of his hoofs, and the way sunlight braided itself in his mane. I inhaled his golden-brown aroma, mixed with the cinnamon-sweet scent of the leather of the saddle. The ride had a calming effect on me, and I forgot my restless morning. I could have continued in that slow-motion tranquility forever without speaking, but Raylene had other things on her mind.

"Don't you just hate living out here like this?" She was leaning on the saddle horn, letting Sal wander at will. "Wouldn't it be nice to live in a city where things *happen?*

"What kind of things?"

She gave me a disgusted look "Well, picture shows, for one thing. I mean more than one to choose from and that have the *current* shows like you read about in *Modern Screen* and *Motion Picture*. The shows are already out of date by the time we get them in Morton. And there are things like fancy restaurants and nightclubs. I can't wait to go to one."

"Good Lord, Raylene, we're Baptist."

"That's another thing. Being a Baptist holds you back."

I thought about it. "Yeah, I guess maybe it does." After a while, I said, "There's a swimming pool in Morton, you know. And a skating rink."

"And how often do you go there?" asked Raylene, with that disgusted tone.

"Well, there's the lake." About eight miles from our house on the way to the school, Monument Lake was said to been the site of Billy the Kid's hideout.

"Always the same people there all the time." Raylene said with a disdainful wave of her hand.

"You'll have to move to some other county if you want to see different people." I was becoming a little bored of her complaining.

"I'd be gone in a minute if I could. Wouldn't you? I mean, I just can't live up to my potential in a place like this."

"Potential? What do you mean?"

Raylene snapped at me. "You don't think I have potential?"

"Of course, you have potential." I was in no mood for an argument. Fortunately, her attention turned elsewhere.

"That looks like somebody sitting in that pickup in front of us."

I didn't reply, but recognized the pickup.

"That's y'all's Chevy." she said. "Must be your daddy." She looked at me and raised her eyebrows in a suggestive manner. "Who could that be with him?"

"A friend, I guess."

"You don't sit in a pickup on a country road with just a friend."

"What are you getting at?"

"Nothing." she said. "I was just wondering."

I headed to the pickup, nudging Sargo's sides with my heels to make him go faster, knowing Sal would pick up her pace to try to stay up with us.

"Hey!" yelled Raylene. "What'd you do that for? You made Sal lunge, and I almost fell out of the saddle."

I didn't care if she fell off her horse. In fact, I kind of wished she would.

As we got closer I saw who was in the pickup with Daddy.

Raylene could, too. "That's old Thaddeus. Why is your daddy talking to that old nigger?"

I didn't answer. I lay the reins against Sargo's neck to turn him around.

"Hey, where are you going?" Raylene shouted. She was doing her best to keep Sal from turning around to follow.

"Whatever they're talking about, it's nothing important." I called back to her. "I'm going home."

"You're just plain weird, Caroline. Come back here. What are you afraid of, anyway? Go home if you want to. I'm gonna go see what's up."

She got Sal to trot away toward the pickup where Daddy and Thaddeus were talking. I knew what they were doing, but didn't want Raylene to know. I followed her anyway.

When we rode up to the pickup, Daddy greeted us with a loose-lipped crooked grin. Thaddeus sat next to him, weaving slightly and holding the almost-empty bottle of Jim Beam they had been sharing.

Raylene leaned down to the open window to greet Daddy. "Hello there, Mr. Campbell."

"'Lo Ruleen." Daddy said.

A puzzled frown marred Raylene's well-made-up forehead. Raylene was probably unaccustomed to seeing anyone drunk. Maybe this was even the first time. "What you doing sitting out here with that old nigger?"

"Oh, jus relaxin'." Daddy said.

"With a nigger?"

Daddy glanced at Thaddeus and back at Raylene before he chortled and said, "Old Thad's a nigger all right, but he's my frin." Daddy said then added, "Ain't that right, Thad?"

"Damn shore is." Old Thaddeus's words were every bit as slurred as Daddy's. He brought the bottle to his mouth, taking in the last swallow of whiskey.

"Is that *whiskey*?" Raylene screeched.

"Come on, let's go." I gave Sargo another nudge with my heels, hoping Sal would follow as we started back the way we'd come. Astonishment seemed to have given Raylene strength. She took control of Sal and forced her to be still while she stared down through the window at Daddy.

"Drunkenness is a *sin*. Y'all both ought to know that." She was clearly agitated with righteousness, and her voice shook a little. Maybe that was more because Sal was dancing around, trying to join Sargo and me than it was from emotion. Only a few minutes ago she had been talking about how our religion held her back.

"A sin it is, Miss." Thaddeus said, weaving a little. "But I reckon 'tis a sweet sin. Not near so bitter as doin' hurt to somebody."

"Sin is sin." Raylene's words came out with a huff of breath that carried the odor of sanctity. Religion wasn't holding her back now. "You ought to be ashamed for drinking that whiskey, and what's even worse, for hanging out with a nigger. Now, that's what I call low life and …"

If Raylene finished that sentence I didn't hear it because the pounding of Sargo's hoofs was too loud. I had kicked him into a run, headed back home as fast as I could go. In a little while I heard her screaming behind me, telling me to slow down. I glanced over my shoulder and saw her hanging on to the saddle horn in desperation while Sal raced to catch up with Sargo and me as fast as her little mare legs would carry her. I slowed Sargo enough for Sal to catch up.

Raylene looked as if she was about to throw up. "What are you doing? You scared the holy crap out of me."

"I told you to come on, and you wouldn't."

"Well for Christ sake, you didn't have to try and kill me."

I wanted to tell her I didn't try to kill her and besides that she was using the Lord's name in vain, but I didn't say a word. I just nudged Sargo into a gentle walk toward home.

"I know you must feel bad." said Raylene, after a while. "It's got to be embarrassing to have a daddy who's a drunkard."

"Daddy's not a drunkard. He just drinks too much sometimes."

"Well he *drinks*." Raylene said. "I didn't even know that. My daddy has never had a drink in his life." When I made no comment, she started up again. "My daddy's a good man. He's even a deacon, you know. Besides being the song leader every Sunday."

"Yeah, I know." I spoke without looking at her. "At the Baptist Church. The church that holds you back in life."

Raylene breathed out another one of her potent huffs. "You don't have to be a smart aleck just because you're embarrassed. It *does* hold you back in some ways, but at least nobody in my family drinks."

"That's twisted logic." I said, half under my breath. Raylene didn't hear. "You shouldn't call Thaddeus a nigger to his face."

"What are you talking about? He *is* a nigger."

"You should refer to him a colored. It's not as offensive. It's not very Christian to hurt somebody's feelings on purpose."

"Will you listen to that?" Raylene said. "The drunkard's daughter is telling me how to be a Christian."

"Forget it." I said, giving Sargo a discreet nudge to get ahead of her.

"I feel sorry for you." Raylene said to my back. Her voice softened. "I know you're embarrassed."

I didn't answer. There was no point in telling her how hurt and demoralized I was each time Daddy went on one of his drunks—how it upset Mother and disrupted the family. All I did was keep riding, looking straight ahead while tears ran down my face.

Once we reached our front yard, Raylene said something about what a nice day for riding it was. She was trying to smooth over our conversation, but I brushed her off, telling her I had work to do.

As she rode away, her last words were, "I'm sorry for you, Caroline. I know it's not your fault. I guess it just makes me realize how lucky I am."

Leading Sargo toward the barn, I saw Dotty at the edge of the draw, holding her shovel, spade side up, staring at something at the bottom, probably deciding where to dig next. As soon as I got the saddle off of Sargo and gave his back a few swipes with a brush, I hurried inside to the room I shared with Dotty, closing the door.

I hoped Mother hadn't noticed that I was home, since I'd entered through the back door and had moved as quietly as possible. No more than five minutes passed before, to my dismay, she knocked on the door and asked if I was okay.

"I'm fine."

"Why are you sulking?"

"I just want to be alone for a while."

"Did you see Doug while you were out and quarrel with him?"

"No, I didn't see Doug."

"He must be upset about you hanging around that Fitzgerald boy."

I wanted to scream at her that I didn't care what Doug thought or was upset about, but all I said in measured tones was, "I—didn't—see—Doug." Then as an afterthought, I added, "I don't feel good, Mother. I think I'm starting my period."

"Oh." she said. There was a pause, as if she thought I was lying. "I'll bring you a heating pad."

"I have one." I said, furthering the lie. "I have it on my stomach."

I could sense her lingering outside the door. She didn't leave until Daddy came in the front. "Dorothy! Where are you?"

"I'm here." Mother answered, and the next thing she said was, "Damn it, you're drunk! I thought you were working in the field."

"Not much I can do until it rains." Daddy said, slurring his words. "Did Caroline get home okay? She was riding Sargo. That horse got too much spirit for a young girl to ride."

"You saw Caroline? In your condition?"

"She was with Raylene. That little smart aleck chewed me out for being with a nigger. I told her—"

"Who were you with?" Mother demanded.

"It wasn't any of her business who I was with, but I told her if Thaddeus was good enough to work all day for me, he was damn sure good enough to have a drink with me."

"Well that explains a lot." Mother shouted from the hallway. "You embarrassed Caroline in front of her friend."

"I didn't embarrass her," yelled Daddy , "Wasn't anything to get embarrassed about."

They stopped yelling at each other when they heard the back door open. Within a few seconds, Dotty was knocking. When I opened the door, she gave me a knowing look. "What's going on?"

I answered with a shrug.

"He's drunk, isn't he?"

I nodded.

CHAPTER 15

Caroline

Mother, Dotty, Junior, and I ate supper without Daddy that night. He was in bed—passed out, I guess. No one mentioned it, but I could tell by the way Mother looked at me that she wanted to ask me what had transpired with him and Raylene and me. All she did was ask me if I was feeling better, and I said I was.

Even Dotty was unusually quiet while we ate. Mother seemed desperate to make the mealtime relaxed and normal.

"Have you found anything interesting out there in the draw?" she asked Dotty. "Any more arrowheads?"

"Nothing new." Dotty said, without looking up.

"Maybe you should find another hobby." Mother offered.

"Yeah, I might." Dotty said, still looking at her plate. She had hardly touched her food except to stir it around with her fork. Her reply shocked me. Archaeology had always been her passion. I kept expecting her to say more about this unexplained change of mind, but all she said was, "May I be excused?" Before Mother could reply, she stood up and left the table.

Mother looked at me with a concerned expression. "What's wrong with her?"

"She's probably just upset because she's not finding anything." I said, although I doubted it. Dotty had gone long periods without finding anything before and had never given up.

"She wasn't with you and Raylene, was she?"

"No, she stayed here."

When the dishes were done, I went to our room and sat next to Dotty on the bed.

"What's wrong?"

She fell back on the bed. "Nothing." But there was a quiver in her voice.

"Don't lie."

She turned over on her stomach, her face resting on her arms. After a while she said, "I hate life." The words were muffled by the bed.

Those words surprised me. It was inconceivable that Dotty, of all people, hated life. She, who was never bored, who always found something interesting. "What brought that on?"

She sat up again, her legs crossed in front of her. "For one thing, everybody thinks Johnny's the one who tried to kill Hutch."

"We've known that a long time. You said you know who did it. Is that what's bothering you?"

"There's something else."

"What?"

She took a deep breath. "Somebody hurt Pearlie. She. . ." Dotty's voice trailed off, and she stood up suddenly and went to the bureau and started digging in the drawers until she pulled out her swimsuit. "Let's go to the lake and go swimming."

"Not until you tell me about Pearlie."

Dotty had already pulled off her shorts, and was unbuttoning her shirt. I know she felt the tension between us as keenly as I did. Finally, she looked at me, her face ashen. "Remember when we thought she was pregnant?"

"I remember when we speculated." I said, cautiously.

"Well, I think she really is."

"Dotty, we shouldn't be gossiping like this, and you know it."

"She was raped."

The words made my ears ring as if I'd been hit. That can't make you pregnant, can it? "How do you. . . Who do you think. . .?" I was unable to think clearly enough to form a sentence.

"The way you know is first you miss a period." said Dotty. "Isn't that true?"

"Dottie—"

"Well, isn't it?" Dotty shouted the question at me.

"Yes, first, you miss a period."

When she collapsed on the bed, I asked, what are you getting at?"

"I'm just upset. I got my period day before yesterday, and it makes me grumpy."

There was something about the look on her face that made me think she was lying. "Maybe you shouldn't go swimming if you have your period."

She jumped to her feet. "I'm fine. I want to go swimming."

"You're acting really weird, Dotty. You're jumping from one thing to another and—"

"It's all connected." Dotty said. "Maybe Hutch got beat up because he raped Pearlie and got her pregnant."

"Oh, dear God. Are you saying Johnny tried to kill Hutch because he raped Pearlie?"

Dotty didn't answer. She just looked at me. I saw fear in her eyes and something else I couldn't identify.

"You have to tell me where you got this idea." I said.

Before she could say anything, there was a *tap-tap* on the bedroom door. Mother's voice said, "What are you girls doing in there?"

"We're putting on our swimsuits." Dotty called. "We're going swimming. Over at the lake."

Mother opened the door, and I turned quickly toward the chest to look for my own swimsuit. "The lake?" she said. "Are you sure there's enough water there? It hasn't rained in a while."

"There'll be at least a little water." I said. "Anyway, at least there'll be people there. It gets lonesome way out here."

Mother put her hands on her hips, cocking her head to look at me. "I get it. You think Doug will be there."

I ducked my head, pretending to be embarrassed. "Maybe," I said.

She laughed. "And you want to take the pickup." she said. "I guess it's okay since your daddy finally got up and took the tractor to the field." She glanced at Dotty sitting on the bed in her swimsuit, shoulders slumped. Mother reached a hand out to stroke her hair. "Go on. I reckon it'll cheer up both of you."

After Mother left the room, I whispered to Dotty, "Well, that was easy." Dotty didn't reply. She picked up her shorts and shirt and put them on over her swimsuit.

After I pulled the pickup out of the driveway, I turned to Dotty. "You've got to tell me why you know about Pearlie being raped."

Dotty was silent for several seconds before she spoke in a low, trembling voice. "I think I saw when it happened."

I almost swerved off the road. "You saw. . .?

"I was out practicing my driving one day. I drove over by that old boxcar off the side of the road. You know, the one on the highway to Muleshoe?"

"You were driving by yourself way over there?" Daddy had allowed me to practice driving before I got my license just as he did with Dotty, but I was only allowed to drive dirt roads, not on the highway.

"Let me finish." said Dotty. "I was just coming up to the boxcar, but I was still kind of a long ways from it. I thought I saw someone coming out of it, but I couldn't tell who it was. Somebody got in a car and drove off. I met him on the highway and just about ran off the road trying to see who was in that car. By the time I was even with the boxcar, I saw Pearlie come out, crying. She started walking, and when she got up to the highway, I honked at her, but she paid me no mind. I yelled and asked if she wanted a ride, but she started running. Left the road and ran across the pasture—like she was ashamed or something. I mean, wouldn't you feel ashamed if that happened to you?"

"I don't know."

"I think you would." Dotty said.

"I don't want to think about it." Sunshine splattered the windows of the pickup, almost blinding me, but I was feeling sick and hardly noticed. "Oh my Lord, Dotty." I whispered after a while. "Why didn't you mention this before?"

"I guess I was scared. Or something. I didn't know what to do. I wanted to drive over to Pearlie's and talk to her about it, but Daddy wouldn't let me have the pickup again. He said I was gone too long the last time."

"Why didn't you try to talk to her when we were working in the field?"

"I tried to, but she kept walking away every time I got close to her."

My heart was pounding in my chest, and we had just turned onto the highway. Ahead of us the white-hot light was playing tricks, making shimmering and swirling mirages on the pavement. They looked like puddles of water but each one disappeared as we got closer. Although I'd grown up seeing these tricks of light all my life, they always made me feel as if I'd entered a strange, unsettling, make-believe world. "Dotty, do you think Johnny found out about it, and that's why he came after Hutch?"

Dotty turned toward me and spoke in an angry voice. "It wasn't Johnny!"

"You have to tell me what you know!"

She didn't answer.

"Dotty. . ."

"I'm not sure I know anything."

"But you said. . ."

"I think I was wrong. Somebody told me something, but I think he was trying to protect Johnny."

"What? Who?"

"Old Thaddeus. He tried to make me believe he was the one. Can you believe that? Old Thaddeus beating up a big guy like Hutch? He was just trying to protect Johnny."

"Because he knows Johnny did it?"

"I don't know! I don't know!" She had turned her face away from me again, and neither of us spoke again until we got to the lake.

Monument Lake is in the middle of pastureland, surrounded by the native grass of west Texas. Short and tough, the grass is not the kind that trembles in the wind. It crunches when you walk on it. It's a defiant sound. As if the grass refuses to die no matter how dry the weather gets. I parked the pickup on the rise above the lake besides some other cars and pickups. There were a few people on blankets and towels along the edge of the water and a few more in the shrinking lake. Most of the surface, except for the edges was polished and still, reflecting the sky, making me feel that if I could step on that surface I would sink into heaven.

I saw Doug as soon as we parked. He waved as I got out of the car. I waved back and surreptitiously searched the shore for Hal, not wanting to admit even to myself I was doing it.

"I see Joanie out there." Dotty said. "I'm gonna hang out with her." She walked to her friend, a little too quickly, I thought, as if she was in a hurry to get away from me.

Doug approached with his powerful gait. His tight swim trunks clung to his slender hips, making his shoulders appear even broader than usual.

"I was hoping you'd be here." He put his arm around my shoulders and kissed me lightly on the lips. "I thought about going by your house and picking you up so we could go together."

"Did you?"

Doug missed the sarcasm in my voice. "Yeah, but I didn't know if you'd be free."

"What do you mean *free*?"

Doug shrugged, "Well, you know. You work for your daddy sometimes." Before I could respond, he said, "Just as well I didn't stop by. We woulda had to drag your little sister along."

"Sorry you feel that way." I said.

Doug frowned. "Hey! What's your problem?"

I turned around, searching for Hal, and Doug grabbed my arm, forcing me to face him. "Oh, yeah, I know you're mad about me for standing you up Saturday night. Not my fault. I had to fix the carburetor."

I waited for him to say he was sorry but he just took my hand and pulled me toward the lake. "Come on, let's get in the water." he said.

I tried to hold back, but couldn't escape his powerful grip. I don't think he even noticed that I was staying a step or two behind him. I was angry that he hadn't apologized for standing me up. Added to that, his remark about having to drag Dotty along annoyed me. I didn't like him thinking of her as extra baggage. I pulled back harder when we got to the water's edge and stopped, allowing its gentle ebb and flow to lick my feet. I was reluctant to plunge in too soon, knowing the water would feel cold on my sun-cooked skin.

"Come on!" Doug grabbed my hand again and pulled me in farther than I wanted. My body ached for a moment at the water's chill, tightening almost to the point of paralysis. When I saw Doug laughing, resurrection set in. I swam away from him until he caught up with me and dunked me underwater. I came up sputtering, my curly permed hair falling in ringlets into my eyes. I could think of nothing but revenge and lunged at him, catching him off guard enough that I overcame his superior strength and dunked him quickly and mercilessly.

He came up laughing. In spite of myself, I laughed with him and squealed when he tried to dunk me again. We played that way for several minutes, and the water and laughter washed away my discontent. When we were both breathless, Doug picked me up and carried me in his arms to the shore. We were both still laughing as he sat me down on a towel and took his place next to me.

It was just at that moment I spotted Hal. He saw me as well and gave me a brief nod of his head just before plunging into the water. I watched until he disappeared underneath the skin of the lake.

"Who is that?" Doug asked.

"His name's Hal. He works for Daddy sometimes."

"Oh yeah, that guy from Levelland. I heard he's some kind of criminal."

"I doubt that's true."

"You trying to defend him?"

My only answer was to roll my eyes.

"I've seen him around." said Doug. "Looks like a smart aleck to me."

"You can tell that just by the way he looks? Have you ever talked to him?"

Doug pushed me onto my back with my head cradled in his arm and put his face close to mine as he spoke. "No, have you?"

"I may have said hi to him." I wondered if he'd heard about me going to the drive-in with Hal.

"Stay away from him." Doug kissed me on the lips. At least that kept me from telling him what I was thinking—that I would talk to and be with anyone I wanted. At the same time, I wondered again why I was being so evasive with him. Irritation boiled inside me, and I tried to sit up, but Doug held me tightly.

"When are y'all coming up for air?" Kent Dunlap was looking down at us, grinning. I pushed away Doug and sat up straight.

"Hey, Kent" Doug said. "Where's your woman?"

"Damned if I know." Kent said. "I went by her house to pick her up, but she wasn't home. Her momma said she went to Lubbock to the doctor." I wondered who his current woman was. He'd dated Raylene, but I'd heard he'd recently started seeing a girl from Morton.

"Doctor?" Doug said and laughed. "She ain't pregnant, is she?"

"I sure as hell hope not." Kent said, laughing along with him.

"You saying there's a chance?" Doug asked.

Kent wiggled his eyebrows suggestively. I looked away, trying to ignore him. I scanned the lakeshore, looking for Hal and Dotty. Knowing her as I did, she was probably already bored and wanting to go home. I was ready to go myself, eager to wash the lake water out of my hair. I couldn't find Dotty, but I did spot her friend Joanie talking to a group of friends.

Dotty wasn't among them. I got to my feet and was about to walk over to the group to inquire about my sister when I saw her several feet away from the others. She was with Bobby Nations, a boy three years older than Dotty. Bobby had his arm around her. While I watched, she turned her face toward his, and he kissed her lips. Holding hands and laughing, they ran into the water. Dotty, who was a much better swimmer than I was, quickly outswam him. I continued to watch until she swam back to him, and he hoisted her up to ride on his shoulders.

Something visceral and primitive exploded like a bomb inside me, leaving the debris of denial. That was Dotty out there, my *little sister.* But those legs dangling down Bobby's chest were long and shapely, if a little too thin, and the top of her swimsuit blossomed with a soft roundness. Why had I never seen her this way before? Up until this moment, she had just been skinny little Dotty who loved digging up arrowheads. How dare Bobby Nations see her now as anything more than that!

"Where you going?" Doug asked. He reached for my hand and tried to pull me down beside him.

"I got to get Dotty home." I said.

"Of course you do." He sounded disgruntled. "Come back to the lake if you can get free." he called to me as I walked away. I didn't turn around and didn't respond. I was still walking toward the lake to rescue Dotty when I literally ran into Hal.

"Oh!" I said, bumping into him.

He laughed and took my hands in his. "Where you headed in such a hurry?"

"I, uh, I was just going to tell Dotty it's time to go home."

He glanced toward the lake. "Looks like she's busy right now."

"Yeah, well. . ."

"Don't bother her. She deserves to have some fun after—"

"After what?"

A nervous smile flickered at his lips. "None of my business. Take her home if you have to."

I pressed him. "What's none of your business?"

"What I mean is, I think she's been kind of upset about all this business about Hutch and Johnny."

"Who hasn't?"

"Yeah." His eyes scanned the shore. "Where's your boyfriend?"

I wanted to ask him how he knew about Dotty being upset lately, but all I said was, "You mean Doug?"

Hal grinned. "There's more than one?"

His remark embarrassed and rattled me. "He's not really my boyfriend. He's a friend, but. . .What I mean is, I don't have a real boyfriend. Not really, I mean."

"Just a friend!"

"Yeah." My heart was beating too fast, and I could feel myself blushing. I knew he had seen Doug kissing me.

He cocked his head slightly and gave me a questioning look. "In that case, want to go to the picture show with me this weekend?"

To avoid his eyes, I looked away. When I did, all I could say was, "Oh my lord!"

The alarm in my voice caused Hal to turn around. "Uh oh!" He'd seen the same thing I'd seen—Pearlie and her two little brothers. They were all wearing jeans rolled up to their knees, and were walking toward the water. It was obvious they were going for a swim.

A voice bellowed from somewhere behind them. "Hey! What y'all think you're doing?" Kent Dunlap was walking with long, determined strides toward Pearlie and her brothers, and Doug was next to him, walking just as fast. "No niggers allowed out here." Doug shouted.

"Get outta here, niggers! This place is for white people." someone else yelled. I couldn't see who it was. By this time, Doug and Kent reached Pearlie and her brothers. Doug held Pearlie by her upper arm and was dragging her away from the water's edge, making her stumble. Her little brothers were crying. When she fell, Kent kicked her. I felt sickened and at the same time, stunned, rooted to where I stood.

I heard Dotty's voice from somewhere behind me. "Leave them alone!" she shouted. She ran past me toward the crowd that had gathered around Pearlie and the boys. Hal had disappeared.

"Dotty! Come back here. You'll get hurt!" I called. I could see her at the edge of the crowd, trying to make her way through. At last, my cowardly paralysis left me and I rushed to Dotty's side. "Don't hurt Pearlie." she said to the boys when she saw me beside her.

"Stay out of it, Dotty!" I said At that moment, I saw Hal helping Pearlie to her feet.

"Go on! All of you." Hal said. "These three are with me."

"You brought niggers here?" demanded Doug.

"Yeah." Hal said, "I brought niggers here."

"You son of a bitch." Kent swung at him, but Hal dodged his fist and came up with a jab at Kent's stomach. Kent fell to the ground, gasping. Doug was on Hal immediately, hitting him in the jaw. Hal staggered backward.

"Stop it! All of you!" I didn't know at first if it was my voice, but Doug turned toward me.

"Get back, Caroline. Stay out of this."

Pearlie was back on her feet. She held a hand of each of her little brothers and was running away from the water. Several people, both male and female started after them.

"Leave them alone." called a loud voice. "They're leaving. No harm done." It was Mike Propps, Raylene's daddy. "Goddamn it, I said leave 'em alone." he yelled again when Kent and Doug kept after them.

The boys turned and Mr. Propps laughed. "You boys done your job. You gave 'em a good scare." He walked toward the boys, and when he reached them, gave each a one-armed bear hug. "Proud of you two." he said. "Them niggers won't be back, thanks to you. No point in pushing it too far, though, and getting yourself in trouble with the law. This way, if anybody gets in trouble, it'll be that nigger-lovin' Hal Fitzgerald that claims he brought 'em here."

Doug and Kent grinned, basking in the praise.

Dotty moved closer to me, pressing against me. "I want to go home." she said.

I put my arm around her and led her toward the pickup.

CHAPTER 16

Caroline

I wanted to talk to Dotty that night after we went to bed. I wanted to press her to tell me more about Thaddeus taking the blame for beating up Hutch, but I knew how sensitive she was about that. I started out by mentioning Bobby Nations.

"You seem to like each other." I said.

"Yeah, I guess so."

"Mother and Daddy think you're too young to date, you know."

"We see each other at school." Dotty said. "He walks me to class, sits with me during assembly, and we hang out at lunch. Obviously, you haven't noticed."

"Well. . ." I didn't want to admit that she was right.

"You're too caught up with the little dramas of your own life to notice anybody else."

It wasn't like Dotty to lash out at me with such fury. Our bickering never seemed this fraught with anger. She turned her back to me and didn't speak.

"I guess you're right." I said after a while. "Maybe I'm too self-centered." She moved her shoulders slightly but said nothing. "I know you're still upset about what happened with Pearlie at the lake." At last I was getting around to what I really wanted to talk about.

"You didn't do anything to help her." Dotty said.

I didn't know how to answer. I thought Dotty should have been grateful that I was protecting her, my little sister. I didn't mention it, though. I didn't want to start an argument with her.

She was quiet for a while before she said, "It's worse than you think." she said.

"What do you mean?" I thought I knew what she meant in spite of my questioning her. Pearlie and been raped, probably by Hutch. Now she was pregnant, and someone—Thaddeus or Johnny or both—had tried to kill Hutch.

Dotty didn't answer. After a few minutes I heard her regular deep breathing, as if she was asleep. I thought she was faking, so I waited until she was ready to talk. It was a long time later, after I'd fallen asleep that her sniffling woke me up.

"Dotty?"

Again she didn't answer. I lay awake for what seemed like hours listening to her intermittent, quiet crying.

Eventually both of us must have fallen back asleep because Dotty seemed as bleary-eyed and numb as I did when Mother came into out room to awaken us for church. Neither of us wanted to get out of bed. We hadn't told Mother and Daddy what happened at the lake. They'd find out about it soon enough. Even without telephones, word had a way of spreading quickly.

"You two must have had a big time at the lake." Mother said as she served us oatmeal. She was already dressed in her blue nylon dress with the lace collar and her black high heels. Daddy had eaten his breakfast and was sitting in his chair in the living room reading the Friday *Lubbock Avalanche- Journal* that came in the mail Saturday. He seldom went to church with us.

"How much water is in the lake?" he called from behind his paper.

"It's gone down some since I was there last." I answered

"Shouting at each other from different rooms is not the way to have a conversation." Mother said, stirring sugar into her oatmeal.

"If it don't rain soon, that lake will be dry and the cotton will dry out worse." Daddy said, ignoring Mother's edict.

In spite of Mother's urging for Dotty and me to hurry, by the time we got the dishes done and were dressed, it was getting late. Mother had to drive the pickup at sixty miles-per-hour once we reached the highway. By the time we got to church, Sunday School had already started. Mother went to the women's class while Dotty and I did our best to slide unnoticed into the wooden slatted chairs in the girls' classroom. It was an exercise in futility, though. Every girl in the class turned to look. Our denomination didn't allow boys and girls or men and women to attend Sunday School class together—something to do with the Apostle Paul saying females weren't qualified to teach males. Dotty once told me she bet she could teach the Apostle Paul a thing or two.

"Glad you could make it, girls." Mrs. Houser said, wetting the tip of her finger with her tongue to turn the page of the lesson.

"Thank you." I murmured. Dotty said nothing.

The room was small, maybe twelve-feet square with a wooden floor covered with linoleum that was supposed to look like tile. There were several unframed pictures on the wall—one of Jesus knocking on an elaborate wooden door, another of him coming out of a body of water with a dove over his head, and still another of Jesus sitting down with children gathered around him.

The lesson was on evangelism. I was called on to read the scripture from the gospel of Matthew about going out and spreading the word of God to all nations. Mrs. Houser said the scripture meant we should take every opportunity we could to talk to sinners about being saved and accepting Jesus as their savior. I'd heard this before. All of us had. I hated it every time that lesson came around because I didn't want to talk to anybody about their religion. People accused me of being nosey, but this was one aspect of everyone's life I considered private.

Maybe everyone else in the room had feelings similar to mine, because when Mrs. Houser asked us for testimonies about the times we'd shared the Word of God with sinners, nobody spoke up. At least, not at first. After a while, Raylene said she had tried to get some boy she met at 4-H camp to listen to the Word of God. I almost laughed out loud. I'd seen Raylene at camp with a boy from Littlefield, and they certainly weren't talking about the Word of God. Mrs. Houser was pleased with Raylene, though, and told her to continue her mission work.

After Sunday School was finally over, we had regular church to get through. The boys were already out of class by the time the girls' class walked into the sanctuary. Some of the boys were outside, probably smoking cigarettes in the parking lot, and some were hanging around the back of the church not wanting to sit down until the girls came in. I made my way to the last pew on the left side of the aisle while Dotty went to the front to play the piano for the services. As soon as I and the other girls sat down, a few of the boys joined us. They'd already claimed their spot next to their chosen girl by the time the cigarette-smelling boys from the outside came in. Doug was among them.

Stanley Dickenson sat next to me and was telling me a funny story about falling off of a steer calf he'd tried to ride and landing in a cow pie. As soon as he saw Doug, he moved over, giving Doug his spot, both acting as if sitting next to me was Doug's right.

When Doug reached for my hand, I pretended to be busy leafing through one of the Broadman Hymnals housed in wooden brackets on the back of the pew in front of us. I'd never done that kind of thing before. Now, though, it seemed that I'd rather listen to a story about falling into manure than to hold Doug's hand.

Doug smiled at me as he took the hymnal from my hands and replaced it in the rack, then he put his arm around me and leaned close to whisper in my ear, "You sure looked great in that swimsuit yesterday."

"Thank you." I said, without looking at him.

"I'd like to see you that way more often." he whispered.

I leaned away from him slightly. "That was awful what happened to Pearlie."

"Pearlie? Oh, you mean that nigger. Don't worry about it. She deserved it for coming out there with white people."

I didn't respond. His sentiment was the same I'd heard all my life, words spoken so often I hardly took in their meaning. Until now.

"Can you believe that bastard Fitzgerald claimed he brought 'em?" He snickered and added, "He's probably one hisself."

I couldn't reply since, by now, the preacher, Brother Rodgers, was reading from the Bible. "From the Gospel of John, chapter four, verse nine: *'Then saith the woman of Samaria unto him, How is it that thou, being a Jew, asketh drink of me, which am a woman of Samaria? For the Jews have no dealings with the Samaritans.'*"

He went on from there, talking about Jeee Zus giving the woman living water which was, of course, a metaphor for the Word of God. I didn't follow the sermon the rest of the hour. I must have stopped listening at the word "Jews." It made me think of Anne Frank, her diary, and of Mr. Rabinowitz, the only Jew I knew. He would be the person to talk to of my concerns about the way Pearlie had been treated, but it would be another week before we would go to town. Another week before I'd have a chance to see him.

Doug was whispering in my ear. "Let's go for a ride after church." he said.

"I can't. I promised Mother I'd help her when we get home."

"Help her do what?"

I glanced toward the pew where Mother and Junior were seated, trying to think how to answer Doug. Both of them seemed as distracted as I was. Junior was squirming in his seat and alternately glancing over his shoulder toward me and scratching the back of his neck. Mother put her hand over her mouth to suppress a yawn, then picked at something on the shoulder of her dress.

I hadn't come up with an answer for Doug when Dotty struck the first note of "Softly and Tenderly." on the piano, and we were told to stand and sing hymn number one-hundred. It was the invitation hymn. We would sing all four verses while waiting for someone to walk up the aisle to the front of the church where Brother Rodgers stood with his arms outstretched, waiting for sinners to come and say they wanted to accept Jesus and be saved from hell.

"Shadows are gathering, death-beds are coming, coming for you and for me." we sang.

Brother Rodgers was murmuring, "Come, sinner come." but no one came, and the preacher dropped his arms at last and reminded us to return at six o'clock for the evening sermon.

When the service ended, a low buzz filled the sanctuary as people filed out of the pews, greeting each other. It was always a cheerful, maybe even relieved sound after the long service was over, and we could all go home to fried chicken or a pot roast that had been simmering while we were gone.

Doug held my hand. "You sure you can't get out of helping your mother?"

I felt my face flush. Was there some kind of double punishment for a person who lied in church? In spite of that worrisome thought, I heard myself saying, "I doubt it. You know how mothers are."

He blew a sigh out of puffed cheeks. "Oh well, I guess it's okay. We'd probably have to take that pesky Dotty with us."

I glared at him. I felt even more protective and defensive about Dotty than usual because of the strange way she'd been acting. "Dotty's not pesky. She's my little sister, and…"

Doug grinned, making him look even more handsome than usual. "I didn't mean nothin' by that." He put his arm around me and gave me a one-armed hug. "I'll see you Saturday. But tell your mother you might be late that night. I'm taking you to Lubbock."

I was completely surprised. Lubbock was eighty miles away. People only went there to see a doctor or visit a relative or maybe once a year to the South Plains Fair. It was always a treat when the opportunity came. I liked shopping in the stores that lined the brick streets downtown. There was Sears and Roebuck, Levines, Halsey Drugstore, and, of course, Hemphill-Wells that was too expensive for people like us to shop. There was a reason it was known as the Neiman's of West

Texas. Besides the stores, there were three theaters. Even if it meant spending all day with Doug, it would be fun

"I feel like giving you a special treat." said Doug.

Guilt clutched at my chest. It wasn't that I didn't like him, I told myself. He was always nice to me, even if he wasn't particularly interesting to talk to. Maybe I was just outgrowing him. Nevertheless, a trip to Lubbock was something I didn't want to pass up.

"Okay." I said and tried to swallow my guilt

He kissed me on the cheek. "See you Saturday." He walked away then turned around with that cute grin on his face. "Don't work too hard today." He laughed. "Remember it's a sin to work on Sunday."

I gave him a wordless wave and tried to smile. He was right. Baptists weren't supposed to work on Sundays, and Mother would never have asked me to. Knowing that only compounded my guilt.

When we got home, Dotty and I helped Mother fry chicken for our noon meal. Junior, as usual, got out of having to help and spent his time trying to teach Jesus to fetch a stick and bring it back to him. We were barely finished with the dishes when we all heard the sound of a motor and car doors slamming. As I walked to the living room, rubbing almond-scented lotion on my hands, I saw Daddy opening the front door.

"Hidee, Hal." he said. "Come in and have a seat."

Hal stepped inside, followed by Junior, who had been playing with his new toy truck in the front yard. "Thank you, Mr. Campbell." Hal saw me, smiled, and ruffled Junior's hair.

"You taking Caroline to town? Can I go?" Junior asked, looking up at him.

"Ask your mama." Hal said.

"Not this time, Junior." Daddy said before Mother could answer. "I think they got business to tend to."

"I got business, too." Junior insisted. "Besides, I like Hal."

"I like you, too, buddy." Hal said. His laugh faded and was replaced with something on his face I didn't understand when he saw Dotty and Mother behind me. "Hello, Miz Campbell."

She barely nodded. All of us were remembering that she had told Hal not to come back. No one said anything for what seemed like a long time. Finally, Hal spoke to Dotty. "Hey there, kid. You doing okay?"

"Yeah." Dotty said.

Mother tried to hide a frown. Daddy had put down the paper and was lighting a cigarette.

"Want to go for a ride?" Hal asked, looking at me again.

I glanced at Daddy, who chuckled. "Didn't I just admit y'all got business to tend to? Go ahead."

Mother looked first at Daddy and me but said nothing. I could almost hear her thinking, *Why didn't you go with Doug?*

"Okay." I said. "Thanks, Daddy.

Junior made an attempt to follow us. "Maybe next time." I said. I could still hear him whining as I got into the front seat of Hal's Ford.

"Where are we going?" I asked.

"Nowhere." He made a big cloud of dust as he pulled away from the house and down the dirt road, driving a little too fast.

"Nowhere? Well now that sounds like fun."

He laughed and kept driving. The afternoon was full of sunshine, white and glaring. A brisk wind blowing across the grassland to the southwest made it too hot to be pleasant. We rolled down our windows, and I let the breeze rip at my hair. Hal kept driving until we came to a stand of elm trees planted in the ten or fifteen years ago to serve as a wind break since there were no native trees on this vast stretch of west Texas plains.

Hal turned off the motor and leaned back against the door, looking at me. "I'm sorry you had to see that ugly scene at the lake yesterday."

"I'm sorry it happened."

"Dotty jumped right in the middle of it." he said with a grin.

"While I just stood back and did nothing." I said. "Dotty is braver than I am."

A lot of people criticized Dotty behind her back for doing that." Hal was silent a moment before he added, "We should all be more like Dotty." Hal said.

"At least we don't put coloreds in concentration camps and gas them, the way the Nazis did the Jews." I said. "At least Americans don't do things like that."

"We don't? You think coloreds don't get killed just for looking at a woman the wrong way? Like that kid in Mississippi."

"You mean Emmit Till? We don't do stuff like that here. Didn't you see Mr. Propps put a stop to that business at the lake."

Hal snorted a derisive laugh. "Propps didn't do it out of the goodness of his heart. He knows Maylock's been looking for an excuse to get him ever since he got drunk and drove into his front lawn. Old Maylock's proud of that Bermuda grass he grows, not to mention his wife's flowers."

"Mr. Propps got drunk? Raylene's daddy?" I was remembering her holier-than-thou attitude about Daddy.

Hal laughed again. "You're kind of naïve, honey. He wasn't the only one drunk and tearing up the streets that night."

"Who else? It wasn't Daddy, was it?" I regretted asking as soon as I spoke.

"No, it wasn't your dad."

"He drinks, you know. He gets drunk sometimes."

"So he drinks too much sometimes. He's a good man."

I looked at Hal for a few seconds, wondering if I was falling in love with him. Wondering if it was even possible to be in love at seventeen. "You're a good man, too."

"And you're beautiful."

"You keep saying that."

"You're blushing."

"Nobody else ever says that to me. I mean, people have said I'm pretty, but beautiful? Women are beautiful, not—"

"You're beautiful." he said, then added, "Let's go to the show in Morton next Saturday."

"I can't. I promised Doug."

"Oh, I see."

"He doesn't own me, you know."

"I never thought he did."

"Maybe the next Saturday." I said. "Or…Well, didn't you tell me they don't just have shows on weekends?"

He laughed. "I don't get paid until Monday that week. How about next Tuesday?"

"Yes." I said. "I'd like that very much."

He reached for me and kissed me full on the lips. A kiss had never made me feel that way before. Certainly not when Doug did it.

Hal must have guessed. When he pulled away, he looked at me and smiled. "I think I could fall in love with you."

CHAPTER 17

Pearlie

Pearlie knew all along that they shouldn't go to the lake. It was just so hot that day, and she let the thought of that nice cool water seduce her into going and taking the boys.

"Act in haste, repent at leisure." Uncle Thaddeus said that all the time. Now Pearlie knew firsthand what he meant.

Little bitty Dotty Campbell—no bigger than a minute—but that didn't stop her from sticking up for what she thought was right. She tried to help them out of the awful mess, and that boy Hal probably saved their lives.

Maybe she ought to be glad for that, Pearlie thought. But she wasn't. It wasn't right that they weren't allowed certain places just because they were colored. When Pearlie said that to her mama, her response was to tell her to hush up and not cause trouble. When she said it to Uncle Thaddeus, he said what we need is a colored Moses to lead us out of bondage. Pearlie didn't know who that might be, but she hoped he came before she died.

It bothered her when Mama said hush up and don't cause trouble. She knew Mama was thinking of Papa in jail when she said that. She also knew that almost anything they did could make it worse for

Papa. Now Pearlie was afraid it had just been selfishness that made her not care about anything except cooling off on a hot day.

Mama was worried sick about Papa in that jail and her not having any money to pay his bail. They all worried about what might happen to them if Papa was sent away to prison. Even Todd and Luthy worried.

Uncle Thaddeus did his best not to let on that he was worried, but Pearlie knew he was. He wasn't sleeping at night. He mostly just walked the floor. He was drinking, too. One day he came home smelling like a still. Only good thing Pearlie could say about that was, when he passed out, he got a little sleep.

Uncle Thaddeus and Mama looked haggard and worried all the time. Pearlie wished there was something she could do to get Papa out of jail, so everybody could rest a little easier. Yet, no matter how hard she tried, she couldn't come up with anything. It all came back to needing money to pay his bail, which none of them had.

Today all of them were going to town, even Uncle Thaddeus. Pearlie hoped that would make her mama perk up some. Mama and Uncle Thaddeus were going to jail to see Papa. Pearlie and the boys wouldn't get to see him. That was Papa's doing. He had said he didn't want his kids to set foot in that jail. It was no place for young ones, he said.

Even if Mama was going to get to see Papa, it hadn't cheered her up much. Pearlie had seen tears running down her face while she was getting dressed. Uncle Thaddeus was already sitting out in the old pickup, waiting for the others. Pearlie wasn't sure if he wanted to get away from everybody and have some time to himself or if he was just in a hurry to get to town. Maybe he thought he would find a bootlegger to sell him more whiskey. Liquor was not for sale legally in Morton. It was, everyone said, a Christian town.

Mama finally got in the pickup, and Pearlie and the boys followed. The boys climbed into the back. Pearlie drove since Mama was so terrible at it, and Uncle Thaddeus just preferred not to drive if he didn't have to. No one spoke except for the two boys. The windows were open because of the heat, and Pearlie and her mother and uncle could hear their racket—a giggle here, a squabble there, motor noises as they pretended to be driving. Mama didn't even bother to tell them to hush up.

Pearlie took a chance and parked the in front of The New York Store instead of next to the gas station so Uncle Thaddeus wouldn't have so far to walk to the courthouse .Mama and Uncle Thaddeus got out, and Mama opened her purse and pulled out a dollar bill. She handed it to Pearlie.

"Go in there and see if you can find a coffee pot." she said. "That old thing we got is rusted out in the bottom." Pearlie took the money and gave her a nod. "If they's anything left over, get Luthy and Todd a play-pretty." said Mama.

That brought a whoop from the boys, and they nearly fell over themselves trying to get out of the back of the pickup. When Pearlie and the boys were inside the store, Pearlie turned to see Uncle Thaddeus holding Mama's arm to help her across the street to the courthouse.

Luthy and Todd took off for the aisle where the plastic horses and other play-pretties were, while Pearlie searched for a coffee pot. She found one for thirty-six cents. It looked just like the one that had rusted. Maybe the new one would last for a couple a years like the old one did. Pearlie started for the aisle where the boys had turned their attention to toy tractors that she knew cost too much money when—of course—she nearly ran into Caroline Campbell.

She was with that boy Hal, the one who tried to help them. Pearlie's first instinct was to turn and head in the opposite direction. It wasn't that Caroline wasn't nice, even if she did ask a lot of questions. She hadn't stood up for them the way her little sister had, but Pearlie brushed that aside because it wasn't unusual. What was unusual was that anyone had stood up for them. Still, Pearlie wasn't in a mood to see Caroline Campbell. It seemed like every time Pearlie got around her, something bad happened.

But it was too late for Pearlie to act as if she hadn't seen her.

Caroline was walking directly toward her. "Hey there, Pearlie. I was hoping I'd find you here. I've been wanting to talk to you."

Hal stood next to her. They looked good together, sort of like they belonged together. Hal gave Pearlie a nod and a smile. Nice looking boy, she thought. If she were Caroline, she'd latch on to him.

"I just read a book I wanted to talk to you about. *The Diary of a Young Girl?*"

"Yes'm." Pearlie said.

"You said you borrowed Mr. Rabinowitz's book and read it too."

"Yes'm."

Caroline smiled, and her new boyfriend looked at her like she was the smartest thing on earth. "Tell me what you think of it." Caroline said.

"It's a good book." Pearlie was afraid she sounded dumb, but was too scared to say anything else.

"Did you think it was sad?"

"People don't have no right to treat other people like they done with the Jews. Uncle Thaddeus told me. . ." Pearlie let her voice trail off. She was wondering what made her blurt out anything in the first place. The book had gotten her to thinking about many different things. It had prompted her to ask Uncle Thaddeus about the Jews. He knew about all sorts of things because he read everything he could get his hands on.

"Go on." Caroline said. "What did your uncle say?"

"That people ain't got no right to treat others bad just on accounta they got different. . ." Pearlie stopped. Talking like that could mean trouble for her. For her whole family.

That boyfriend Hal spoke up. "Different religions, you mean?"

"Or different color a skin." The words were out of Pearlie's mouth before she knew it. She seemed to have lost all self-control.

Caroline and Hal looked at each other, making Pearlie wonder what they were thinking. Finally, Caroline said, "I wonder if that's the lesson we are supposed to learn from this."

Caroline always talked like that—so serious it sometimes seemed funny. This time it wasn't so funny.

Before Pearlie could reply, that boy spoke up again. "It ought not to take a war to teach us that lesson."

"It ain't very Christian to treat people that way." Pearlie didn't know if she said those words out loud of if she only thought them. All she knew was that the conversation was about to make her cry.

"Pearlie. . ." Caroline's face was all scrunched up. "Pearlie, I. . .I'm sorry about what happened to you and your little brothers out at the lake."

Pearlie turned away. This was getting to be more than she could handle.

Caroline spoke again. "That book just made me wonder if. . . ."

Pearlie hurried away. She didn't want trouble, and this kind of conversation was headed that direction. She found Luthy and Todd and ushered them to the front of the store so she could pay for the coffee pot and toys. When she saw Caroline standing nearby talking to Mr. Rabinowitz, she slowed her pace. Hal, she noticed, was at the far side of the store looking at motor oil. Why couldn't Caroline look at motor oil and Hal stand at the cash register?

As soon as Caroline saw Pearlie, she asked her a question. "Did I upset you, Pearlie? I truly didn't mean to."

"No ma'am." she said, clearly lying.

"We were talking about Anne Frank's book." Caroline explained to Mr. Rabinowitz. "Pearlie compared the way colored people are treated to the way Jews were treated."

Pearlie felt her heart drop. She was desperately afraid Mr. Rabinowitz was going to say something to her, but he spoke to Caroline instead. "And what do you think?"

"We don't put people in gas chambers." Caroline said.

"It didn't start out that way with the Jews." Mr. Rabinowitz said. "But we weren't treated as equals." He leaned on the counter, propped up on his elbows. His shirtsleeves were rolled up, and Pearlie could see he had something on his arm, the arm with the battered hand. At first, she thought it was a dirty spot before she realized it was a tattoo, except this one wasn't pretty. She was embarrassed when he saw her looking at it. Pearlie tried to look away, but it was too late. "You're looking at my tattoo." he said.

"No, I wasn't." Pearlie said. Your tongue will blister if you tell too many lies, Grandma said. It was too late to think about that.

"They branded us like cattle in those camps." he said.

"Everybody? Even women? And children?" Caroline asked, which was exactly what Pearlie was wondering.

Mr. Rabinowitz stared straight ahead for a bit, then took a deep breath and stood up straight. "The ones they didn't kill first." His voice sounded like he was choking.

When Caroline started to ask her next question, Pearlie wished she would just shut her mouth. "Your wife and children, did they—?"

"I believe my wife went to a gas chamber as soon as she got to the camp. The kind I told you about, Caroline. I'm not sure how my girls died. Maybe typhus." He looked at Pearlie when he said that. It made her feel sick, like she was going to faint.

"Oh, my Lord, Mr. Rabinowitz!" Caroline said. "Why'd they do that? Just because they were Jews? Like Anne Frank? It doesn't make sense. What I mean is, just because a person isn't. . ." She didn't finish what she was trying to say. She just looked at Mr. Rabinowitz like she was begging him to tell her it never happened.

But Mr. Rabinowitz looked at Pearlie instead of Caroline. "No, it doesn't make sense, does it?"

Pearlie didn't know how long that boy named Hal had been standing there, maybe because she was too caught up in what Mr. Rabinowitz was saying, but at just that moment Hal put his arm around Caroline, who looked like she was about to cry. Hal kept his arm around her as he walked her out of the store.

"What wrong with that white gal?" asked Luthy.

Pearlie didn't answer. She handed the money her mama had given her to Mr. Rabinowitz.

"What wrong with that white gal?" Luthy asked again.

Mr. Rabinowitz said, "She's trying to figure things out. What she doesn't know yet is that trying to understand something impossible to understand can eat away your soul."

CHAPTER 18

Caroline

When Hal and I left, we met Mrs. Houser going into The New York Store. With an embarrassed expression on her face, she made the excuse that every place she'd looked was sold out of canning jars. She kept glancing over her shoulder as if hoping no one else would see her in the store.

Hal kept his arm around my waist as he led me back to his car, parked about a half a block away in front of the Rose Theater.

We had planned to go see *Dial M for Murder*, but I had told Hal I wanted to see Mr. Rabinowitz first. Hal didn't protest. I think he knew why, because I'd been talking to him about Anne Frank's book. When we got in the car, Hal pulled me closer to him, and the next thing I knew he had his arms around me and was kissing me for the second time. I'd never been kissed by anyone except Doug. This was different. I mean really different. I don't want to sound sappy like those women who get swept off their feet in those pulp romance magazines Mother buys sometimes, but. . . well, let's just say I liked it. A lot.

"The picture show's already started." Hal said. "You still want to go?"

I shook my head. I had wanted to see *Dial M for Murder* for months because I loved Grace Kelly, and I wanted to be just like her, but now was not the time.

Hal drove west out of town toward the road leading home. He stopped next to the row of windbreak trees a few miles out of Morton.

Besides slowing down the wind, during a sandstorm they were supposed to keep sand off of the highway. They never did much good as far as I could tell, but I knew they served another purpose, although I'd never had any experience of my own in that regard. Not until now.

Hal stopped the car behind the row of trees and pulled me close again. "I've wanted to do this for a long time." he said, kissing me. We stayed longer than we should, and almost went too far until I pulled away.

"I'm sorry." I said. "I can't."

"I know." Hal moved away from me a little and put his head against the back of the seat. He was silent for a while before he said, "That book got to you bad, didn't it?"

"Have you read it?"

"No." He was looking straight ahead, not at me.

"Don't you like to read?"

He turned to me. "Sure. It's hard to find time when I'm working. Even when I had to read school assignments."

I was trying to imagine what it would be like not to have time to read. "I wish life were different for you." I said. "What I mean is, I wish you had parents and didn't have to depend on. . ." I stopped talking. I was getting in deeper than I wanted to.

"Don't feel sorry for me." It came out sounding like a command.

"I didn't mean to..."

"I know a little bit about what happened to the Jews during the war." he said, cutting me off. "Haven't read any books but I've spent some time talking to old Rabinowitz."

"I just don't understand why things like that—the Jews, I mean—I don't understand why things like that happen."

"People don't like other people who are different from them. It scares them, and their fear turns into hate."

"I could never be that way." I sounded more self-righteous than I'd meant to.

"What about Pearlie and her little brothers? Her whole family? Her whole race?"

His words hit a nerve. For a second I felt guilty and then defensive. "I don't hate Pearlie or anybody in her race."

"Yeah, but you're scared of them."

"Of course, I'm not." I was unable to keep a tinge of anger out of my voice. "Why would you say that?"

"Because it's true. Colored folks look different on the outside. That makes a person think they might be different on the inside, and we don't know how different, so that makes it scary."

His words made me uneasy. "I don't know if that's true."

"Then how come Pearlie's not your best friend and Raylene Propps is?"

"I've known Raylene all my life." I said with an indignant huff. "Since before we started to school."

"You've known Pearlie long enough to be friends."

"You just don't know how it is around here." I said, feeling defensive.

"Maybe, but tell me how come Pearlie's not your best friend."

"Oh, come on, Hal, you know why."

"Sure, I do." he said, "but I want to hear you say it."

I looked at him several seconds, trying to make the words form in my mind. "Well, it's because she's. . ."

"She's what?"

"Different." I said, knowing instantly I'd walked into a trap.

"Yep."

"It's the same reason you never dated her." I was glad to have thought of that. It was a stab at vindicating myself.

"Yep." he said again. "Same reason. Same as what happened to the Jews."

"No, it's not!" I almost screeched the words. "I'm not interested in killing anyone or even hurting them just because they're different."

He twisted the key and started his car's motor. "I'm thinking it probably started that way in the war. Then it turned to hate and then slaughter."

"No." I said, "I'm not. . ." I stopped speaking, knowing that whatever I said would sound lame. Hal drove out of the grove of trees and headed toward home. We rode without speaking all the way home.

Hal came by again on Friday, the day before I was supposed to go to Lubbock with Doug. Mother frowned when she saw his car out front, but she watched me going out to talk to him without saying a word. She seemed to have given up on keeping him away.

"I heard Johnny Davis is out of jail." Hal said when I got into the car to talk to him. We were still parked in the front of the house, and I was well aware that Mother was watching us from the front window.

I turned to look at Hal, surprised at what he had just said. "Where'd you hear that?"

"At the gas station in Morton. Guy that owns the station said he saw Johnny walking out of the courthouse. The sheriff was with him and somebody else he didn't recognize. Johnny and the other guy got in the car and drove off. He figured the guy was taking Johnny home."

"Did they find him not guilty?"

Hal shrugged. "Don't know. Maybe somebody just paid his bail."

"Who?"

"Don't know." Hal changed the subject again. "Want to go with me to the show this weekend? *Dial M for Murder* will still be on. Maybe we can see it this time. That is, unless we think of something else to do."

He looked at me, moving his eyebrows up and down in a gesture that was half clowning and half suggestive. I laughed. "I can't. I've already made plans."

"Damn!" he said. "I forgot about your date with Doug. He reached to pull me closer to him so he could put his arm around my shoulder. Mother was still in the window, watching us, although she was pretending not to be. He didn't even get as far as kissing me, though, and in a little while, I went back inside the house.

I thought about Hal almost constantly the rest of the day—even all day Saturday as I was getting dressed for my date with Doug. It wasn't just the way Hal kissed me, although I thought about that a lot, but it was also what he had said: *It probably didn't start that way, then it turned to hate and slaughter.* I remembered the expression on Pearlie's face when Mr. Rabinowitz looked at her and said, *No, it doesn't make sense, does it, Pearlie?*

I was angry at myself for being so upset. None of that had anything to do with me. I never hurt a Jew or a colored person in my life. I felt sorry for people who were mistreated, but there was nothing I could do about it. I just had to put it out of my mind and concentrate on going to Lubbock with Doug. After all, I didn't get the opportunity to go to a big town like Lubbock more than three or four times a year.

When he came to the door just before five o'clock, he was dressed in a new pair of jeans and a fancy Western shirt that stretched across his broad shoulders. He wore boots, giving him an extra inch of height, and his dark hair was carefully combed except for a stray piece curled on his forehead just above his eyes that were as blue as heaven. He was so sexy it made me catch my breath, just like all the other girls who knew him.

"You ready?" he said though the screen door. I pushed it open and held it, expecting him to step inside as he usually did. This time, he hesitated.

"Come on in." I said, "I want to get a sweater. Those theaters in Lubbock have too much air conditioning." As I moved away toward the bedroom to fetch my sweater, I noticed Doug standing awkwardly with his hands in his pockets. That seemed odd. He always came inside and spoke to Mother and Daddy.

Dotty was in our bedroom when I entered to look for my sweater. She'd taken off the shorts she'd been wearing and was looking through the bureau drawer. She threw a clean bra on the bed and pulled a T-shirt off over her head. "I'm late." she said, going to the closet and pulling out her poodle skirt. "Stayed out at the draw too long."

"Late for what?" I asked.

"You're not the only one with a date tonight."

"You have a date? With who?"

"Whom." she said.

"Bobby Nations?" I said, ignoring her grammar correction.

"Mmmhmm."

"You're too young."

"Who are you? My mother?"

"Caroline? You about ready?" Doug called from the living room. He'd never done that before. He'd always been content to talk to Daddy while waiting, but Daddy hadn't come home yet.

"You better get out there." Dotty said, slipping off her tiny bra and reaching for the clean one she'd taken from the bureau. "Your lord and master is calling."

"He's not my lord and master." I said, snatching my sweater from a shelf in the closet. I didn't wait for her reply if there was one. I left the bedroom, hurrying toward the living room and calling goodbye to Mother, who was busy in the kitchen. She called out for me to be careful and have fun.

Doug still stood near the door, hands in his pockets, looking oddly miserable. As we drove away from the house, another car approached, stirring up a billow of dust on the dirt road. It was not until we were even with the car that I saw it was Bobby Nations coming to pick up Dotty. I felt an emptiness in the pit of my stomach. I had meant it when I told her she was too young. Why couldn't Mother see that? Never mind that I was only a little older than Dotty, when I had my first date. That was different. I had always been more mature than Dotty.

"You're awful quiet." Doug said, glancing my way. "You upset?"

"I'm fine." I said. Doug looked straight ahead, keeping his eyes on the road. "You seem upset yourself." I didn't care, really, and I don't know why I even said anything, except it seemed awkward not to be talking the way we usually did. Why couldn't I have kept my mouth shut and been content to ride in silence thinking about Hal and Pearlie and Mr. Rabinowitz and what Hal had said about hate growing into something worse?

"Yeah." Doug said finally. "I'm upset for the same reason you are."

I was caught off guard, and had almost forgotten what I'd asked him. "What?"

"I'm upset for the same reason you are." he repeated.

"Oh." I couldn't think of anything else to say. It both puzzled and disoriented me for him to think he knew what I was thinking about the war and Mr. Rabinowitz and Pearlie.

"About your dad." Doug said.

"My dad?" I felt as if I were fighting my way back from an alternate world.

"What he did for that nigger."

"I don't know what you're talking about."

Doug turned toward me with a puzzled frown. "You really don't know?"

"Don't know what?" By now, I was feeling shards of panic along with confusion.

"He paid the bail for Johnny Davis. Now that son-of-a-bitch murderer is out again, free to kill a white man. Or woman."

"Daddy paid his bail? Are you sure?"

"It's all over Morton." he said. "That's all anybody's talking about."

I started to say something to Doug, I'm not sure what. Maybe something about how wonderful I thought it was for Daddy to do a thing like that. Or maybe something about how surprised I was that he would do it. Or how risky it was for anyone to pay Johnny Davis's bail. But I said nothing. I just sat there looking at Doug with my mouth half open.

"I know, sweetheart." Doug said. "It's hard to believe. Not just 'cause Johnny's a murderer, but he's a nigger!" He reached for me like he was going to pull me closer to him, but I backed away from him. "I shouldn't have told you." he said when he saw my reluctance.

"No. No, I'm glad you did." My voice sounded odd to my own ears.

"Well, don't worry. I won't let it come between us." He chuckled. "I thought for a minute out at the lake that you was going to try to help that nigger girl, but I know now you was just upset about the fight. Girls are like that."

I stared at him, speechless.

"My ma was kinda upset when she heard what your dad done." he said, "but I told her it didn't have anything to do with you. I told her you're no nigger lover and you think for yourself."

"Yes, but I—"

"I told you not to worry about it." he said, reaching for me again. This time he managed to pull me closer while he was still driving. "Let's talk about something else." He let his arm drop enough that his hand could touch my breast.

"Don't do that." I said and moved away again.

"You're my girl. I got a right."

"No, you don't have a right. Not unless I say so."

His face contorted with anger. "What the hell's wrong with you? You never stopped me before."

I turned away, eyes fixed on the rows of green cotton plants in fields next to the road. The motion and speed of the car made the long green rows look like they were running away from something.

"So you're going to pout." he said.

I didn't reply.

After several seconds, he spoke again. "I know you're disappointed in your daddy. I don't blame you. If my dad—"

"I'm not disappointed."

"You're sure as hell acting like something's bothering you."

I turned toward him. "Okay, you're right. Something's bothering me."

He smiled and grabbed my arm, again pulling me across the seat as he drove, so that I was once again next to him. He told me I would always be his girl, no matter what my daddy did. I didn't respond. After a while, he spoke again.

"You love me, don't you?"

"Sure." I said, though I wanted to say no. I don't know why I didn't. I told myself it was because I didn't want to start an argument or didn't want to hurt Doug's feelings, but the real reason was that I was pathetically weak with no backbone whatsoever.

Long before we got to Lubbock, I could see the town beginning to bloom in multicolor in the early darkness and eternal flatness. The bed of lights stretched out over an area that looked enormous. The town had more than one hundred thousand people and was the closest thing to a city I'd ever been in. As we entered the town, traffic lights winked at each other as if sharing a joke about country bumpkins driving into the city. Downtown, most of the stores were closed except for a few cafes, the movie theaters, and Halsey Drugs on the corner of Broadway and Avenue L. Doug's car bounced and rattled on red brick streets, but I hardly noticed. I was watching marquees on the front of theaters. The Chief was showing *The Man With The Golden Arm*, and the State advertised *The Tall Men*.

"A cowboy show!" Doug said. "Let's go see that one." As he drove past the theater, I saw a picture of Jane Russell standing with three tall cowboys. Jane's hands were on her hips, and her skirt was split, showing one leg all the way up to her thigh.

"Let's see what's on at the Lindsey." I said. Doug gave me a grimacing look and circled around. I already knew what was showing there. I'd seen it in the Lubbock paper.

"*Rebel Without A Cause*." Doug said, reading the marquee. "That's not a Western, is it?" We had stopped in front of the theater, the motor still running.

I gave him an evasive answer. "James Dean is the star."

"Who's that?"

"He's good." I said. "I think you'll like it."

"What's it about?"

"Kids in California."

"I don't like California people." Doug said. "They act foreign."

"Let's give it a try." I said and tried to smile.

"I don't want to give it a try." Doug put the car in gear and moved away. "We'll go see that cowboy show. You like Westerns, don't you?"

I didn't answer. I waited for Doug to drive back to the State and park the car. I didn't wait for him to open the door for me. I let myself out and walked at a fast pace toward the theater.

"Hey, wait up, sweetheart." he said with a little laugh. He caught up with me and put his arm around my neck, walking in step with me. "You're gonna love this show."

"Yeah." I said.

I hated the movie. I'm sick of cattle drives and Indian attacks and women with big breasts, but I acted nice and even let Doug put his arm around me and kiss me goodnight when we got home.

I hate myself.

CHAPTER 19

Thaddeus

A few hours earlier

Thaddeus sat in an old chair just under the portico in the front of the shack where he lived with his niece and her family. He watched the blades of the windmill in their repetitive dance to the silent music of the hot June wind. He wished for rain. He would have prayed for it, except that he had learned long ago that God doesn't listen to men like him. Worst of all, though, he was sick at heart for what happened to Johnny. Thaddeus blamed himself for that. He knew he was the one who should be in jail now, not Johnny.

He'd told George Campbell everything that had happened that day when they were drinking together. Pearlie hadn't told him everything that happened to her, just that Jasper Hutchinson had hurt her and she was afraid to tell Johnny and Mozelle. Thaddeus had guessed the truth, though, and when Johnny took him to town to buy a supply of bootleg whiskey that he would resell later, they happened upon Hutch outside of town. Thaddeus was just drunk enough to beat the bastard nearly to death. Johnny had tried to stop him, of course, but nobody could stop him when he was mad. Now the blame had fallen on Johnny. Thaddeus had tried to protest, but Johnny had convinced the sheriff that Old Thaddeus was too drunk to remember what happened.

Thaddeus was making himself sick trying to find a way to fix that. He didn't know how, he just knew it had to be done.

Most people called him Old Thaddeus, but he didn't feel old. Even the constant ache in his left knee, an all-too-frequent cough, and the gray hair on his head couldn't make him think of himself as old. Not that he was a young kid chasing women, and not that he could do anything about it even if he caught one. It was just that he couldn't think of himself as old when everything—people, dogs, horses, life in general—still interested him enough to try to learn more about all of it.

Thaddeus looked out across the leather-brown earth that had been plowed into rows for cotton. The green plants had grown tall and taken on the translucent look of a Coca Cola bottle left out too long in the dry heat. Thinking about it made him wish for something cold to drink. Maybe a bottle of beer or ice to pour whiskey over. He had no beer, cold or otherwise, and no ice. It was too hot to pull out one of the bottles hidden in the shed—whiskey he bought cheap from a Mexican in Morton who sold it for a small profit to farmers out in the country who were thirsty for what the law forbade. He'd been bootlegging whiskey most of his life. At times it meant the difference between food and hunger, not just for him, but for Mozelle and Johnny and the three kids. Mozelle was his niece, or more precisely, his great niece—his brother's granddaughter. She and Johnny and the kids were the only family he had left. The others had drifted away, either into death or a new town where they hoped to make a living or escape the law—or the lawless. Thaddeus had no children, although his wife had died trying to give him one. He was thankful to have Mozelle and Johnny and their three children. Now Johnny was in jail, and it was hard on all of them. Guilt stabbed Thaddeus again.

He turned away from the fading cotton plants to look in the other direction toward a blood-red sun dropping over the edge of a winding sheet of crisp grass that refused to die. He watched, wondering how the sinking sun could make the sky look so unruly, all painted with red and peach colors.

Just before the colors faded, Thaddeus looked away from the phenomenon out of a superstitious conviction that it would bring on bad luck for a man to watch the sun disappear altogether. He picked up the two-day-old newspaper he'd been reading. He kept up with the news of the day as best he could by listening every night to Ed Murrow on CBS. But he relished the opportunity to get a more in-depth look at things by reading the paper that Dorothy Campbell dropped off from time to time when she remembered to do it. She usually left it on the front porch of the shack on her way someplace else. It was always at least a couple of days old. It seemed important to Thaddeus to know what was going on in the world. Even when it sickened him—Emmit Till, for example. If anything like that ever happened to one of Mozelle and Johnny's kids. . . He wouldn't think about that. Maybe he ought to stick to just reading things in books—philosophy maybe, or history.

Thaddeus missed reading books. He'd had a job as a night watch-man at a library once when he lived in Oklahoma City until he got replaced by a white man. While he was there, he'd devoured as much of the library's fare as was possible. The last book he'd read was a book Pearlie had brought home. That was *The Diary of a Young Girl*. Pearlie said that Jew in Morton loaned it to her. That didn't surprise Thaddeus. Gersham Rabinowitz was a good man. Kind of odd, but a good man nevertheless.

Thaddeus figured Rabinowitz had a right to be odd, given what he had been through during the war. Never wanted to talk about it much except to Pearlie and, according to Pearlie, that oldest Campbell girl.

Thaddeus had been sitting on the very same steps he was sitting on now when Pearlie sat down next to him and told him about that book she'd just read. Asked him questions he found hard to answer, like why some people hated others on account of their race.

"Some folks is just scairt of coloreds. Maybe Jews too." he'd told her.

She'd frowned at him and said, "That no reason to be scairt. I never tried to hurt nobody and I's colored."

He agreed with her, but for her own benefit, he had to add, "Don't suppose Rabinowitz ever tried to hurt nobody either."

"Then why they scairt?" she asked.

Thaddeus had to think a minute before he said, "Must be on accounta they don't know much. They can't understand why God made some things different from others, and it makes 'em worry that maybe the way they got made was the wrong way. They just ain't sure enough a themselves so they get mad."

"That don't make no sense." Pearlie had said.

"No, I reckon not." Thaddeus said. He'd watched Pearlie walk away from him, a frown on her face like she was doing her best to figure it out.

Now he was thinking that if she gets half a chance, that girl's gonna make something a herself one a these days.

He shook the paper and folded it to make it easier to hold. The big story on the front page was about Governor Shriver trying to fight some law congress had passed to end school segregation. Separate but equal schools, the governor said, still served the State of Texas and the entire country best, even if the rest of the country was following a new law. Thaddeus read the story to the end after it jumped to page A8.

He spat over his shoulder and turned back to the front page. Winston Churchill, he read, was spending time on a yacht, now that he was retired. The yacht was owned by a fellow called Onassis. Thaddeus wasn't even sure what a yacht was, and he lost interest in the story before he finished.

He was perusing the paper for something more interesting when he was distracted by the sound of an approaching motor and the perturbed barking of the skinny dog the boys called Booger.

It didn't take him long to determine that it was George Campbell's pickup waddling down the road in a veil of dust. He was coming to the Davis shack either to hire some of them to work or to buy a bottle of Old Crow. Thaddeus hoped it was the latter. It was too damned hot to work.

He kept his eyes on the approaching pickup. In a little while, he could make out that there were two people in the cab. Somebody else who wanted some bootleg whiskey? Even before the pickup stopped in front of the shack, Thaddeus saw that it wasn't another customer with George. It was Johnny!

Thaddeus got up from his chair in the shade and limped toward the pickup. "By God, Johnny! How did you get out?"

"Mr. Campbell done paid my bail."

Thaddeus turned toward George, too astonished to speak at first, but he finally managed to ask, "Where the hell did you get the money for that?" He regretted it immediately. It wasn't his place to be asking a white man about his finances.

George laughed. "You worried I'm cuttin' into your business? You worried I started bootleggin' myself?

"You ain't got the knack for it." Thaddeus said, laughing along with George. "If you tried, you'd be in jail yourself by sundown tomorrow." He didn't fail to notice that George hadn't answered his question. Thaddeus's best guess was that he'd had to borrow the money to pay the bail. This time of year, dry land farmers in west Texas barely had money to buy groceries.

Johnny had already entered the house. Thaddeus could hear the surprised and excited squeals of Mozelle and the kids.

"We sure enough thank you for gettin' the boy out." Thaddeus said, offering George his hand.

"Glad to do it." George ducked his head and sounded embarrassed as he shook Thaddeus's hand. "Well, I reckon I better be heading home."

"Not yet." Thaddeus said. "Come with me."

George was hesitant at first, but curiosity got the best of him. Thaddeus walked to the shed and stepped inside long enough to fetch a bottle, handing it to George.

George shook his head. "I ain't got the money right now to pay—"

"Don't need no money." Thaddeus said. "My thanks for what you done for Johnny."

George hesitated again, looking first at the bottle and then at Thaddeus. "Well. . ." He took the bottle and gave the lid a hard twist and handed it to Thaddeus. "You first, old friend."

Thaddeus took a long drink from the bottle and shuddered slightly as he handed it back to George, then accepted one of the Lucky Strikes from the pack George offered.

They were still sitting on the ground in the shade of the shed half an hour later when Mozelle came out to find them.

"Shoulda known!" she said, looking at the bottle which was only half full now. She laughed. "Wish we could do more, but I thank you,

Mr. Campbell, me and the kids, Johnny, all of us thanks you." All three children stood back several yards, looking on timidly, not speaking.

George grinned, a cigarette dangling from his lips, and tried to say something in reply, but the words didn't come out right. Mozelle laughed again and turned toward the children. "Y'all go on back in the house. Your daddy will be done with his bath by now." Pearlie and the two boys turned toward the house and Mozelle followed. "I'll keep some supper warm for you, uncle." she said over her shoulder. "You're welcome to stay for supper, too, Mr. George."

"Good woman, Mozelle." Thaddeus took another swallow from the bottle.

"Ev' man needs a good woman." George said in a slow slur. "You ev' had one?"

"Mor'n one." Thaddeus said. "Mozelle, though, she be one of a kind."

"Yep." George said. "They're all one of a kind. All a mystery." The word came out sounding like mishtree. He tried once or twice to correct it but never got past the *M* before Thaddeus interrupted him.

"She worries 'bout them kids and Johnny all the time. Hell, she even worries 'bout me."

"Wommmen like to worry."

"No, that ain't right. They don't like it; they jus caint hep it."

"Yep." George reached for the bottle.

"I worries too." Thaddeus said. "'Bout Pearlie."

"You tol' me, but you fixed that didn't you? Beat up the bastard that hurt her." George leaned back against the shed and hit his head against it with a thud that got muffled by a gust of wind.

"Didn't like Johnny gettin' the blame."

"You tol' me that, too. Hell, Thad, forget about it. Johnny's outta jail now."

"Ain't permanent." Thaddeus said. "After they has a trial, they'll put him back in for good, 'les I tells the truth."

"Johnny don't know 'bout Pearlie." George said. "He thinks you was just drunk and lookin' for a fight."

Thaddeus's only reply was a *hmpff* that made whiskey-stained spit dribble from his mouth before he added, "He done more than hurt that girl, Mr. Campbell. I'm talkin' rape."

"Ah hell, no." George tried to focus his eyes on Thaddeus. "You sure?"

"Ain't sure a nothin', but if I ever find out. . ."

"Don't tell Johnny."

"Hell, no. Ain't tellin' nobody. No tellin' what Johnny'd do to that sum bitch if he found out the truth."

"Sheriff." George said. "You ought to tell Sheriff May. . ." He tried to say Maylock, but that wouldn't come out either. It didn't matter. Thaddeus just laughed a hard-sounding laugh, like something scraping off skin.

"You forgettin' Pearlie colored?"

George looked at Thaddeus bleary-eyed, saying nothing.

"Rapin' a colored ain't no crime. Coloreds don't tell the sheriff nothin'."

CHAPTER 20

Caroline

I slipped in the front door, doing my best not to awaken Mother and Daddy, making my way to the bedroom I shared with Dotty. I was surprised to see that the light was on and she was buttoning the front of her pajamas.

"What are you doing up so late?" I asked.

"Getting ready for bed." Dotty was folding back the covers and fluffing her pillow.

"You know what I mean. What were you doing out so late with Bobby?" It sounded more like nagging than I meant to.

She looked at me and grinned. "Probably the same thing you and Doug were doing."

I took off my blouse and threw it at her. "Then you must have had a miserable night."

"Uh oh." she said, throwing the blouse back at me. "Y'all had a fight."

"Not exactly. I just don't want to see him anymore. I think maybe I've outgrown him."

Dotty laughed. "Hal Fitzgerald."

"What's he got to do with it?' I was pretending to look in the chest of drawers for my pajamas.

"You're in love with him." she said. When I didn't reply, she said, "See, I told you."

"Are you in love with Bobby?" I asked, hoping to change the subject.

"I'm too young to be in love." She was quiet for a moment before she added, "At least it was a good picture show. *Creature From The Black Lagoon.*"

"Good lord, Dotty, I thought you didn't like scary picture shows."

"Well, it was in three-D." she said. "Never saw one of those before. We got these glasses to wear, see, so things would look like they were coming at us right off of the screen."

"Three-D, huh? I've never seen one either."

"You ought to. It was fun."

"We should have gone to Morton instead of Lubbock."

"Okay, tell me what happened between you and Doug." Dotty said.

Mother's voice came from the bedroom next door. "You girls turn off the light and go to sleep."

I turned off the light and got into bed. Before I could get settled, Dotty jabbed me with her elbow and whispered, "What happened between you and Doug? Did you tell him you're in love with Hal?"

"Of course not." I whispered back. "I'm just tired of him. Besides, he spent the first part of the night complaining that Daddy paid Johnny's bail." That was not entirely true, of course. Doug hadn't dwelled on the issue, but I didn't want her to bring up my being in love with Hal again. I wasn't ready to admit it.

"Oh yeah." Dotty said. "That's all anybody wanted to talk about in Morton. Nobody thinks it was a good idea for Daddy to do that. They say Daddy's a nigger lover and Johnny will murder somebody for sure now that he's out of jail."

"Johnny would never murder anybody."

"I know that. You know that. Daddy knows that, but we're still pariahs."

"Where'd you learn that word?"

"Oh, come on, Caroline. You think I'm a child?"

"Hush and go to sleep, you two." called Mother, this time sounding more annoyed and impatient by several degrees.

"You *are* a child." I whispered.

Dotty jabbed me with her elbow again, harder this time, before pretending to go to sleep.

The next morning Mother was in a bad mood, and Daddy had a hangover which explained Mother's bad mood. Daddy sat at the breakfast table drinking coffee and looking at his plate of eggs as if he might be afraid the yellow and white mixture was going to rise up and bite him.

Mother, who was already dressed for church and covered with an apron, wordlessly placed plates and flatware on the table for Dotty and me, glancing at Daddy's plate. "If you're not going to eat that, throw it away. Don't just sit and stare at it." Then, she added in a decidedly unpleasant tone. "And if you're not going to church, which I'm sure you're not, get out there and fix the gate. The damn horse got out three times while you were gone."

Dotty and I exchanged a raised-eyebrow look. We could count on one hand and have at least four fingers left over the times we'd heard Mother swear. Except when she was calling for Jesus to come to the house and he wouldn't come, then she'd cry out, "Jesus Christ, get yourself over here!"

"Sure." Daddy stuck his fork in an egg yolk. A thick yellow rivulet ran down to the edge of a curled-up mass of bacon.

We ate in silence for a minute or two before Daddy spoke. "You two girls have a good time last night?"

"Oh, yes." Dotty said. "I saw a three-D picture show."

"What's that?" asked Junior. He had just entered the kitchen, still in his pajamas.

"Three-D. No kiddin'?" Daddy said.

"I heard you bailed Johnny out of jail." I said.

He looked at me with a surprised look I hadn't expected. "Where'd you hear that?"

"Doug." I said. "Seems everybody's heard about it."

"Yeah." Dotty repeated. "Everybody's talking about it."

"Well, I'll be damned." We were used to hearing Daddy swear, so his words didn't faze us.

"Why'd you do it?" I asked.

Daddy's blue eyes seemed to bore holes in my own. "It's a man's right to bail outta jail. Specially since he didn't kill Hutch. Didn't kill anybody."

"No, he didn't." I said.

"So every body's talking." Daddy said. "I guess that makes you girls ashamed of me."

"Nope!" Dotty said almost before he had the words out of his mouth.

"I shamed a myself." Junior said. "Peed the bed again."

"Junior!" Mother screeched, dragging him back to his bed room.

I shook my head. "No, Daddy, I'm not ashamed of you." I said, in a voice so quiet I'm not sure he heard it.

Daddy stabbed at his eggs again. "So I got some people mad. Not surprised at that."

Mother returned and picked up my plate along with Dotty's. "Hurry up and brush your teeth and get dressed. We don't want to be late for church."

Dotty called dibs on being first in the bathroom. I was alone in the bedroom making the bed while Dotty was in the tub. The bedroom door was open, and I heard low voices from the kitchen. I couldn't make out everything they said, but I did hear Mother's scolding voice saying something like, ". . .staying up all night getting drunk with niggers." I couldn't make out Daddy's response.

Mother was stone-faced and silent as she drove the pickup to church.

Dotty, sitting in the middle holding Junior in her lap, turned to Mother. "I guess you're mad at Daddy."

"I love your daddy." Her voice was clipped

"Yeah, but you're still mad at him." Dotty said. "I'm proud of him for getting Johnny out of jail."

"I'm proud of him for that, too." said Mother. "Your daddy is a good man, and Johnny didn't need to be in jail."

"I want to see the jail." Junior said.

"No!" Mother said. "Don't mention that word again."

After a while, I said, "He must have got drunk again, and that's why you're mad at him."

Her answer was sharp and chopped-off. "Yes."

"You think it's a sin to get drunk?" asked Dotty.

"I think it's disgraceful." Mother said. "It's an embarrassment to me and to you girls, too. After all, this is a Christian community."

"Is Daddy drunk?" Junior asked.

"Sure, it's a Christian community." Dotty said. "A Christian community that thinks Johnny Davis ought to stay in jail just because he's colored."

Mother turned her eyes away from the road long enough to look at me and Dotty with an expression I couldn't read.

"Why can't I see the jail?" asked Johnny.

Mother's answer was a deep sigh.

We were too late for Sunday School, and it was almost time for the church service to start. The first thing I saw in the parking lot was Hal's black Ford. It was parked in the spot where Doug usually parked next to his parent's Oldsmobile. Mother didn't notice at first, but Dotty did. She punched me in the ribs with her elbow and said, "Well, look who's here."

"Who?" Mother asked. She still hadn't noticed the car.

"Handsome Hal." Dotty said and giggled.

Without another word, Mother walked into the church behind Dotty and me, holding Junior's hand. Dotty hurried to the piano in front. I skipped the back row where all of the teenagers always sat and went to the next to last one where Hal sat alone. Mother glanced at me over her shoulder with a look of disapproval.

Hal smiled when I sat next to him, and I reached for his hand. That seemed to surprise him at first, but he gave my hand a squeeze and looked toward the front of the church, pretending to be interested in the morning announcements.

"What are you doing here?" I whispered.

"I came to see you."

He knew I'd be here. He wanted to be with me. I had no idea what any of the announcements were about, and neither did I have any inkling about the subject of the sermon. All I remember for sure is that Hal put his arm around my waist when we stood to sing a hymn.

I could feel at least a dozen eyes looking at us from the pew behind us, but I never turned around. I had a pretty good idea what they would be whispering to each other as well. They thought I belonged to Doug, and they were either expressing their surprise at my brazen act or condemning me in unchurchly language for betraying the mighty captain of the football team. I felt nervous and brave at the same time.

When the service ended, I moved into the aisle ahead of Hal. None of the kids in the back row had stood. They all looked at me, heads turning in unison as I walked by. I was relieved to see Doug was not there, not in the usual space the two of us sat in each Sunday. Kent, who was on the end, stood and followed me out.

"Hey!" he said in a loud voice that made me turn around. "What do you think you're doing?"

"I've just listened to a sermon, Kent. What are you doing?"

"I don't like what you're doing to Doug. He came in late and had to leave. Couldn't stay here and watch his woman—"

"Excuse me, Kent. I have to go." I walked away, but felt as if the entire congregation was watching.

"You're just like your no-good daddy, you know that?" Kent called.

I turned to face him. "What do you mean by that?"

"Nigger lover." Kent said.

"Let's go for a ride." Hal said, taking my arm.

"Okay, but I have to tell my mother." When I turned around to find her, she was only a few steps behind me. The entire congregation it seemed, was staring at us. "I'm going with Hal for a little while." I said.

"You know your curfew." She glanced at Hal, and I would have sworn she gave him the slightest of smiles before taking Dotty's hand in one of hers and Junior's in the other. She pulled them toward the pickup as quickly as she could.

"Don't do anything I wouldn't do!" Dotty called. I wanted to throttle her, but instead looked straight ahead, hoping Hal wouldn't see my burning face.

He laughed and pulled me closer. "I don't think your friends approve." he said when he started the motor.

"I don't need their approval." I said. "Besides, it's only because of the high and mighty Doug McCallick that they care what I do. Nobody dares to go against him."

"Except you." he said, grinning.

"There's something else going on." I said. "Everybody knows about Daddy bailing Johnny out of jail. You can tell they don't approve."

"You just said you don't need their approval." Hal said.

"Where are we going?" I asked.

"Want to go roller skating?"

"The rink doesn't open until two o'clock."

"I'll bet we can find something to do until then." He laughed when he saw the surprised look on my face. "You don't have to be afraid of me." he added.

"I'm not afraid of you." I said, "but I *am* hungry."

The drive-in lot was already crowded when we got there. Doug's car was among those parked at the various stations. I know Doug saw us as we drove in. I watched as the carhop, a cute blonde I didn't know and who was most likely from Morton High School, walked up to Doug's window to take his order and those of his two passengers—Kent and a girl I didn't know. Doug was obviously flirting with the carhop, and she was enjoying it, alternating between giggling and leaning toward him to give him a coquettish look as she took their order. All the while, Doug kept glancing to see if I was noticing.

"Your boyfriend is putting on quite a show for you." Hal said.

"It's quite a show, all right, but he's not my boyfriend."

Hal looked at me and grinned as he rolled the window on his side of the car up slightly so our carhop, a different one who was not as cute, could attach the tray. "You've been dating old Doug for a long time, and it seems everybody around here thinks the two of you are an item." Hal handed me my hamburger and cherry Coke. "Also, seems like he's a popular guy. Even your mother and daddy like him."

I stole one of his French fries and popped it in my mouth. "You seem to know a lot about me. Why don't you tell me something about you? The only thing I know is that you came here from Levelland after you graduated from high school."

"You know I went to jail. Everybody seems to know that."

"Well. . .I heard something like that."

"It was in Levelland." he said. "With a bunch of guys. I was dumb. All of us were. One of us got the idea to use the pistol one of the guys kept in his glove compartment to shoot out some streetlights. I guess I was in the wrong place at the wrong time. Anyway, I spent a night in jail."

"That's it?" I laughed. "That makes you a criminal?

Hal shrugged. "To some people, I guess."

"So tell me more about you."

"Nothing else to tell."

"You didn't want to go to college?"

Hal was silent for what seemed like a long time before he answered. "Never crossed my mind." I could tell by the look on his face that was a lie. "I needed to go to work." he added. "Just like my brother. Then my sister got married. It was a relief to our mama."

"What do you mean by that?"

He shrugged and laughed a short, dismissive sound. "I guess she was just worn out trying to raise us."

"Oh." I was dying to know more, but tried to curb my curiosity. I knew he must be thinking I ask too many questions.

Hal wadded up the paper his hamburger had been wrapped in and threw it on the tray. "You ready to go skating?"

I handed my own greasy paper to Hal and glanced at Doug's car. He was pulling away from the lot, racing his motor to a roar and spraying gravel behind his wheels. "No." I said. Doug would be at the rink, and I was in no mood for more of his juvenile antics.

"I don't feel like skating either." Hal said. "Let's drive out to the lake."

"The lake? But I don't have a swimsuit."

"We don't have to swim. We can just walk. "

"Okay." I said. "We can walk, but don't make me do all the talking."

He nodded and started the motor.

Once at the lake, he took me by the hand, leading me toward the shore. Only a few people were there. That both surprised and pleased me, but I knew our relative privacy wouldn't last long. The warm Sunday afternoon would bring a crowd to the lake after Sunday dinner dishes were done.

The sun dripped yellow pieces of itself into the lake's surface and ran in streaks, making the surface look like an impressionist painting. The water would be warm but still cool enough to offer a reprieve from a day that was quickly turning itself into a kiln that would try to cure us all to ashes. That made me wish we'd brought our swimsuits. Even the miniscule waves reaching the shoreline invited me with their soft chatter.

Although I had earlier urged him to talk, it was enough now just to be with him, holding his hand, watching the water.

"I saw you playing in the water with Doug that day we were here, and I was jealous." he said.

I turned my eyes away from the lake to look at him. "Jealous?"

"Yeah, I guess I was." He picked up a pebble and made it skid along the water's surface.

"No need to be."

He turned suddenly to look at me, a question in his eyes.

"I. . .I won't be going out with Doug again." I said. He kept his eyes on me, still not saying anything, and I found myself staring at his sensuous mouth.

"You won't?"

I shook my head slowly. Now his eyes were flecked with the color of the sun.

"Does that mean. . .?"

"Yes." I said when it didn't seem he would ever get the question out.

He put both his arms around me. I looked up at him expecting, wanting him to kiss me. He did, gently on the forehead. "You make me feel like a whole person." he whispered. "I don't ever want to lose you."

I could barely hear those last whispered words because the wind abruptly came up and blew them away toward the changing surface of the lake.

CHAPTER 21

Gersham Rabinowitz

Dust blew across the street's asphalt and lapped up onto the sidewalk in front of The New York Store. A few cars were parked on the square in front of the courthouse, most belonging to workers at the county offices. One car was parked in front of the drugstore. As Rabinowitz stood looking out the front window of his store, he saw the sidewalks were empty. It was too hot for anyone to be out, and most of the farmers were on their tractors plowing along the rows to form clods that would help keep the soil of their farms from blowing away the way it did during the dust bowl of the 1930s.

The wafting sand triggered an unwelcome memory of the way vapors of gray dust would gust out of blankets when he and other prisoners in Brudy, a subcamp of Auschwitz, were forced to shake out their blankets in lieu of washing them. Rabinowitz routinely made a concentrated effort to not think about it. Still, at times, unbidden images came to mind, most frequently the scene of his wife and daughters being taken away. He learned months after his liberation what had happened to them. A quick and fatal shower cleansed his wife of the need to suffer starvation, lice, bleeding feet, typhoid. But Rabinowitz's daughters died a slower death. His mind screamed when he thought of what followed for all of them—a mass grave of bodies twisted and warped.

Rabinowitz rubbed at the embedded numbers on his forearm that seemed to tingle when he remembered too much. He forced himself to turn back to his store where invoices and bills awaited. His office was sweltering hot, but still a good place to bury oneself in mind-numbing bookkeeping—profit and loss, taxes and fees, utility bills and plumbing repairs. He welcomed the numbing.

Rabinowitz had been a musician before the war, First violin in the orchestra in Gdansk. But at Brudy, a heavy steel girder had crushed his right hand when he and the others on the work crew were trying to help transport it in the rain. Up until the injury, untreated except for an inadequate bandage, the thought of his music waiting for him and a miraculous rescue of his wife and daughters had kept Rabinowitz sane.

But there was no rescue for his family, and the music left him when he saw how disfigured his fingers became. His hand was fit for nothing more than to lift steel girders, and it became more disfigured as he was forced to continue working.

Oddly, he thought now, the pain in his hand saved his life. Pain and bleeding blisters reminded him that he was alive and that he could not give in to hopelessness. Hope had brought him finally to America and to a tiny store in the middle of the expansive nothingness that was Texas—the opportunity his wife's cousin had provided with a promise of a life in the golden realm that was America. Rabinowitz did not complain. He was a long way from Brudy and from mass graves full of children's bones. He made a decent living and even had a few friends. He had music as well. Not the twangy songs that played constantly on the few radio stations he could receive, but a phonograph and a collection of records. He could listen to Vivaldi, Corelli, Mozart, Tchaikovsky. And when he did, he sometimes even allowed himself to cry.

The air in his office grew more stifling, and he loosened his tie, running a finger around his damp collar, thinking maybe he would stop wearing a tie in summer like the druggist up the street. But the salesmen in St. Claire's Department Store always wore ties, so he did as well, even though The New York Store was considered second-rate. It was impossible for a store like his to keep up with a corporate chain store. Nevertheless, Rabinowitz would wear his tie, because he had his self-respect. It had outlasted Brudy. If he lost self-respect now, all would be lost.

When he could stand it no longer, he made his way back to the front door and outside where the hot wind could hit his face. He stayed, face to the wind, until it came to him that the wind was eternal here in his new home—eternal, old, and yet ever changing, like the land. The realization was oddly calming.

When he opened his eyes and turned away from the wind, he caught sight of a couple walking out of the drugstore. They were holding hands and laughing as they walked away. Caroline Campbell and the Fitzgerald boy. They looked as if they belonged together, as if nothing could ever separate them. He remembered having that feeling himself once, a long time ago.

Rabinowitz was about to go back inside his store when he saw Sheriff Maylock walking down the front steps of the courthouse, ducking his head against the wind and tightly holding his Stetson in defiance. He sauntered onto the lawn, avoiding the sidewalk leading from the steps and then jaywalked across the street toward the drugstore.

"Howdy, Mr. Rabinowitz." the sheriff said when he saw him standing in front of his store.

Rabinowitz nodded in response.

"Kinda quiet in town today, ain't it?" said Maylock. Before Rabinowitz had a chance to respond, he added, "Independence Day coming up pretty soon. That'll bring people in."

"At least for a day." Rabinowitz responded.

Well hell, a day's better'n nothing." Maylock said.

"Yes." Rabinowitz said.

"Then after that, we got a big trial coming up. That's better'n a circus."

Rabinowitz made no comment. He was thinking of Pearlie and her family.

"George Campbell might a bailed that nigger out, but he can't save him from a guilty verdict and a stretch in prison."

Rabinowitz had to pull hard against the pressure of the wind to open the door to The New York Store, but he did it quickly and stepped inside, not wanting to think about prisons.

He had not yet made it all the way back to his office when he saw Caroline and Hal enter his store. They were still holding hands, and the expressions on their faces made him reluctant to spoil the moment by asking if he could help. In the next moment, Caroline turned her eyes away from Hal long enough to speak.

"Hello, Mr. Rabinowitz." She gave him her pretty smile, but something about her also made her appear edgy.

"Good afternoon, Caroline, Hal."

"I need to buy some work socks." Hal said. "You know the kind— nice and thick."

"Of course." Rabinowitz walked toward the aisle where they were displayed, remembering that he had seen the two of them walking out of St. Clair's where they must have looked for them first.

Hal picked up a pair, checked the size, and took three more pair. "I'll take these." he said, handing them to Rabinowitz and following him to the front counter.

Rabinowitz punched the keys on the ancient cash register he'd bought secondhand. The old machine was elaborately decorated with iron scrolls, flowers, and leaves and was heavy enough to make Rabinowitz worry about the plate glass on the top of the counter where it perched. "That'll be forty cents." Rabinowitz said over the cash register's ring as the drawer popped out.

"Can I ask you something?" Caroline asked while Hal dug in his pockets for the money.

Rabinowitz glanced up at her, trying not to smile. Caroline Campbell always had something to ask. She reminded him of his younger daughter who also had been full of questions, but Lisle's hair had been dark and curly and her eyes the color of toasted almonds. "Of course, you may ask." he said, not wanting any more memories to assault him.

"I couldn't help overhearing what Sheriff Maylock said to you about the trial." She hesitated a moment before she added, "He mentioned my daddy."

"Yes, he did." Rabinowitz said, thinking how Lisle would have said, *He mentioned my father,* not daddy. But this was Texas and the past was long gone. He noticed Caroline's eyes again and saw the uneasy look. Caroline knew what people were saying about George

Campbell. How angry they were that he'd paid bail for a colored man. He wanted to tell her how he admired her father's courage, but she was speaking again.

"He said Daddy couldn't save Johnny from a trial and from prison. Don't you think that sounds like he's declaring Johnny guilty before he even has a trial? It doesn't seem right, does it? That an officer of the law would prejudge like that? Isn't that illegal?"

Four questions fired off quickly. She was a challenge.

"Yes." Rabinowitz said, "he's condemning Mr. Davis without a trial. No, it's not right for an officer of the law for anyone else to do that, and yes, I suppose it's technically illegal. But it happens all the time, I'm afraid. Not just here. All over the world."

"But that's not right, is it? Don't you think we ought to do something about that? Isn't it true that everybody in America has a right to a trial? An honest one, I mean."

"You're going to take on the whole world someday, sweetheart." Hal said before Rabinowitz could respond. "You're just the one to do it, too." he added as he picked up his package and took Caroline's hand, leading her out. "But you'll have to do it later. I got to get you home so I can get to work."

Rabinowitz watched them leave, Caroline looking at Hal and saying something he couldn't hear. He wanted to tell them to forget about Johnny Davis and Homer Maylock and the world's many injustices. He wanted to tell them just to laugh and hold hands and buy ice cream at the drugstore while they were young. Before the world came crashing down around them. He had known so many when he was young himself, who could have been warned about the same thing and would not have listened.

CHAPTER 22

Pearlie

It was dark and stifling in the bedroom where Pearlie lay trying to sleep in the bed with her two little brothers. There was more than the heat to keep her awake. It was a terrible truth that lay inside her. She was pregnant. Hutch had done it to her. Forced it on her. She'd never been with any other man.

It had been too many weeks now that she had looked for the blood stain on her panties. Nothing—except the swelling soreness in her breasts and the sickness every morning.

She'd done her best to hide the sickness from her mama and everyone else in the house, and she thought she'd been successful. She could sneak out every morning to the toilet that stood behind Uncle Thaddeus's shed without anyone noticing. There had been only one time so far that she hadn't made it inside the privy before throwing up, but no one had been outside of the house to notice.

The sickness came every morning but didn't last long. At least there was that. She'd been able to work the cotton fields of whatever farmer had hired them so far without missing a day. When she was younger, she'd heard Mama and some of the women talking at Zion Baptist Church in Morton—the Nigger Church, as the white people called it. They said if a woman could throw off the morning sickness easy, she would have a strong, healthy baby.

Pearlie didn't want any kind of baby that was part Jasper Hutchinson. She wished sometimes that she could get sick enough to empty out everything inside her, including the baby. But that was only wishing. She knew there was more than one way for babies to come out—the natural way and another. But people said it was a sin to do it. Besides, it cost money.

She wished she could talk to Mama about it, but she didn't dare. Papa would be sure to find out. He'd somehow learned about the first time Hutch had done it to her, and he'd hunted him down, finding him out in the country where Uncle Thaddeus had beat him up. Papa was the one who said they had to drop Hutch off at the hospital. Pearlie knew that was true because she'd heard Papa and Uncle Thaddeus talking about it when they'd thought she wasn't listening. Each of them took the blame and refused to let the other have any of it.

Uncle Thaddeus had warned Papa that trouble was certain to come of what he'd done, but Papa argued Hutch had been too drunk to remember who done it to him. As it turned out, Papa was right, and he was the one who was blamed.

Papa was out of jail, thanks to George Campbell, but there was still the trial ahead. Most likely, he would be sent to prison. She worried that Papa or Uncle Thaddeus would go after Hutch again if they found out she was pregnant. Maybe do something worse than beat him up. Then they might be sentenced to the electric chair.

All of that kept Pearlie awake and worrying night after night. That, along with the sickness, left her tired and listless. Mama even mentioned it one day, but Pearlie brushed it off, telling her it was something she ate. She wished she had told Mama it was the curse making her feel that way, but she hadn't thought of it at the time.

The night was stifling, with no breeze blowing through the open window next to where she slept. She swung her feet over the edge, getting out of bed as quietly as possible so as not to wake the boys or Uncle Thaddeus, snoring in his own bed across the room. She crossed the front room where Mama and Papa slept, Mama on her side with her arm slung across Papa's chest. Pearlie tiptoed to the front door, left ajar also to allow air into the room through the screen.

The screen door screeched when Pearlie pushed it. She stopped, rigid and unmoving, fearing that the sound had awakened her mama and papa. A quick glance assured her they were still asleep, still in the same position—both still breathing the heavy rhythm of sleep.

She slipped out the screen door and propped it open with the toy truck the boys had left on the front step so it wouldn't make a sound as it closed. Small, white caliche rocks were scattered across the packed earth that served as a front yard, giving out a weak glow in the moonlight and nipping at her feet as she walked across them. She stopped just before she got to the section-line road in front of the house and stood staring up at the expanse of stars Uncle Thaddeus said was called the Milky Way. Pearlie used to wonder if a person would pass through that when going to heaven. She wasn't thinking of heaven now.

She was staring into a dim nothingness when she felt something touch her shoulder. She turned to see Mama in her nightgown standing slightly behind her.

When she spoke, her voice was low, quiet. "How far along? Six weeks, maybe?"

Pearlie hesitated before whispering, "I reckon."

"Couldn't be nobody but Hutch, could it?"

Pearlie shook her head. She wasn't sure her mama could see her well enough in the darkness, but she had to know there had been no one else.

"We got to try to keep it from your papa."

Pearlie wanted to ask how that would be possible. She would be growing a big bump soon enough. Everyone would know. But Pearlie couldn't speak. The paralyzing fear had returned.

"You and me both know what he'll do if he finds out."

Pearlie's head was pounding, and the world spun around her. She reached for her mama to steady herself. Mama put both her arms around Pearlie, but it was an odd, stiff embrace.

"We got to get it outta there." Mama said.

Pearlie pushed away from her. "Get it outta. . . You mean. . ."

"They's a woman in Morton. I heard about her one time when. . .Name's Buela. People calls her Black Buela. We got to find her."

"But, Mama. . ."

"Hush, child. You know how it has to be, so just hush up now."

The next morning Mama told Papa she needed to take the pickup to town on account of she was out of cornmeal. Pearlie knew that wasn't true. She'd seen Mama wrap the round box of meal in a towel and carry it outside. She must have hidden it somewhere because she came back in without the towel or box.

Papa wanted to know why she had to go all the way to Morton just for cornmeal when she could get it at the store next to the gin in Stegall that was only six miles away.

"Why you think I'm out in the first place?" Mama said. "That Stegall store been out of cornmeal for two weeks."

That was also a lie. The Stegall store, while its stock was meager, always had cornmeal. Papa gave in and said he'd drive her to town, but Mama wouldn't let him.

"People see you there, they gonna yell out all kinds of nasty things at you. Got to let things settle down a little bit 'fore you go to town. Pearlie can drive me. She's real good at it now."

Papa gave up arguing when Uncle Thaddeus told him the windmill needed fixing and we were about to run out of water. He said the two of them could get it done before nightfall if they started early.

When Pearlie got in the driver's seat of the old pickup, she was shaking so much she could hardly drive. If her mama noticed, she didn't mention it. She didn't speak at all until Pearlie managed to murmur, "Mama, I'm scairt."

"I know, child." Mama said.

"I don't know how to. . .how to go about getting a baby outta—"

"Hush, now!"

Heading toward town, Pearlie managed to speak again. "Where we go once we get there?"

Mama just shook her head. Pearlie took that to mean she didn't know where to go either. That made Pearlie even more nervous, and she almost ran off the road into the ditch. Mama just braced herself with her hands on the dashboard.

Pearlie slowed her speed when they reached town and glanced at her mama, waiting for instructions. Mama gave no instructions even when Pearlie circled the square for the second time, worrying all the while that she would be arrested for driving without a license. When Pearlie glanced at her mama she saw that she was chewing her lip.

"Park there!" Mama pointed to an empty space in front of The New York Store. Pearlie pulled into the slot, and when Mama opened her door to get out of the car, Pearlie did the same. "Stay where you are." Mama barked and hurried inside the store.

Pearlie waited while fear roared in her head. She had no idea how long her mama stayed inside the store but was too numb even to feel relief when she saw her come out onto the sidewalk.

"North end of town." Mama said when she was in the car. "Take that street that runs beside the picture show all the way out to the rodeo grounds."

"Did Mr. Rabinowitz tell you where—?"

"Just drive!" Mama said. She didn't speak again except to tell her which narrow dirt street to turn on and when to stop in front of a weathered house that was turning mouse-colored under peeling paint.

Pearlie turned off the motor, looking down at her hands folded in her lap. Mama waited for a few seconds before opening the pickup door, getting out, and motioning with a tilt of her head for Pearlie to follow.

A black woman opened the door when Mama knocked. She had a broad face with eyes that Pearlie thought looked angry. Her hair, showing only a little gray, was cropped close to her head. "Yeah?" she said, pushing the word out in a gust of tobacco-tainted breath.

"Miss Beula?" Mama said.

"Yeah."

"Mr. Rabinowitz said—"

"Come in." Beula held open the screen door for them to enter. The room was small with crumbling linoleum on the floor. A sofa, sagging in the middle, and two easy chairs were shoved to one side of the room opposite a metal television set perched on a table. Two antennae sprouted from the TV and pointed opposite directions. Beyond the room, Pearlie could see an old-fashioned kerosene range in the kitchen with a chrome table and chairs in the center of the room.

"So the Jew sent you." Beula looked at Pearlie as she spoke, her eyes moving over her body as if sizing her up.

"Yes, ma'am." Mama said. "He say—"

"How far 'long is ye?" she asked, still looking at Pearlie.

"I don't know." Pearlie's voice was breathy with fear. She didn't know why she couldn't tell the woman she was about six weeks along. The words just wouldn't come out.

"I reckon she be gettin' into her second month pretty soon." said Mama. She must have known all along. Pearlie thought.

"'Bout right." Beula said, inspecting Pearlie from a distance. "Ain't too far since she ain't got much of a bump. That good."

Good? Pearlie thought. Nothing was good anymore. Tears were running down her cheeks and she felt like she might throw up again.

"Don't worry none." Beula said, surprising Pearlie with a hint of sympathy. Black Beula goin' to fix you up jes like that Jew tol' ye." She turned away to the kitchen. "Have a seat. Make yourself to home." she said, throwing the words over her shoulder.

Pearlie sat on the sagging couch, away from the opening to the kitchen. She couldn't see what Beula was doing, but she heard movement. She smelled kerosene when Beula put a match to a burner on the stove.

Before long, Mama sat down beside her and picked up her hand, holding it in her own. "I know it ain't natural, but we got no choice. You knows that, don't you?"

"Yes, ma'am." said Pearlie. After a pause, she added, "Will it hurt?"

"I 'spect so." Mama said. "But I be here with you, and the Lord be watchin' over you."

"You think he will? Even if what's happenin' is a sin! You sure the devil ain't lickin' his chops, waitin' for me in hell?"

"Oh, Pearlie, don't you be talkin' like that." Mama put her arm around Pearlie and pulled her close, letting her rest her head on her bosom the way she did when Pearlie was a little girl. "The devil ain't gonna get you for this. He too busy getting' ready for Hutch. The Lord know you his child. He know what you got to do."

Mama's words comforted her some, even though she wasn't sure Mama believed them herself. Pearlie stayed cuddled next to her mama until Beula came back into the room.

"Come on in." she said. "Everthing's ready.

Pearlie and Mama stood, Mama still holding her hand.

"Best you stay in here." Beula said, looking at Mama.

"I'm coming with her." Mama said.

Beula shrugged. "Suit yourself." She walked into the kitchen ahead of them and picked up a damp dishcloth draped over a pump and wiped her hands with it. "Take off your drawers and get on the table." she said to Pearlie.

Pearlie stepped out of her panties, folded them, and handed them to her mama. Then she sat on the edge of the table.

Beula frowned at her. "You gotta lay down and spread your legs out. No, not like that. I ain't fixin' to fuck you. Prop your knees up so I can get inside you." She watched as Pearlie did her best to comply. "Oh, shit." Beula said. "Your shakin' so hard you're making the table shake." She turned away and took a whiskey bottle from shelf. "Drink this." She shoved the bottle toward Pearlie.

Pearlie looked at her, still on her back on the table. "I ain't never drunk no—"

"Drink it!" said Beula.

Pearlie looked at Mama who nodded. Pearlie brought the bottle to her lips.

"Two big swallers." Beula said.

Pearlie gulped the liquid twice, and Beula pushed her back flat on the table. She wasn't sure what happened next, except that Mama was at her side, holding her hand. She later had a vague memory of Beula with a straightened coat hanger in her hand, holding it over the flame sputtering on the stove. She must have waited a while to let the wire cool and to let the liquor seep into Pearlie's veins, but Pearlie had no clear memory of that.

She remembered hands spreading her private area, the invasion of the wire, a scraping feeling, a pain that made her stop breathing. She heard a scream, felt more scraping, and a warm wetness between her thighs. Beula used the same dishcloth she'd used to wipe her hands to dab between Pearlie's legs just before she turned away, shook something off of the wire into a bucket near the stove, and propped the wire in a corner to be used again.

How did they get home? Pearlie couldn't remember as she lay on the bed, questions whirling in her mind. Mama must have driven all the way. A miracle they got home at all. Did she ever buy cornmeal?

How had Mama paid Beula? Did Mr. Rabinowitz loan her the money? How long was the cramping going to last?

Finally, she slept. After Pearlie woke the next morning, Papa asked her how she felt and told her she ought to be more careful about what she ate. She smiled and said she sure would be more careful, but she couldn't forget that odd look on Papa's face, the bloodless look of his lips like he knew the truth.

CHAPTER 23

Caroline

Day after day, the summer sun poured dry, scorching misery on the fields and crops, accompanied by hot wind. The Fourth of July was no different, but we were determined to defy it with a trip to Morton to see the parade and rodeo. It would be a welcome respite since, in spite of the miserable weather, weeds had made relentless invasions in the fields, and for the past week Dotty and I had been forced to battle them with sharpened hoes as our weapons.

Dressed in new jeans and red, white, and blue shirts that Mother had made, Dotty and I crowded into the pickup seat with Mother and Daddy for the un-air-conditioned ride to Morton. Junior, also dressed in a red, white, and blue shirt, sat in Mother's lap.

"It's hot." whined Junior. "When we get to town, I want a grape snow cone."

"We'll see." Mother said.

Junior sighed. "I gotta have one 'cause I feel sick. Sick as Pearlie."

"You're not sick." Mother said. "You're just hot."

"What's wrong with Pearlie?" I asked.

"She's sick." Junior said.

"How do you know that?" Daddy asked.

"Luthy and Todd told me she's sick in bed on account of affections."

"On account of what?" asked Dotty, frowning.

"Affections."

"I think he means infections." I said. "What kind of infections, Junior?"

"The kind that makes you sick." Junior said.

"I wonder if she's contagious." Mother said. "I don't think you ought to play with those little nigger boys until we find out what's going on."

"Did she go to the doctor?" Dotty asked. I saw that her face had gone white. It made me wonder if she was afraid of catching something.

"Don't know. Maybe. Can I please have a grape snow cone?"

He kept up his banter about snow cones the rest of the way to town until Mother told him if he didn't quit begging, he wasn't getting one. Neither Dotty nor I said anything the rest of the way.

Sweat rimmed the collar of my new shirt by the time we got there. It brought forth the odor of home permanent chemicals in my hair. Relief came like a smack on the face when we could finally got out of the crowded pickup to allow the wind to hit and dry us. Along the western horizon, a bank of clouds stretched from north to south, far enough away to be unmoved by the wind or to offer any shade. Parking spots near the square were already filled, and we had to walk from an empty lot on the north side.

Daddy pushed his hat down firmly on his head and took Junior by the hand to look for a snow cone vender. Mother, Dotty, and I wrapped flowered cotton head scarfs around our hair as protection against the wind. Firecrackers blasted in rapid succession from somewhere in front of us.

By the time we got to the edge of the square where the parade would pass, the sidewalks were lined with people at least three deep. In the distance, we could hear the dissonant clamoring of the Morton High School Band, tuning instruments. Daddy along with Junior, whose face and shirt were already grape-colored, joined us while we waited. The wind calmed, and the distinctive scent of horses wafted toward us. I pushed the scarf off my head to rest around my neck, and Dotty did the same. Mother kept hers on as a precaution.

People were looking at us. When I noticed, most of them turned away, unwilling to make eye contact. Only one or two men stopped to shake hands with Daddy or to nod at Mother. Daddy's charitable deed had indeed made us pariahs.

Dotty put it another way. "People act like we're Ishmael with leprosy."

"Just hold your head up." Mother said. "We've got nothing to be ashamed of and everything to be proud of." She set an example by holding her head so high she would have drowned if it ever rained.

The crowd was growing while we waited, and everyone seemed to forget about the leprous Campbells and stretched their necks to the west where the parade was assembling.

A group of coloreds were on the opposite side of the street. I searched for Pearlie but didn't see her or Johnny. Her mother was there with the boys and Old Thaddeus.

Hutch walked up to them, his arm in a sling, and a bandage plastered on his head. From where I stood, it looked like he had a black eye. While I watched, he spat on the sidewalk near where Pearlie's mother was standing. Some of it got on her shoe. Old Thaddeus grabbed her arm and pulled her away from Hutch. It looked like Hutch tried to take a swing at Old Thaddeus, but he missed. Old Thaddeus and Pearlie's mother just kept walking away. The boys followed as Hutch laughed loud enough that I could hear him all the way across the street. A man I didn't know came up to Hutch, laughing as well, pounding Hutch on his back as if congratulating him. Another man shook Hutch's hand. A few steps away from the group, two women smiled and nodded.

"Did you see that?" Dotty asked.

Mother shushed her and put an arm around her shoulder. "Don't pay them any mind."

I couldn't help looking. Watching them fawn over Hutch as if he was some kind of celebrity made me feel sick. I was glad when the discordant sounds coming from the band were replaced by an almost harmonious *Battle Hymn of the Republic*. Someone shouted, "Here they come!" and we all turned to see a brand new 1956 Ford pickup, brilliant turquoise in color, with a man in a big black hat in the back standing and waving to the crowd. Banners draped along the sides of the pickup bed were printed with the words, *Jake Bonner, Mayor*. Following him were more pickups carrying various other politicians—Cochran County commissioners, the city clerk, city counselors all throwing candy to the crowd. Then came Sheriff Maylock and his deputy, both on geldings whose sorrel coats had been brushed until they gleamed. Floats sailed by, some with men and women dressed in costumes from another century, some with children singing *Texas, Our Texas* alternating with *The Star-Spangled Banner*. Men removed their hats and women placed their hands over their hearts. Interspersed among the floats were people on horseback. Finally, the band marched by stepping high as they played *Yankee Doodle* and then *The Eyes of Texas* while a girl in a short, pleated shirt and white boots twirled a baton, pitching it high into the air to cheers from the crowd.

When more floats and more people on horseback passed by, Dotty called out, "Look, Caroline, there's Hal!" I saw him the same instant. He was wearing a new hat and new boots and riding a pretty *grua* mare who seemed to be stepping in time to the music each time she lifted her forelegs in a prancing movement.

All five of us waved to him, and he waved back, grinning. In the next moment he had moved out of the parade formation and was riding toward us. In what was one fluid movement, he leaned over in the saddle to put his arm around my shoulders and kissed me on the mouth. Just before he maneuvered back in the saddle, he said, "Meet me at the rodeo grounds. I'm riding saddle bronc."

A murmur rippled through the crowd, and I couldn't keep my eyes off him as he moved back into the parade.

"Now that was romantic." Mother said. "Brazen, but romantic."

"Just like in the movies." Dotty said.

Even Daddy was chuckling, but I was too caught up in the moment to speak. All I could do was watch Hal until he turned the corner to go around the square.

"That was that new guy, Hal Fitzgerald, wasn't it?" a voice behind said. I turned to see Raylene. I hadn't seen her approach.

"Yes." I said. "That's Hal."

"So I guess it's true." Raylene said. "You've been unfaithful to Doug."

"I'm not unfaithful to anybody!"

"You're crazy if you lose Doug. There's not a girl in the whole county who wouldn't kill to date him."

"Including you?"

Her face turned pink. "Don't be silly."

"Well, isn't it true?"

"Of course not. I'm going out with Troy, and I intend to be faithful."

I had to close my eyes to keep from rolling them all the way back.

"I guess you just can't be faithful to anybody, can you?" she asked.

"Maybe not." I said. "I really hadn't thought about it." That wasn't true. I *had* thought about it and decided that I didn't want to date Doug. The only guy I wanted to see was Hal.

"Are you going to the rodeo?" she asked.

"Sure." I said. "We always go to the Fourth of July Rodeo."

"Doug will be there. I saw him with Kent a little while ago."

"I'm sure he will."

Raylene frowned as she leaned toward me. "I can't believe you'd just dump poor Doug like that. He worships the ground you walk on."

"Doug worships the ground Doug McCalick walks on."

Raylene frowned and shook her head. "What in the world has happened to you and your family?"

"My family has nothing to do with my decision to stop seeing Doug."

Raylene's mouth twisted. "First, your daddy gets drunk with a nigger, then he springs another dangerous one out of jail, and now you've taken up with some stranger with a criminal record who just rolls in out of nowhere."

My first instinct was to spew out the fury of the storm inside me but before I could speak, the sound of a firecracker nearby startled me and set my heart to pounding like artillery in my chest. Finally, I managed to calm all the ferocity I felt. "We've all gone to hell." I said. "All of us."

Raylene stared at me with her mouth open before she marched away in a huff.

"See you at the rodeo." I called to her back.

The rodeo grounds were at the edge of town, and the big show wouldn't start until early afternoon. It provided one of the few times we ate in town. We could buy hot dogs or hamburgers at the stands outside the arena.

Mother, Dotty, Junior, and I waited in the bleachers while Daddy went to get our hamburgers and hot dogs. While we were waiting, I saw Hutch with his bandaged arm and wounded face making his way up the bleachers toward us. I felt a sudden void in my chest when he sat down next to Mother and grinned at her. I was on the opposite side of her, and I could smell liquor on his breath.

"Too bad a pretty lady like you got stuck with a goddamned son of a bitch like George Campbell." I sensed Mother cringe as she tried to back away from him. I was about to tell him to go away and leave us alone when he spoke again. "You better tell that bastard you married to keep his eyes open. He's gonna pay for what he done."

"Get away from here!" Mother said, pushing his broken arm.

Hutch flinched before he said, "I got my ways, and I got friends. We'll make him and that nigger wish they'd never been born."

"I said get away!" Mother said, pushing him even harder. "Leave us alone!"

"Go away, you son of a bitch." yelled Junior.

By this time, everyone around us had turned to watch the commotion. No one came forward to help Mother, though. She didn't scold Junior for his language. Instead, she pulled him up on her lap.

At least Hutch didn't stay long. But he'd gone no more than two steps when he turned and pointed a finger at Mother. "Remember what I said."

Mother's breath was coming in short, fitful gasps. I put my arm around her. "It'll be okay," I said. "He won't come back." Dotty sat so still she seemed to be frozen to her seat. I still had my arm over Mother's shoulders when, no more than two minutes later, Daddy came back with our food.

"What did Hutch want?" he asked, his face flushed with anger.

"Nothing." Mother said.

"Then why did the son of a bitch come up here and sit next to you?"

"Son of a bitch." Junior said.

"Hush, Junior." Mother said. "I wish you'd watch your language in front of the kids." she said to Daddy. "Junior picks up all your bad language."

"Well, what did he say?" Daddy demanded.

"He was drunk, so I couldn't make out what he was saying." Mother said. "Something about who's riding in the rodeo today, I guess."

I held my breath while I watched Daddy. Dotty looked at me from the other side of Mother. We waited, hardly breathing, as Daddy looked in the direction Hutch had gone. "He damn sure better not come up here again." he said, handing hotdogs to me, Dotty, and Junior, and a hamburger to Mother. He sat next to her as Dotty moved away to give him room. I felt a mixture of relief and worry.

After that, I kept my eyes on the stalls where the rodeo contestants would gather. Beyond, the bank of clouds we'd seen in the west had begun to bunch together and stretch themselves across the sky. Enough of them had reached the dome of the sky to provide some respite from the sun.

When I finally spotted Hal, I stood and waved to him until he saw me and waved back. Only a few seconds later a speaker blared, the announcer's voice welcoming us to the Cochran County Fourth of July Rodeo. A scratchy recording of the Star-Spangled Banner blasted out of the speakers next, and everyone in the crowd stood as two horsemen rode to the middle of the arena, one holding the Lone Star Flag and the other the Stars and Stripes, both flags stirring slightly in the breeze. They rode to the end of the arena and back, and immediately another horse and rider emerged from the stands. This time it was a girl about my age riding a beautiful zebra dun mare and carrying another American flag. She bent over the mare's neck as she raced at a full run all the way around the arena, the flag flying in a straight line on her left side while the crowd raised its collective voice in a loud cheer.

After the opening ceremony, calf roping would be the first event, and it's usually one of my favorites. I love watching the coordination of rider and horse as the calf is roped, then turned on its side by the cowboy in a re-enactment of the way calves were once captured for branding. Now they are usually herded into a branding shoot and locked in for the few seconds it takes to apply the hot iron to their flank. In spite of my fondness for the event, I had a hard time paying attention. My gaze kept wandering beyond the gate where the cowboys gathered, but I couldn't find Hal again.

Bull riding was next. The rodeo clown made his appearance before any of the bulls and their riders showed up. Dressed in baggy pants and suspenders, with his face painted a garish red and white, the clown performed hand springs and exaggerated pratfalls for a brief time before the first rider and bull were announced. The clown stood out of the way when the bull and rider emerged from the shoot. When the rider hit the ground, landing on his back hard enough to knock the air from his lungs, the clown immediately ran toward the bull, fulfilling his true purpose—to distract the snorting, frothing creature away from the rider until he could be helped back to his feet.

The crowd roared with laughter as the clown goose-stepped away from the bull before breaking into a full run and finally climbing the fence and hanging over it like a rag doll while the bull snorted and plowed the ground with his right front hoof. The clown hung there until two cowboys on horseback herded the bull back into the pens behind the gate.

There were more bull riders and then bulldogging, where riders jumped from their horses to grab steers by the horns to wrestle them to the ground. That was followed by barrel racers—girls my age who raced their horses at full speed in a cloverleaf pattern around strategically-placed barrels. I watched this event carefully, since it was a sport in which I longed to compete. Unfortunately, we couldn't afford a horse for me, and Daddy's Sargo was too valuable as a working horse to be used for sport.

Although I enjoyed barrel racing, I was happy when it finally ended because saddle bronc riding was next. Hal would be riding. I was nervous. Saddle bronc riding is more dangerous than the bareback bronc competition because of the likelihood of the rider becoming entangled in the stirrups and saddle straps.

Two riders came before him, and neither was able to stay on the horse for more than four seconds. A rider has to stay on for eight seconds to be considered for the winning slot. The rider's form and the ferocity of the horse's bucking counts as well.

My entire body tensed when his name was announced. "Hal Fitzgerald of Morton, a newcomer to the Cochran County Rodeo." the announcer called out. "He's riding Storm Cloud."

Storm Cloud came out of the gate fast, his head down and kicking up his hind legs while he tried to sway from side to side. Hal held onto the rigging and threw his right arm out for balance. The crowd went wild when Storm Cloud jumped high, bringing all four of his hoofs together under him as he pivoted in a half circle then bounced and kicked when he landed. Hal's hat flew from his head, but he didn't look up. His right arm was a single, thin wing keeping him from flying off.

My chest was too tight to breathe. Surely, he'd ridden for more than eight seconds—a full minute, maybe. Without realizing I was going to, I came to my feet, and in the same instant Hal's butt lifted from the saddle, and his entire body turned parallel to the ground, an arrow of flesh flying straight, until he fell hard on his back. I stepped forward, almost flying off the edge of the bleacher, except that Mother caught my shirt in her hand and pulled me back. She said something to me, but I couldn't distinguish the words because the speaker was booming with the announcer's voice, telling us the ride had only lasted seven seconds.

I could no longer see him. Several men had gathered around Hal as he lay on the ground. "I'm going down there." I called over my shoulder to my family as I pulled myself free of Mother's grasp and bounded down the steps. By the time I reached the bottom of the bleachers, the men had pulled Hal to his feet. One handed him his hat just before Hal moved away, limping toward the gates.

I saw him just as he emerged from the corrals and ran toward him, calling his name. He was still limping, but when he looked up and saw me he grinned. When I reached him, I threw my arms around him.

"Are you all right?"

"Sure." he said and grimaced, "'cept it hurts my pride that I didn't ride that bastard."

"You were wonderful."

That made him laugh. "Here, I got something for you." he said and reached to pull the stiff paper contestant number from the back of his shirt then pinned it on the front of mine. Let's get out of here."

"And go where?"

"I don't know." he said. "Let's just go." He walked gingerly, his back straight and stiff as we made our way to his car. We drove away from the rodeo grounds and all the way past the one stoplight in town where we turned onto the highway toward Muleshoe.

"Are you sure you're going to be okay?" I asked.

"I'm feelin' good right now." He winked at me.

"Where did you get that horse you rode in the parade?"

"Borrowed him from a friend just outside of town." He winced and straightened his back.

"Shouldn't a doctor check your back?"

"Nope." he said, reaching across the seat to pull me next to him. "I told you, I'm feelin' good. You ask too many questions, you know that?"

I smiled and laid my head on his shoulder. Above us, the clouds were bunching into cream puffs and frothy meringue, some towering into peaks—the kind of sky that made you want to run your finger through it and lick off the sweetness.

"I didn't know you were a cowboy." I said.

"I'm not." he said and laughed.

"You sure rode like one on that Storm Cloud."

"I didn't ride the son of a bitch. I got bucked off before eight seconds."

"Where'd you learn to ride broncs?"

"More questions." He squeezed my shoulders.

"Well, are you going to answer?"

"That guy I worked for in Lubbock before I came here. Now, he was a real cowboy. I bet he coulda stayed on that horse."

"You're a good cowboy. Maybe you ought to make it a profession. You know, follow the circuit."

"You trying to run me off?" He looked down at me and grinned.

"No! I just thought. . .well, I just thought you'd make a good one."

He moved his arm from my shoulders as he slowed the car, looking to his left as if searching for something. "I don't want to be just a cowboy, but I would like to be a veterinarian."

I moved away slightly and looked at him. "Really?"

"You're surprised."

"Well, yeah, I guess I am. What I mean is, it takes. . ."

"I know what it takes. A college education and money to pay for it. I know it won't be easy, but that's what I'd like to do."

"I thought you said you hadn't thought about college."

His answer was a noncommittal shrug.

"That would be wonderful." I said. A few drops of rain hit the windshield, and I could see that the clouds had darkened.

"You'll be going to college in the fall."

"Yes." I said. "I will."

"It will take me longer than that to save enough money. I'll be an old man before I can start. Maybe twenty-four, twenty-five. Here it is!" he said, turning off the highway onto a dirt road.

"You just turned off into the middle of a pasture. Where are we going?"

"Have you ever been to the national wildlife refuge that's between Morton and Muleshoe?"

"No." I said. "I've lived here all my life, and I've never been."

"It's something to see. Never been touched by a plow. Must be what this country looked like a hundred years ago."

"Like the pasture around our house."

"Yes, but a bigger stretch. And there's a bunch of playa lakes out here that fill up when it rains." He stopped the car on the top of a small hill. "Look at it." he said. "An ocean of grass."

"It's beautiful." The vastness of my homeland had never become commonplace to me. The vista stretching to the horizon and beyond to eternity always made me feel I was without limitations.

"That's where those cranes you told me about flying over your house stay in the winter. Maybe we can come out here later in the year and see them."

I didn't respond. I was thinking about being gone later in the year.

"I forgot for a minute." he said, as if reading my mind. He was looking out at the expanse of grass.

A fox ambled across the grass in front of us and stopped long enough to stare. He stayed only a moment before he moved away, disappearing behind a clump of mesquite. "You don't want me to go." I said.

Hal turned toward me suddenly. "Of course I want you to go. It's what you want, and I wouldn't stop you for anything in the world. It's what I want, too. For both of us."

I leaned forward and kissed his cheek. He caught my head and caressed it, looking into my eyes. A flaming torch of lightning seared the sky in front of us and thunder exploded a second later.

"That was close!" Hal said.

"We'll be safe in the car." I said remembering Daddy had once told me a car with rubber tires was a refuge from lightning. Just as I spoke, rain rushed at our windows. The parched earth took in the rain and delivered up a scent of welcome. "It won't last long." I said.

"Probably not." Hal replied. We'd both frequently seen these little squalls in dry years. They flirted with us for a while then moved on to bestow favors on someone else.

Within minutes, I realized the rain was showing no sign of stopping. It spit at the windows and ran down the glass in rivulets that glowed when more lightning leapt out of the clouds. Soon, the streaks of rain became a dark blanket shrouding the world.

"We gotta get off of this dirt road before it's too late." Hal said.

Dirt road was hardly the way to describe what Hal was trying to navigate. It had already turned into a river of mud. Hal drove a slow pace to try to control the car, but it kept slipping side to side.

The windshield wipers were no match for the shroud of rain covering us, and soon it was impossible to see anything ahead. Hal stopped the car when he ran into a clump of mesquite and realized he was no longer on the road.

"We got to wait this out." he said. "We're gonna wind up in one of those draws that crisscross the prairie if we don't."

I was shivering, not only because of the rain-cooled air but because the torrent of rain coupled with jagged flames of lightning and explosions of thunder were scaring me. Hal moved to my side of the front seat and wrapped his arms around me.

"You're cold." he whispered. "Let me get you warm." I snuggled into his embrace, welcoming the heat of his body against mine. We stayed that way for several seconds until he raised my head from his shoulder and kissed me. We kissed again and again, each kiss becoming more passionate until he whispered, "Let's get in the back seat."

"We shouldn't."

"I know."

We looked at each other for a few seconds before I raised myself up from the front seat and crawled in back. He followed and took me in his arms again. "Are you sure?" he asked as we fumbled with our belt buckles.

"No." I said, my voice trembling, but I reached for him and helped him push his jeans over his hips.

"I don't know how to do this." I said.

"Don't worry."

"What if I don't do it right?"

He pulled me closer. "No more questions."

CHAPTER 24

Caroline

It was past three o'clock in the morning by the time Hal drove me home. It had stopped raining, but the smell of the storm lingered. He walked me to the front door and whispered, "You'll be in trouble, won't you? Should I go in with you?"

"Good Lord, no!"

"Are you sorry?"

My voice was trembling. "No, are you?"

"Not a bit."

He kissed me lightly. "I'll always think of you when it rains."

I laughed. "It won't be all that often if you stay in west Texas."

He kissed me again and went to his car while I gathered up my courage to go inside. There were no lights on, but I expected Mother and Daddy to be sitting in the dark with anger burning on their faces.

No one was in the living room, and the door to Mother's and Daddy's bedroom was closed. I tiptoed past their door and into my bedroom. It was as dark as the rest of the house. The bed was still made. I felt a clutch of fear in my chest. Where was Dotty?

Just as I turned on the light, Mother appeared in the hall wearing her nightgown and robe. She didn't speak, but I saw anger and worry on her face.

"I'm sorry." I said. "I know you were worried, but we got stuck in the mud."

Daddy appeared behind her, wearing only his khaki pants, his chest bare. "Where the hell were you?"

"At the nature preserve. It started raining real hard while we were there, and…"

"You didn't have permission to go there." Mother said. "In fact, you left without telling us where you were going. Didn't it occur to you that we would worry?"

"I know I should have, but Hal just got the idea to go to the nature preserve, and…well, I'm sorry. I should have told you. I guess I just didn't. . ."

"Didn't what?" Daddy said.

"Didn't think."

"You damn sure didn't think." he said. "Your mother and I worry when you're not home."

"We drove up the road as far as we could go looking for you." Mother said. "We couldn't…"

"I should have been more considerate." I said, interrupting her.

"…even make it to the highway because it was raining so hard." she continued.

"I know. It was some kinda rain."

"We got stuck in the mud, and your daddy had to walk in the rain to get Johnny to help get us out. In the middle of the night, mind you."

I looked down at my hands, not knowing what else to say.

"Johnny damn near burned the motor out of his old pickup pulling us out with a chain." Daddy said. "Woke up all them nigger kids.

I raised my head. "Did you see Pearlie?"

"No." Daddy said. "I don't think she's doing too good. She probably ought to be in the hospital, but they don't like to take in niggers."

"Get in bed." Mother's voice was sharp. "We'll be getting up early tomorrow."

"Yes, ma'am." I said. "Where's Dotty?" The question had been burning inside me since I opened our bedroom door.

"She spent the night with Joanie." Mother said. "At least she asked permission."

"Oh!" I couldn't think of anything else to say.

"You should have done the same. Since you didn't, you won't be going out for two weeks."

"Yes. ma'am."

"I hope it was worth it."

I didn't answer. I got into bed and turned away smiling, because it was.

By the time I woke up the next morning, Dotty was back home. I expected her to be gloating because I was in trouble, but she was oddly quiet as she helped Mother in the kitchen. Maybe she hadn't heard about my late night.

"Did you have fun with Joanie?" I asked.

She looked up at me, her hands still in the dough bowl where she was making biscuits. Her expression was startled. "What?"

"Joanie. You spent the night at her house, didn't you? Slumber party?"

"Not really a party. Just the two of us." After a while, she added, "You were with Hal, weren't you?"

"Yes. We got stuck in the mud because of all of that rain."

"I see you got his contestant number on your shirt." She went back to rolling out the dough. While she finished the biscuits, I got out eggs and bacon. We had breakfast ready by the time Mother and Daddy walked in the front door. Junior was riding Daddy's shoulders.

"It rained a big un last night." Junior said. "We went out and looked at the cotton. Looks good." he added, sounding like a grownup.

They had both left their mud-caked shoes on the front step, and all of them were smiling. Their good mood was a relief. The rain had provided what the dry, thirsty cotton plants needed and what the rest of us needed as well.

Hal came to see me the next day. I knew he would want to make sure I didn't regret what had happened. The problem was that I wasn't allowed to see him. Mother went to the drive way to meet him before he got out of the car to tell him I wasn't allowed to see him or anyone else for two weeks. Dotty tagged along and reported their conversation back to me. She said Hal apologized for getting me home late and said it was because we got the car stuck in the mud on a dirt road near the game reserve.

"At least your stories match." Dotty said. She didn't smile. She was still in an odd mood. Maybe she'd had a fight with Bobby.

"Of course, they match. It's the truth."

"Sure, it is."

"What did Mother say to him?"

"She just told him to stay off of dirt roads when he's with you, except of course the road from here to the highway."

"That's all?" I asked, feeling relieved. "At least she didn't tell him not to come back."

"Not yet." Dotty gave me a look that was scrutinizing and shrewd. "Do you think she knows?"

"Knows what?"

"You know what I mean."

"No, I don't."

Dotty snorted and walked away.

Mother had to break her rule about me staying home for two weeks, because by the end of the first week, she ran out of flour. She sent me to the Stegall store to buy some for her. I was eager for any excuse to get out of the house, even if it was nothing more than going to that little store. When I got back with the flour, I didn't tell Mother that I had seen Hal at the store or what had happened after that.

The two of them kept asking me if there was something wrong. Of course, I told them no, and I might have had to endure more of their prying if Homer Maylock hadn't shown up at our front door with his deputy in tow.

Mother greeted them with a worried hello. She, as well as Dotty and me knew they wouldn't have been there unless there was trouble.

"George around?" asked Maylock. He was standing on the front step, but he wasn't making a move to come inside, although Mother was holding open the screen door.

"He's out in the field." she said. "He and Junior decided to go back out there to check on that west end that got washed out in that big rain we had last week. He'll be back in a little while." She studied his face a moment. "What's going on?"

Maylock looked down at his muddy boots. The deputy pushed his hat back a little and rubbed at his head. "I'm afraid I got some bad news." Maylock said.

Mother's hand went to cover her mouth. "Oh, my Lord." she said. "What—?"

"Jasper Hutchinson was killed sometime last night or early this morning. Murdered." he added.

Mother looked like she was going to faint. "Oh no!" she said, letting go of the screen door. Maylock caught the door before it closed all the way. "Who did it?"

"Don't know." Maylock said.

"I guess you know that nigger that beat him up is out on the loose, thanks to somebody we both know." the deputy said.

"Shut up, Larry." Maylock said, throwing his words over his shoulder to the deputy standing behind him. Maylock turned his attention back to Mother. "We don't want to come in your house with our muddy boots, Dorothy. We're just going to have a look around while we wait for George to come back."

"Look around? What do you mean? Why do you want to look around here?"

"Aren't you supposed to have a warrant or something to do that?" I asked.

Maylock shot me a stinging look. "Not if all I'm gonna do is have a look at them Hereford calves your daddy bought a few weeks back. I'm thinking of investing in some myself."

We all knew he was lying. He was as good as accusing Daddy and Johnny Davis of murder.

CHAPTER 25

Hal

H e couldn't sleep.

He knew all about the dead man.

He'd had to go to work after he saw Carolyn at the store. He worked until it was too dark to drive a tractor, then he'd driven around a while, then he'd taken the long way home because he wanted more time to think about Caroline as he drove. He'd passed the usual turn-off to Morton and was headed toward the nature preserve when he had to slow down because his headlights went out. He'd known for several days that there was a short in the wiring, but hadn't gotten around to fixing it. Before, the lights would flicker, this time they went out completely. Must have been the dampness.

Since the eastern sky was streaked with birthing pains of dawn, he kept going, telling himself he could make it home without needing his lights. He'd only gone a few yards when he was able to make out the dark and ethereal shape of the abandoned railcar and Hutch's car in front of it.

Hal stopped his car, grabbed a flashlight from the glove compartment, and ran toward Hutch's car, slogging through the mud that was still there after the heavy rain. He wouldn't think about what happened next. It took a great effort to push it out of his mind, and even then, some things wouldn't be erased. He could still see Hutch on the floor of the railcar in a pool of blood, still see his face when he shone the light on him. The face of a dead man.

Hal couldn't remember all that happened until he walked through the mud again and got into his car. He sat there for a long time, shaking, trying to think. When his mind cleared enough to realize that if he sat there long enough someone might come by and see him, he started his car and drove toward Morton. Once he made it back to town, he parked his car across the street from the courthouse and sat in the dark for another long time, knowing he needed to tell the sheriff everything.

Hal was still shaking as he made his way up the courthouse steps. He pushed on the door, but it was locked. There were doors on three of the four sides of the building. He walked around the building, trying all of them, but none would open. He went back to his car, thinking that maybe there was a god and he had spared him from having to tell the sheriff anything.

By the time he was back in his rented room, the feeling of relief had left him.

He didn't sleep at all that night. He got up after an hour and went to Audrey's Cafe, the only thing open that early. She was just unlocking the front door when he arrived.

"You're up mighty early." she said.

"Yeah." he said, making his way to a booth.

Audrey brought him coffee without his ordering it. "You look like hell." she said, setting the cup and saucer on the table. "Lots of booze last night, huh?" When Hal shook his head, she laughed. "Sure, it's booze. A night of lovin' don't leave you lookin' like that."

Hal tried to smile at her, to send a signal that everything was all right with him, in spite of the way he looked. He dumped sugar in his coffee and swallowed it before it cooled, burning his tongue and throat. He was vaguely aware of more customers entering the café.

One of them got his attention when he spoke in a loud voice. "Goddamn nigger killed Hutch!" The speaker was a big man with the same weathered skin most men on the high plains had, making it difficult to determine his age. He wore faded jeans and a wide-brimmed Western-style hat like all the other men.

"Yeah, Dub, we heard." A male voice came from the booth behind Hal.

"I coulda told you it would happen." Dub said in his booming voice. "Coulda told you when that goddamn George Campbell bailed the son of a bitch outta jail." He slid into the booth behind Hal and shouted in an even louder voice, "Bring me some coffee, Audrey."

"Heard there was two men done the killing." the other man said. "Somebody said it was a white man."

"Well I'll be damned." Dub said. "I'll bet my new tractor the second son of a bitch was that nigger-lover Campbell."

"No suspects yet." said the other voice.

"Formality." Dub said. "You know how ol' Maylock is. He'll have both of them bastards in custody by tomorrow."

Hal left the café as quickly as he could and drove all the way to the Campbell place so he could warn Caroline and her daddy about what he had heard. He also wanted to see if Caroline and Dotty were all right, but Mrs. Campbell wouldn't even let him get out of the car, and refused to talk to him. He drove back into Morton, but didn't want to go to his two-room apartment and sit there alone with nothing but his radio and the TV that received only two channels on a good day. He wouldn't go to work today. Even the thought of it was impossible. He parked on the square in front of the courthouse and sat there, staring at the steps and the double doors at the top of them and wrestling with the idea of going in to talk to Maylock.

With a resigned sigh, Hal got out of his car and slammed the door behind him. Halfway up the steps, he stopped, turned around, and went back down. Before he got to his car, he walked diagonally across the street. With no plan in mind, he headed toward The New York Store.

When he entered, Rabinowitz was busy with a customer, both of them standing next to a display of work boots in the shoe department. Rabinowitz looked toward him and nodded. "Be with you in a moment."

Hal stood still for a few seconds before turning back toward the door. He was about to push it open when Rabinowitz called, "Hal! Give me a minute." The words boomed out like a command. Hal stopped and turned around, surprised at the man's tone, but he gave Rabinowitz a slight nod and moved toward a display of costume jewelry

It would be wonderful to be able to afford to buy Caroline something nice, he thought, but not this. Not colored glass glued to cheap metal. He moved toward a shelf full of toy trucks, thinking of Junior. He was still looking at them when Rabinowitz called again, this time in a more normal voice.

"Hello, Mr. Rabinowitz." Hal put out his hand to shake Rabinowitz's.

"You know about the killing." Rabinowitz said. When Hal nodded, Rabinowitz added. "You know who they're blaming."

"Johnny Davis and George Campbell." Hal's voice sounded tired, even to his own ears.

"Both of them?" Rabinowitz frowned. "I didn't know that."

"I'm worried." Hal said.

"You should be. 'More dangerous than monsters are common men ready to believe and act without asking questions.'"

"You quoting Shakespeare or the Bible or something?"

"Anne Frank." Rabinowitz said.

"Caroline read that book." Hal shook his head. "I oughta do something, but I don't know what."

"Come with me to the back. I'll give you a cup of coffee." Rabinowitz had started

walking toward his office at the back of the store.

"I'm plumb full of coffee. You got anything stronger?"

"No. And even if I did, I wouldn't give it to you. You're still a kid."

Hal felt his face burning, but he said nothing and followed Rabinowitz. In the office, when he handed Hal the coffee, he accepted it and sat in a chair in the corner. The coffee was strong and bitter, like it had been sitting in the pot for a while. Hal took one sip and set the cup aside. "I. . .know when it happened." His voice shook as he spoke, but it was something he had to say. Gersham Rabinowitz was the only person he could think of to talk to about it.

"Explain that." Rabinowitz's voice was calm, like a teacher asking Hal to explain the answer to an algebra problem.

"It wasn't Johnny or Mr. Campbell." he said in a shaky voice.

"How do you know that?"

"Well, it couldn't be, could it? Neither one of them is the kind that would do that."

Gersham looked at him with a look that almost made him shake. Finally, he spoke. "You know who did it."

Hal didn't want to speak. He wasn't even sure he could because of the awful tightness in his chest, but the words blurted out anyway. "No, I don't. How could I? I mean. . ." He stopped speaking, too frightened, too angry, too confused to say more.

Rabinowitz breathed a deep sigh. "Some of us always try to protect the vulnerable ones. We want to make things better." He looked away, then back at Hal. "It's better than hate." he said. Hal wasn't sure what Rabinowitz was getting at, but before he could say anything, Rabinowitz sadly shook his head. "I lived in a world based on hate the Nazis created. All I can tell you is that there are lots of things better than hate, but some of them can get you killed.

CHAPTER 26

Caroline

I thought I was losing my mind. I needed to get away, but Mother wouldn't let me go out again. The only place I could go was to the chicken house to gather eggs. I even begged Daddy to let me go to the field to hoe out the weeds in the cotton, but he said there was no need. "Weeds will be coming up soon enough because of that rain, but it's not time yet." he said.

When he saw tears in my eyes, I later heard him telling Mother. "Maybe it's time we let her out of the house." he said, laughing. Mother laughed too, but still wouldn't let me out.

The best thing about that was their laughter. Sheriff Maylock had been out to talk to Daddy several more times, and each time he came, Mother and Daddy got quiet and distant. They would retreat into their bedroom to talk, leaving Junior for Dotty and me to watch. Dotty wasn't much help. She spent most of her time out at the draw that was too muddy even to walk in now.

It wasn't so hard watching Junior at first, since he spent most of the time in the mud puddle in front of the house. When it dried up at the end of the week, he became restless. More than once he knocked on the door to Mother's and Daddy's bedroom, demanding to be let in. Mother's reply was always, "Just a minute, Junior. Caroline, find something for Junior to do."

"Why they won't let me in?" Junior demanded.

"Because they're talking about important things." I told him.

"What?"

Dotty looked at me and walked out to the back again, leaving me to come up with a lie. "They're talking about cotton."

Junior gave me an angry frown. "No. They're talking about Mr. Maylock."

"What makes you think that?"

"Because Mr. Maylock is going to put Daddy in jail, and Luthy and Todd's daddy, too."

"No, he's not!" Dotty said, suddenly reappearing. Apparently she'd decided not to dig. At the same time, I grabbed Junior's hand and tried to lead him toward the kitchen, promising him a butter and sugar sandwich.

"How does he know that?" Dotty whispered to me while we sat at the table watching Junior eat his sandwich. Dotty looked as if she was about to be sick.

"Don't know." I said. I felt as if I might throw up.

"But he's not going to jail." Dotty whispered to me. "Daddy said the sheriff doesn't know who did it. Just because Daddy is friends with Johnny doesn't mean…"

"Why are y'all whispering?" asked Junior.

"Because we have a secret." Dotty said.

There was a suspicious look on his buttery sugary face. "What?"

"If it's a secret I can't tell." Dotty said.

"Yes, you can."

"It's a surprise. For you." Dotty said.

"What is it?"

"We can't tell." Dotty said "But you'll like it."

Junior took another big bite from his sandwich and chewed a long time. "Can we go see Daddy and Johnny when they're in jail?"

"You hush up that kind of talk." I said. "Mother and Daddy don't want you to talk about jail."

Junior wore a somber expression as he glanced at me, then Dotty, then back at me. I thought maybe he was about to cry but all he said was, "Can I have another sandwich?"

Either Junior took my warning seriously or he had an extremely short attention span because he didn't mention Daddy or Johnny going to jail again. He even forgot about the surprise Dotty had lied about. Sheriff Maylock stopped coming to the house as well. I wasn't sure why. I hoped he was convinced Daddy and Johnny had nothing to do with it.

Mother's and Daddy's moods improved, too. Everything was returning to normal except for me. I felt trapped. I needed to see Hal. But he wouldn't be likely to show up for a while. Not after Mother had sent him away. Maybe that was a good thing. Maybe I should never talk to him again.

By the following week, the weeds had stuck their heads out of the earth to attempt forbidden communion with the cotton plants. Daddy drove over to Johnny's house to hire him and his family to chop them out. He said the Davis crew could take care of the weeds this time, and Dotty and I didn't have to help, since it would only take a few days. That way, he said, we wouldn't be too tired to go to the summer revival meeting at church.

I wasn't all that crazy about revival meetings any more than I was about chopping weeds out of the cotton, and I certainly didn't want to go now. I felt too sick to go. Besides that, if you've been to one revival, you've been to them all. They last for at least one full week with services every night. There is a guest preacher, sometimes from another church or sometimes one that makes revival circuit preaching his career. The subject for every sermon is sin. The guest preacher always tries to scare people into repenting and being saved. They also come along with our preacher, Brother Rodgers, to various members' houses for dinner every day at noon. We've had our share of them.

If it's a sin to hate revival meetings, maybe I can be redeemed by admitting some of the preachers have been kind of interesting. One summer, we had a revival preacher who had been a cowboy back in the days of the open range, before ranches had been broken up into farms. He told stories about his adventures. Most of them were un-Christian, but he said he had surrendered his life to Jesus, so we knew he was okay. I wished I could feel the same.

Instead of the usual sins, this one preached about the land. To him, the biggest sin of mankind was plowing up the grass and turning the prairie into farms. We should have left it the way God created it, he said.

Another revival preacher that stopped by our house was a water witch. He could take a mesquite twig that he'd carved into a fork and walk along with it in his hands until the base of the fork turned down to the ground. That meant there was water underground. I asked a lot of questions, and to get me to shut up, he gave me the forked stick and told me to try it while he went to the house for ice tea. Sure enough, I found water, but there was already a well a few feet away. I guess I'm a witch. I'm feeling it more and more.

At the current revival, I knew the visiting preacher wasn't going to be so interesting because he'd been our revival preacher before. He was the ordinary kind who was against sin of all kinds. That made me worry about going to church every night for a week because of what I'd done.

The first Monday night of the revival. Daddy stayed home, but the rest of us went to the church. By the time we got there, several cars were parked around the building, and the sanctuary was filling up. The room sounded like bees swarming around a hive, since it was still five minutes before services. As soon as the four of us entered, the buzzing stopped. Mother hesitated a moment, then grabbed Junior's hand and started toward one of the pews close to the front. Dotty and I followed. Dotty went to the piano, and I sat with Mother and Junior rather than sitting in the back pew with the other teenagers. Under the circumstances, it felt as if we needed to stick together.

The sound in the room never returned to the original level. It was more of a breathy *whoosh* of whispers. Mother stared straight ahead, but I looked around the room, hoping not to see Doug. I spotted his parents, Jess and Vera May, sitting on the front row close to the piano. They had turned their heads to look when we entered. Doug wasn't there, not with his parents and not in the back row with the other teenagers. I was relieved, but not surprised. He attended on Sundays only because his parents insisted. That usually got him a reprieve from having to go to revivals. The Campbell kids weren't so lucky.

Within a few minutes, Raylene's daddy, Mr. Propps, the music minister, got up from his seat and went to the front holding his hymnal and told us all to turn to page 423. We sang "Let Others See Jesus in

You" while Dotty pounded it out on the old upright. After the song, Dotty left the piano bench and sat next to me, saying, "If these people think anybody can see Jesus in the way they act, they're a bunch of damned hypocrites."

I almost dropped the hymnal. I had never heard Dottie swear before. In fact, I don't think I'd ever heard a girl swear. Although all the boys and men I knew used colorful language, girls didn't. We were too Baptist for that. Dotty caught the hymnal as it slipped from my grip

She had sounded uncharacteristically bitter, and when I glanced at her, she was staring ahead while Brother Rodgers intoned, "Do others see Jesus in you?" The look on Dotty's face would have made me laugh under different circumstances. Dotty was trying not to laugh, and she covered it up by pretending to have a coughing fit. Mother opened her purse, retrieved a peppermint drop, and handed it to her. Junior, of course, immediately pretended to be struck by the same affliction with a spasm of coughs. Mother looked down at him and told him to hush.

The pastor said a long prayer asking the Holy Spirit to come down upon us, saying the same thing over and again in different ways, like the Holy Spirit was too dumb to get it the first time.

We had to stand up again and sing another song, "Take Me As I Am." It's about being full of guilt and begging the Lord to forgive us. It was the kind of hymn that made me feel even more miserable. Finally, the pastor introduced the revival preacher, Brother Jake, whose real name was Jason Schulz. Brother Jake launched into his sermon, fanning the fires of hell and waving his arms like a drowning man. He was sweating and swiping at his shiny forehead with a crumpled handkerchief by the time he signaled Mr. Propps and Dotty to start the invitational hymn, "Jesus is Calling."

Brother Jake stood in the front with his hands out stretched and speaking in a low and mournful voice that sinners must answer the call and be saved. A few people came forward, weeping and declaring their urge for salvation, but by the time we finished the hymn, Brother Jake was disappointed at the small number who had come forward. We had to sing all four verses of "Why Do You Wait?" Junior started his fake cough again, and Mother gave in and handed him a peppermint to shut him up. Dotty looked bored sitting at the piano and she hit the wrong note several times. That was actually startling. Dotty never messed up at the piano.

We sang all four verses again. All of that for just one more soul. It was Lola Patterson. She was probably in her seventies and had been a member of the church as long as I could remember. She'd already been saved, she told the congregation, but she wanted to rededicate her life to Christ because she was such a terrible sinner. That sure made me wonder what her sin was. Whatever it was, it wasn't as bad as mine. Dottie just stared. If she'd been sitting next to me, she would have jabbed me with her elbow when she heard dear old Mrs. Patterson was a sinner, and I would have jabbed her back.

The service went on forever, and it started to feel as if everyone was looking at us. Maybe they wanted us to walk up to the front and confess our sins or what they thought was Daddy's sin. We always have to stand during the invitation to salvation, but at one point, Mother sat down like she couldn't take it anymore, making me wonder if she'd been thinking the same thing I had.

At last the music stopped, and the pastor announced that the two people who had come forward to express their desires to be saved would be baptized at the end of the revival in Propps' big tank, along with any other people he was certain would come to accept Christ as their personal savior before the week's end.

I just wanted to go home, and I made my way to the aisle, hoping Mother wouldn't stay and talk with the other women the way she usually did. She didn't. She walked toward the door, looking straight ahead. It was only when Mrs. Houser spoke to her that she hesitated.

"I'm praying for you and your family, Dorothy. I know none of it's your fault." said Mrs. Houser.

"And just what is it that's not my fault?" Mother's strained voice was a sound I'd never heard before.

"Oh, hon, you can't help what your husband does."

"What my husband does? What do you mean?'

"You know what he done." Harriet Jacobs said, moving toward Mother and Mrs. Houser. "He got that colored man outta jail, then the nigger killed Hutch. Some say George was in on it, and both of 'em will be arrested. That new boy Caroline's been going out with? He's a suspect, too. Listen, Dorothy, you need to keep better control over your girls. No telling what they'll end up doing if..."

"Harriet!" Mrs. Houser said in a scolding voice. "You oughtn't to upset Dorothy like that."

"Well, she ought not to deny what's obvious. It won't do her soul a bit of good."

"Let me worry about my soul." Mother said. "You just worry about your own." She headed for the door, holding Junior's hand and walking so fast she was practically dragging him. Dottie and I followed close behind. My heart was banging at my chest so hard it hurt. Why would Hal be a suspect? And Daddy was at home when it happened. Now my head was hurting, along with my chest. Everything was confused. Everything was wrong.

In the pickup, Mother backed out of the parking space, spinning the back wheels and spewing dirt and gravel on anybody who happened to be in the way.

"We won't be coming back to this damned church." she said, tears falling down her cheeks. "I'll become a Methodist before I'll come back here."

CHAPTER 27

Homer Maylock

His thick fingers made it difficult to pick the aspirin from the little tin he kept in his shirt pocket, so he emptied the tin on his desk, scooped four of them into his hand, and washed them down with a drink from the bottle of bootleg whiskey he had confiscated two days before.

Maylock had spent the almost two weeks out at the murder scene, combing through everything from the debris and blood on the floor of the railcar where Jasper Hutchison's body had fallen to the row of trees and the mesquite brush and yucca plants beyond. Now he had a headache, not to mention a sick stomach. The murder was still an open case, but he could close it within a day. He knew who had killed Hutch. That was what was making him sick.

Maylock replaced the bottle in the bottom drawer of his desk and locked it. He was trying to scrape the aspirin back into the tin when his secretary, knocked on his door.

"What is it, Janice?" It came out sounding as irritated as he felt.

Janice opened the door part way and stuck her head into the room. "Someone here to see you."

"Who is it?" he asked, giving up on the aspirin. Most of them had landed on the floor.

"I don't know. Some nigger."

"Send him in." Maylock kicked at the aspirin on the floor, then looked up. "Hello Thaddeus. What is it you want?" Thaddeus had already confessed to him that he was the one who beat Hutch up the first time, and he told him why. Maylock wasn't inclined to arrest Old Thaddeus, but he was still mulling it over in his mind.

Thaddeus stood near the door, reluctant to approach Maylock's desk. "I come to tell you 'bout Johnny."

"Shit!" Maylock said under his breath. "What about Johnny?"

"He in the hospital."

"Somebody beat him up? I don't have time to go looking for who ever done it. I got a murder on my hands." Neither the aspirin nor the whiskey seemed to be doing him much good so far. Blood pounding in his head was making it hurt worse.

"That what I want to talk to you about." Thaddeus said. "I knows what people are sayin' but Johnny never killed that boy Hutch. He been in the hospital since before it happened."

Maylock sat up straighter. "How do you know that?"

"'Cause I'm the one that taken him to the hospital."

Maylock stared at him. "How do you know what time the killing happened?"

"I just knows that it happened sometime after that big rain."

"Uh huh." Maylock said, studying the man's face.

"Johnny got in the hospital before that. Next morning. After the rain.."

"Can you prove that?"

Thaddeus nodded. "I was there when it happened. When he cut his toes off. Nearly bled to death before I could get the pickup ready and get him to Morton to the hospital."

"What do you mean, cut his toes off?"

"Three of 'em. On his right foot. He was tryin' to get his old pickup ready to go to town. He was fixin' the brakes that went out on him when he had to pull George Campbell outta the mud. Pickup fell off of the jack. Drum hit his foot. Sliced off three toes I seen 'em there. Layin' in the dirt and grease next to the brake drum. Mozelle come out and picked 'em up."

Maylock felt an even stronger wave of nausea. "How'd you get him to the hospital if the pickup had a wheel off?"

"Had to put the damn thing back together by myself. Pearlie helped me best she could." Thaddeus took a handkerchief from his back pocket and wiped his forehead and his mouth. "Damn near bled to death before I could get it back together. Woulda died if Mozelle hadn't tied a rag around his leg to stop the blood. I reckon he's gonna lose his foot, and it'll be that old butcher we got here in Morton that does it. He even admits Johnny ought to go to that big hospital in Lubbock but they ain't no way we can pay for that."

"Where's Johnny now?"

"Still in the hospital." Thaddeus said.

Maylock was thinking about severed toes and a sawed-off foot. He knew before Thaddeus told him that Johnny was in the hospital. He also knew about the accident. News traveled at lightning speed in a small town. Maylock also knew Johnny wasn't the killer, and he didn't have to cut his foot off to prove it.

The sheriff stood up from behind his desk. "Thank you, Thaddeus. Go home and tell Mozelle not to worry about Johnny getting arrested."

Thaddeus stared at him a moment, his eyes wide in disbelief before he finally managed to tell him thank you.

When Thaddeus was gone, Maylock moved from his desk to the window overlooking the square, crushing aspirin under his boot in the process. A few people milled around outside the stores — women walking into St. Clair's and coming out with packages wrapped in brown paper; Caroline Campbell parking her daddy's pickup across from the courthouse. He switched his attention to two kids sitting on the curb outside the drugstore licking at ice cream cones. Watching people from his high vantage point usually helped him clear his mind. Not this time. He still didn't know how to do what had to be done.

He stared at nothing in particular for several minutes before his attention moved back to the boys in front of the drugstore. The more he watched them, the more he lusted for some of that dripping cold chocolate. While he watched, he noticed the Campbell girl was still sitting in the pickup. He wondered why she didn't just get out and do what she had to do. While he was still watching, she got out of the pickup and walked up the sidewalk toward the courthouse. He was pretty sure what was coming next.

Back at his desk, he riffled through papers without looking at them and argued with himself about unlocking that bottom desk drawer again to get the whiskey. He was still thinking about it when Janice knocked on his door again.

"Yeah, send her in."

Janice opened the door and stuck her head in just as she had before. "How'd you know it was a female?"

"Come on in, Caroline." Maylock called, ignoring Janice's question. Janice gave him a curious frown and stepped aside for Caroline to enter. "Have a seat, little girl, and tell me what's on your mind."

Caroline didn't sit. She stood in front of his desk and looked down at him. "I want to talk to you about the murder." She was doing a good job of keeping her voice even and strong, but clenched fists gave her away.

"Uh-huh. What about it?"

"Johnny didn't kill Hutch."

"You sure about that?"

Caroline took a long time to answer. "Yes sir, I'm sure." she said finally.

Maylock knew that if he was cop that was worth a damn he would ask her for information to back that up, but all he said was, "Thank you Caroline." He thought she would leave then, but she stood still, looking at him like she wanted to say more. His mind was spinning as he tried to think of a way to get rid of her or at least to distract her. "How about. . .uh, how about Hal Fitzgerald?"

Her eyes widened. "Hal?" Her voice sounded choked.

"Have any idy where he went after the rodeo?"

"After the rodeo?" By now all of the color had drained from her face. "That's not when you said Hutch was killed."

"Wasn't asking about Hutch, I asked about Hal. Where'd he go after the rodeo?"

"He was with me."

Maylock waited several seconds, never taking his eyes off her while waiting for her to say more. He saw a slight quiver on her mouth.

"We drove out to the nature preserve."

Maylock said nothing.

"You know, between here and Muleshoe? And it started raining and we couldn't make it out."

He nodded. "So you just sat there in the car waiting for it to quit raining so you could leave."

She took another breath and did her best to keep it from shuddering. "Yes. That's. . .that's pretty much what we did."

"And your folks were out looking for you all night." I hear.

"Well, part of the night."

Maylock nodded. "Does your daddy know you're here now?

Caroline shook her head. "I told him I was going to see Raylene Propps."

Maylock frowned. "What's going on with you, Caroline? Lying to your daddy, staying out late with boys?"

She looked at him with wide eyes and a pale, blood-drained face. She didn't seem to be able to speak.

Finally, he loosened the noose. "Thank you, Caroline. I appreciate you coming in." Caroline still didn't leave. "I have something to uh. . ."

Maylock stood. "I got work to do, Caroline. If you'll excuse me." He took her arm and led her toward the door. She tried to say something, but his own booming voice drowned out whatever it was she wanted to say. "I got important work, Caroline. If I have any questions, I'll call on you." He walked her all the way to the outside door that led to the hallway, ignoring the questioning look Janice gave him.

Back in his office, Maylock sat at his desk, dropped his aching head into both of his hands, and stayed that way for a while. He glanced down at the locked desk drawer one more time before abruptly standing. Walking out of his office, he spoke to Janice without looking at her. "Be back in a few minutes."

Outside the courthouse, he crossed the street and went in the drugstore and ordered a double dip chocolate ice cream cone. He was sitting alone in one of the booths and had only taken a couple of licks when Hal Fitzgerald entered. Maylock stiffened. He'd hoped for a few minutes of peace. Now he'd have to talk to Hal.

Maylock nodded at the young man and watched as he went to the counter and asked for a package of Lucky Strikes. After he'd bought the cigarettes and started to leave, Maylock spoke, "How you doing, son?"

Hal stopped and looked at him with an expression more troubled than surprised. "Fine, sir. How are you?"

"Have a seat." Maylock said, motioning toward the opposite side of the booth he sat in.

"I appreciate the offer, but I got to..."

"I said have a seat." Maylock said without raising his voice. Hal hesitated then sat across from him. "Want some ice cream?"

"No thanks."

"Something to drink?"

"Nothing, thank you."

Maylock took the last bite of his ice cream cone and reached for a paper napkin in a shiny metal holder next to the wall. "I hear you came by to see me a few nights ago after the office was closed." He watched Hal's face for a change of expression. Nothing changed except for a slight twitch in his left eyelid. "You're wondering how I knew that." Still no response. "I seen you walk up the steps and try the door. Surprised you didn't know the whole courthouse is closed that time of night."

Hal unwrapped his Lucky Strike pack and offered it to Maylock.

"No thanks. Them things will kill you." Maylock said.

Hal took out a cigarette and held it in his mouth without lighting it. He looked at Maylock, waiting.

"I was over at the gas station when I saw you." the sheriff said. "What was it you wanted?"

Hal took a packet of matches from his pocket, opened it and struck a match against the edge with one hand. He drew deep to light the cigarette. "Nothing." he said through the cloud of smoke.

"You wasn't by any chance wanting to tell me about what you seen out there at that old railcar, was you?"

The blood drained from Hal's face. "What makes you think I saw anything?"

"Oh, I'm sure you must have. Them tire tracks alongside the road in front of the railcar where the body was found? They was from your tires. Had to be, judging from the mud I seen caked on 'em."

"I had muddy tires, all right. I got stuck out there at. . ."

"Out at the nature reserve with your girlfriend. Yeah, I know."

Hal stared at him, not speaking. He took another drag from his cigarette and let the smoke drift from his mouth like a sluggish drainpipe.

"You're lucky George Campbell didn't kill you." Maylock knew he had Hal sweating now, in spite of his expressionless face. He knew that look in the eyes. He'd seen it before. Maylock enjoyed the moment then shouted over his shoulder to the soda jerk behind the fountain. "Hey, Greg, bring me a coke." He looked at Hal. "You want one?" Hal shook his head.

"What kind of coke?" Greg called.

"Pepsi." Maylock turned back to Hal. "Them new boots you bought? They're sure 'nuf nice boots, but they make what you call distinctive prints in the mud. They was all over the place around old Hutch's body when I went out there."

Hal put out his cigarette in the ashtray on the table and looked away, staring at the opposite wall. Finally, he spoke. One word. "Yeah."

"Yeah what?"

"I was there."

"Is that what you wanted to talk to me about when you stopped by the courthouse?"

"Yeah, but I changed my mind."

"Why's that?" Maylock slurped his Pepsi through a straw.

"Because I don't want to talk to you."

"Don't give me that kind of double talk, boy."

Hal put his hands over his eyes for a moment, rubbing at them as if he might make Maylock disappear. "All I can tell you is I didn't do it."

"I think you can tell me more than that. Come on back to the office with me where it's more private." Maylock stood up, threw change on the table and turned toward the boy behind the counter. "I'm takin' this here glass with me since I ain't finished yet. I'll bring it back next time."

"Yes, sir." Greg said without looking up from his task of cleaning the soda fountain.

As Maylock followed Hal out of the drugstore, he was wishing he hadn't eaten that ice cream. He was sick about what he knew was coming next, and sweet ice cream in his stomach only made it worse.

CHAPTER 28

Hal

Maylock lead the way into his office and sat down behind his desk, motioning Hal to sit in the chair in front of it.

"All right, son. We got to talk about this. You got to tell me. . ." He stood up abruptly and excused himself. "Be right back." he said, hurrying to the door.

Hal didn't know what to do with himself when Maylock left. He looked at the walls. They were painted an ugly gray with two framed certificates to his left and a picture of Franklin Roosevelt hanging to his right. It occurred to Hal that Maylock should have a picture of President Dwight Eisenhower on that wall. He didn't bother contemplating why the sheriff didn't hang the current president's picture there. He was too busy worrying about what he was going to say when Maylock got around to asking him why he'd been walking around that murder scene. Telling him the truth was out of the question. He knew that.

Finally, Maylock came back wiping his mouth with a paper towel. His face had turned an odd color matching the paint on the walls. Once again, the sheriff sat down in his chair, tossed the damp paper towel a few feet to his right, landing it in a dark green metal wastebasket. He puffed out his cheeks and let the air out slowly. To

Hal, that seemed to be a signal that Maylock dreaded talking about this as much as he did.

"All right, damn it. Tell me the truth." Maylock said.

For one fleeting second, Hal thought of playing dumb and asking, *The truth about what?* But he was in no mood to play games, and Maylock wouldn't go for it anyway.

"I saw Hutch's car in front of that railcar, so I stopped the car to see what was going on. I saw Hutch laying there dead."

"That's not all."

"Well, I saw somebody running away, but didn't see who it was."

"You're lying."

"I didn't see who it was."

Maylock's eyes burned with enough anger that Hal felt the scorch. Finally. Maylock spoke. "You son of a bitch."

Hal felt hot and cold at the same time and something—his heart maybe—jumped to his throat, choking him. "Okay, I killed him."

Maylock gave him the same blazing look and spoke the same words. "You son of a bitch."

Hal kept his eyes on Maylock, doing his best not to let him see how scared he was.

"Why?" Maylock said.

Tongue-tied, Hal tried to speak, but finally he managed in a shaking voice, "Because of what he done."

Another long pause. "You gonna tell me what it is you claim he done?"

"To the girls." A strange feeling came over Hal when he spoke this time. It was as if he were outside his body, watching himself sitting there with Maylock staring at him.

"What girls?"

"Pearlie and Dotty." Hal said, or at least that part of him sitting in the chair said that. The other part, the watching part, simply watched.

Maylock kept his eyes on him, and nodded his head slightly.

He knows, Hal thought. The sheriff knows everything.

"How old are you, son?"

"Nineteen." An odd question.

"You likely to be drafted soon."

Hal didn't reply. Where was this going?

"Ever thought of joining up before they draft you? Maybe go overseas?"

"It crossed my mind." Hal still felt confused. "But. . ."

"I think it would be a good idy." Maylock said. "I know you ain't got no daddy, son, but take my advice like it was from your daddy."

Hal frowned. What in hell was he getting at?

"I know what you're thinking." Maylock said. "You're thinking about your girl. But hell, Caroline's gonna go away to college pretty soon. I 'spect you know that. You spend a few years in the army, she spends a few years in college. Y'all can get together again after that."

"Look, sheriff, I don't know what in hell you're getting at. I thought you was going to lock me. . ."

"What I'm getting at is that I got a murder on my hands. I got no witnesses. You hear that? I got *no* witnesses, and I got no suspects for who killed that son of a bitch, and he *was* a son of a bitch. You think

I don't know what Hutch done? You think I don't know who killed him? And listen to me, I questioned you, but I didn't learn a thing, you understand? Even if I thought it would do any good to follow up, I can't do it if you ain't here. If you're off serving your country."

Hal looked at him, unable to speak.

"Now, I know you love that little Campbell gal, but I kinda think it would be better if you didn't write to her while you're gone. That's on accounta. . .well, just take my word for it. Understand?"

"Yes, sir." Hal said. It sounded like someone else was speaking.

"Now get outta here." Maylock said. "I got a murder case to work on."

CHAPTER 29

Caroline

I remember the day as if it were yesterday. Hal came to see me the day I got off of Mother's probation. As soon as I saw his car pull into our driveway, I ran out to meet him. Mother later told me that was highly improper to show such enthusiasm.

Of course I didn't care, and he didn't either. He got out of the car as soon as he saw me and put his arms around me. He held me close to him and didn't seem to want to let me go.

"I love you more than life itself." he said.

"I love you, too." I found it hard to continue. Finally, I said, "I got something I ought to tell you."

"Not now." he whispered, and he kissed me on the forehead the same way he did that day at the lake—the day I first knew I loved him. He still had his arms around me when he said, "Let's go for a ride."

"Sure. I'll tell Mother. Be right back."

I thought we would go to the lake. Or maybe all the way to Morton to the drive-in. He drove toward our field where the cotton had grown tall enough to make the expanse look like a plush green carpet. I saw weeds coming up along with the cotton and knew that within days Dotty and I would be back in the field with our hoes.

Hal turned off the road onto the turn row at the end of the field—the spot used for turning the tractor around to plow another set of rows of cotton. He stopped the car about midway on the edge of the field.

"I'll be leaving soon." He paused, holding me with his eyes. My throat tightened. "You'll be leaving, too, to go to college."

"No." I said. "Listen to me Hal, I have to tell you…"

"I joined the Army."

I was stunned. Hal must have seen it on my face. He reached for me and pulled me close. I settled into his arms, head on his shoulder. Being near him seemed to give me strength. "Why did you decide to do that? Was it because you thought you'd be drafted? It won't be for too long will it? Where will you be?"

He laughed. "So many questions." He touched my face, cupping it in his hands. "Yes, I would probably be drafted soon, so I decided to get it over with. I signed up for three years."

"Three years! That's a long time. You could have just done two."

"Only if I was drafted."

"Then you should have waited." I glimpsed something in his eyes when I said that. It was dark and haunting. I didn't understand what it was, but it frightened me a little.

"Every time I try to get a job outside of farming I'm asked if I have my military duty out of the way. They kind of put you on hold if you don't. Besides, you'll be in school for four years at least."

I felt tears welling in my eyes. "I'm not going. I can't, because—"

Of course you're going to college." He sounded oddly angry. He started the car. "I have a month before I have to report to Fort Ord for basic training."

"Where is Fort Ord?"

"Someplace in California."

I felt dazed, as if I'd been hit on my head. "California? That's so far away. What if I never see you again? Will you be close to the ocean? Will you have to go overseas?

"More questions."

"I'm sorry. I just. . ."

He turned toward me an odd look on his face. "I love you." I couldn't help thinking there was more he wasn't telling me, and I think he knew there was something I wasn't telling him.

By fall when the fields had turned the color of white sea foam, ditches were full of stray bits of cotton that had blown from trailers on the way to the gin, and the air had taken on the sweet bacon-smell of burning burrs. I left for college in Lubbock and enrolled in journalism and political science classes. Hal left for faraway California. Pearlie and her family, including Johnny with his footless leg, moved to Morton. Dottie abandoned her digging site in the draw in back of the house, never to set foot there again.

The murder case was never closed but never again investigated.

Hal never wrote to me.

CHAPTER 30

Caroline

Sixty years later

I'm sitting on the front porch of the house in which I grew up—the porch I added on when I moved back after all those years as a journalist, a wife, a mother, and now a grandmother and a widow. Looking back, I can say it was a good life. Not perfect, and I spent a lot of it in psychologists' and psychiatrists' offices, but it was good enough. Hal was not part of my life except for that one summer, but I never forgot him. Now that I'm old, I think of him more often. I was hurt, yes, and I cried a deluge of tears. For him and for other things. I don't know that I forgave him for never writing, for never trying to contact me at all, but I got past it.

It is cool here on the front porch with a slight, sweet-smelling summer breeze caressing my skin while I watch the clouds, big white puffy ones, tumbling over each other in a sky so blue it looks fake.

I wait for the family. They'll be here soon for an old-fashioned family reunion in celebration of my birthday. I'm expecting children and grandchildren, Junior and at least some of his big family, along with Dotty and her husband. They all wanted to come here in the middle of nowhere where everything has changed to celebrate my birthday—a milestone year.

Many of the people from here sold out their small farms to big corporations and moved away. When the population declined, the school closed, modern technology replaced old-fashioned cotton gins that used to dot the countryside. Even Morton has declined to not much more than a gas station and the courthouse. All the buildings are boarded up on the square—the Rose Theater, the drugstore, St. Clair's, The New York Store. But the family wanted to come here, nevertheless, I suppose because of roots and because I am the one remaining ghost they remember.

Junior is the first to arrive. He pulls up in a new Volvo he's driven all the way from Nebraska. His wife and one of his daughters and her three children are with them. He comes more often than the rest of the family. Last year it was a Lexus he drove. He is the only one of us who stayed in agriculture, and he's made money. I think he owns half the land in the Midwest. His wife Linda, who grew up on a farm near Lubbock, shows me pictures of their new great-grandson, born recently to the son of her older daughter. He looks like Junior, I say, but Linda insists he looks like her.

My son and daughter arrive with their spouses and some of their children, who are no longer children, but young men and women, curious to see this old place on a forgotten road and the old woman who lives here.

"Where's Aunt Dotty?" my daughter Kennedy asks. Just minutes ago, Linda asked if Dotty was coming this year.

"She said she'd be here." I say. I don't get to see Dotty as often as I'd like. She writes mystery novels and lives in Santa Fe. Not so far away, but she has a busy life. "You know Dotty." I add. "She's always late."

"I heard she's bringing a surprise for you." Vicky says. That's Junior's daughter, the one with all the kids.

"She would." I say with exasperation. I had instructed everyone *not* to bring gifts. At my age, there's nothing I need or want. Certainly nothing to clutter my house more than it is already.

It would be like Dotty to disregard my wishes, though. She went to the University of New Mexico to study archaeology back in the sixties when she finished high school. UNM was said to have the best archaeology college in the area, and she could hardly wait to get there. She seemed to be enjoying it, but she dropped out at the end of her third year and became a quintessential hippie, living in a commune in the mountains. Mother was still alive then, and it almost drove her to apoplexy. Dotty left the commune when that phase of American life ended. She married an environmental lawyer in Santa Fe. Mother was never sure that was an improvement. Dotty never finished her degree, but she writes moderately successful mystery novels about Native American ruins and salted archaeology sites.

Before long, my son and daughter arrive.

"Where can I put the potato salad, Mom? There's no room in the fridge." Kennedy calls from the kitchen.

I get up to help her make room in the overflowing refrigerator. At the same time, my son Tom, who is firing up the charcoal grill for hamburgers, asks me when I'm going to spring for a new gas grill and move into the modern world.

The turmoil of a big family is in full swing when Dotty shows up with her surprise. At first, I don't recognize the attractive black woman with her until I see her eyes.

"Pearlie?"

"I didn't think you'd recognize me." She seems shy, as always.

"It's been a few years." I say. I embrace her, and she returns my embrace. "Where did you find her?" I ask, turning to Dotty.

"Are you surprised?" Dotty asks instead of answering my question.

"I couldn't be more surprised." I'm looking at Pearlie again. She's tall and thin, dressed in chic white ankle pants and a silk blouse. By now all of the family has gathered around her, looking at her with curiosity. Only Junior knows who she is. He explains to everyone that Pearlie and her family used to live nearby in a house that collapsed from disuse and harsh weather a long time ago.

"Dotty and I got together in Santa Fe," Pearlie says

"You live there?" I ask Pearlie.

She laughs. "No, I live in Maryland. I came to Santa Fe as a tourist. I knew Dotty lived there, so I looked her up. She told me about your birthday gathering, and well. . .here I am."

"Maryland? How did you end up there?"

"It was Gersham Rabinowitz's fault I ended up in Maryland." says Pearlie. "Remember him? The New York Store?"

"Of course, I remember, but how…?"

"It's a long story," Pearlie said,

"Come along." I say, leading them toward the front porch. "Leave the kitchen to the young ones. We have to talk."

"Yes." Pearlie says, "I want to talk." She gives Dotty a look I don't understand. When we are on the porch, she settles into one of the white rocking chairs I bought at Cracker Barrel in Lubbock. Dotty goes to fetch glasses of ice tea. Pearlie is quiet for a while, looking at the sky.

"That sky." she says. "It's overwhelming. I'd forgotten how it dominates this part of Texas Maybe because there's nothing else to look at." She's quiet again until Dotty shows up with three glasses of tea on an old metal tray that used to be Mother's. "I tried to stay in touch with you." she says.

Something tightens around my chest. "Pearlie, I couldn't'—"

She interrupts me. "You saved my life, Caroline."

"No, I—-"

"You and Mr. Rabinowitz. He saved my whole family, if you want to know the truth. Gave Daddy a job in his store stocking shelves because no farmer would give him a job after the accident. Paid him enough to support us. I guess you didn't know that since you were away at college. You didn't even come home in the summers much."

"I was working summers." I say, "For the *Avalanche Journal* in Lubbock. If I hadn't had a job, I couldn't have afforded the tuition."

"I knew you became a reporter." she says. "Suits you."

"Gave me a license to ask questions." I say, still hoping we could change the subject.

Pearlie laughs and Dotty pushes a puff of air from her lips. "Like you needed a license." she says.

"Mr. Rabinowitz sent me to college." Pearlie says. "Howard University in Washington, D.C. Paid for most of it. Everything I couldn't pay for with a job as a waitress. That's how I ended up in Maryland, so far away from Texas. I taught history in a high school there until I retired a few years ago."

"I should have stayed in touch." I say again, overcome with guilt, but at the same time knowing it would have been impossible for me.

Pearlie and Dotty exchange another look. "Dotty and I did stay in touch."

I'm stunned, even a little hurt because I'd been left out. I look at Dotty. "Why didn't you tell me you two were in touch?

Dotty bites her lip and says nothing.

"I thought. . ." Pearlie began. "We thought. . . well, we were too scared. At least I was."

"Scared? I don't understand."

"I know the truth." Dottie says. "Pearlie told me."

Pearlie reaches a hand to cover my own. I find it impossible to speak, and a knot has formed in my stomach.

"Jason Hutchinson." Dottie whispers. It's okay."

I'm thinking that I don't want to hear this. Hutch was killed a long time ago. Hal disappeared soon after. I can't relive all of that. Not now. Still, I can't stop myself from speaking in a hushed voice, words I have screamed in the past. "Yes! Yes, I killed him."

Dottie shakes her head, and I see tears in her eyes.

Pearlie speaks. "It was an accident. You have to know that, but I would have helped you kill him if I could have. Before it happened, Dotty and I got the crazy idea that we were going to kill him and bury him in that draw behind your house where she used to dig up old stuff all the time. But she was just being crazy. Neither of us meant it." Pearlie pauses a moment then adds, "He raped me More than once."

"I know." That's all I can say, and then I look at Dottie and see that tears have wet her cheeks. "He raped me, too." she said.

"Dotty!" I can't say more. My throat has become paralyzed.

"He tried it again. It was one night when I was supposed to go home with Joanie. Only, neither of us went home. We stayed in Morton after the rodeo. Do you remember that rodeo, Caroline? It was the one when you ran off with Hal Fitzgerald without telling Mother and Daddy where you were going?"

I can't speak. I can only nod.

"We were just horsing around in town. Joanie had some beer. I think she stole it from her daddy. We only had one bottle between us, and we hadn't even finished drinking it when Hutch pulled his car up beside us where we were parked on the edge of town." Dottie stops speaking and looks away. Pearlie is still holding on to her hand.

Dottie continues. "Hutch opened the car door and grabbed me, forced me into his car. Joanie was scared. She sped off in her car. I don't blame her. Maybe I would have done the same thing."

"No, Dottie." Pearlie said. "You would have never left her there if you'd been driving."

Dottie seems not to hear her. "He took me to that old railcar. You know the place."

The old car is still beside the road, one side completely collapsed now. Remembering makes me tremble.

"That's where they found his body." Dotty continues. "That's where you. . ."

"Where I killed him." I say because Dotty is unable to speak the words. "I was at the store. Mother sent me there to buy flour. When I was driving home, I saw Hutch's car in front of that old rail car, and I saw him struggling with Pearlie, trying to force her inside. By the time I parked and ran inside, he had her on the floor." I glance at Pearlie, not sure if I should continue, but she tells me to go on speaking. "There was an old beer bottle on the floor. I picked it up and hit him against his head." Pearlie's hand tightens around mine. She walks to the edge of the porch." It broke, but I just kept at it. I. . .I must have cut. . .cut the jugular vein in his neck. I watched him die. I didn't know what to do. . ."

"We sat in the pickup together." Pearlie says. "Both of us scared. Caroline said people would blame me if they could, but she wouldn't let them. She said she'd never let her best friend take the blame. She called me her best friend. Me! A black girl. I was never the same after that." She begins to cry, and Dotty and I both wrap our arms around her."

"I didn't take the blame either." I say." I was never charged."

"I spent years in therapy." Pearlie says, "but it still. . ."

I laugh. "I know about therapy." I say.

We stand there for a while, the three of us in a huddle. Finally Pearlie backs away and looks down at her hands. "I never told anyone Hutch got me pregnant. There was this woman in Morton—Black Buela she called herself. She helped me out of it. Mr. Rabinowitz paid for that, too."

I'm remembering Pearlie's illness, her "affection," as Junior called it.

"Butcher job." she says, pulling away. "Almost killed me. I could never ... never have children."

"Oh my God, Pearlie..." I say.

"I wanted to kill him for that." Pearlie says, "I wish it had been me who. . ."

"Oh Pearlie!" I reach for her again, but she shakes her head.

"What he did to me. . .and to little Dottie. . ." She stops speaking for a moment before she adds, "That boy, Hal Fitzerald was his name, your boyfriend, Caroline, I think he knew about what. . .what happened to Hutch."

I shake my head. "No! He couldn't possibly know." I glance at Dottie. She's dialing someone on her smart phone. How inappropriate, I think, not like Dottie at all.

Finally, Pearlie speaks again. "Hal knew who killed Hutch. That's why he went away. Maylock sent him away because he knew. Maylock and Hal did that to save you."

"How do you know that?" I'm demanding answers. There are missing pieces to this puzzle, pieces of incomprehensible shapes. "About Hal, I mean, and why he went away? About Maylock knowing?"

"Hal told me." Pearlie says. "When the internet came along, I tracked him down."

I force myself to be calm. I want to ask her where he is. What he is doing. I'd thought of trying to find him, but forced the idea out of my mind. He hadn't cared enough to stay in touch, so I had to let bygones be bygones.

"You know how he knew? Because he saw that rodeo tag he gave you on the floor of the rail car." Pearly says. "He's kicked himself ever since because he didn't pick it up. Said he was too rattled, and by the time he went back to get it, Maylock had been there and took it. Maylock knew you'd been wearing it. You know how he was. Eyes in the back of his head."

I sink into one of the rocking chairs. I'm stunned. Not sure what anyone is saying by now.

"He'll be here any minute." says Dottie.

I don't comprehend. I give her a questioning frown.

"Hal." she says. "That's part of your birthday surprise. I asked him to come. He's been parked in his car about a quarter of a mile away. Down where the mail boxes used to be. He was just waiting for my call."

Pearlie smiles for the first time since we began our talk. "We had to prepare you first."

The rain has begun to fall in intermittent splatters. I spot his car. A roar of thunder announces his arrival. In the front drive, Hal Fitzgerald stops, opens the door, and steps out of the car into the rain.

His hair is white now and his waist a little rounder. The rain falls harder, but he is still walking toward me. He's drenched when he reaches me, but I see his haloed eyes, his sensuous mouth. I reach out my hand. He takes it and holds it close to his heart.

"I think it's going to rain." he says as water runs down his face.